Bounty

Brantley Walker:
Off the Books

By Nicole Edwards

The Walkers

Alluring Indulgence

Kaleb
Zane
Travis
Holidays with The Walker Brothers
Ethan
Braydon
Sawyer
Brendon

The Walkers of Coyote Ridge

Curtis
Jared (a crossover novel)
Hard to Hold
Hard to Handle
Beau
Rex
A Coyote Ridge Christmas
Mack
Kaden & Keegan
Alibi (a crossover novel)

Brantley Walker: Off the Books

All In
Without A Trace
Hide & Seek
Deadly Coincidence
Alibi (a crossover novel)
Secrets
Confessions
Bounty

Austin Arrows

Rush
Kaufman

Club Destiny

Conviction
Temptation
Addicted
Seduction
Infatuation
Captivated
Devotion
Perception
Entrusted
Adored
Distraction
Forevermore

Dead Heat Ranch

Boots Optional
Betting on Grace
Overnight Love
Jared (a crossover novel)

Devil's Bend

Chasing Dreams
Vanishing Dreams

Misplaced Halos

Protected in Darkness
Salvation in Darkness
Bound in Darkness

Office Intrigue

Office Intrigue
Intrigued Out of The Office
Their Rebellious Submissive
Their Famous Dominant
Their Ruthless Sadist
Their Naughty Student
Their Fairy Princess
Owned

Pier 70

Reckless
Fearless
Speechless
Harmless
Clueless

Sniper 1 Security

Wait for Morning
Never Say Never
Tomorrow's Too Late

Southern Boy Mafia/Devil's Playground

Beautifully Brutal
Without Regret
Beautifully Loyal
Without Restraint

Standalone Novels

Unhinged Trilogy
A Million Tiny Pieces
Inked on Paper
Bad Reputation
Bad Business
Filthy Hot Billionaire

Naughty Holiday Editions

2015
2016
2021

BECAUSE NAUGHTY CAN BE OH SO NICE®
NE LTD

Bounty

Brantley Walker: Off the Books, 8

NICOLE EDWARDS

Nicole Edwards Limited
A dba of SL Independent Publishing, LLC
PO Box 1086
Pflugerville, Texas 78691

This is a self-published title.

BOUNTY

Brantley Walker: Off the Books, 8

Nicole Edwards

Cover Details:

Image: © givaga (97508779) | 123rf.com
Design: © Nicole Edwards Limited

Interior Details:

Formatting: Nicole Edwards Limited
Editing: Blue Otter Editing

Audio Details:

Image: © givaga (97508779) | 123rf.com
Narrators: Tor Thom & Charley Ongel

Identifiers:

ISBN: (ebook) 978-1-64418-059-4 | (paperback) 978-1-64418-060-0 | (audio) 978-1-64418-061-7

BISAC: FICTION / Mystery
BISAC: FICTION / LGBTQ

CHAPTER ONE

Friday, April 29, 2022

"Whose ridiculous idea was this anyway?"

Brantley Walker glanced over at his cousin Sawyer, a slow smile forming. "The guy who said he's never bowled before."

Sawyer's dark eyebrows popped up toward his hairline before he dramatically looked over at Reese, then back to Brantley. His voice was pitched higher when he said, "The guy who's kickin' *all* our asses right now?"

Brantley took a long pull on his beer, let his smile widen. "That'd be the one."

"He's a swindler," Sawyer accused.

"I think you mean a hustler," Kaleb corrected.

"A fraud," Sawyer griped, his smile bleeding through despite his efforts to pretend he wasn't amused.

Kaleb laughed. "No, I still think hustler's the right word."

Brantley shot a smirk at Reese. Six feet five inches of prime alpha male, wearing dark jeans and an untucked charcoal-gray T-shirt, was standing with his hands on his hips, looking like sin on a stick. Reese Tavoularis, the man who claimed he didn't know how to bowl, had just gotten his sixth strike in a row, and the way his eyes glittered told him Reese had more hidden talents than he was letting on.

"Beginner's luck," Reese quipped, his lips twitching as he glanced between the others.

"My ass," Sawyer countered, putting his hand above his eyes as though shielding them as he craned his neck and peered around the bowling alley. "Where's the rest of your PBA league hidin', huh? That them down there? They recordin' this for TikTok? I bet they are, the fuckers."

Brantley barked a laugh. His cousin certainly hadn't lost his dramatic flair over the years. As far as bowling went, Brantley didn't care one way or the other who won. He'd come because Reese had suggested it. Since their Fridays were usually spent at Moonshiners, he figured it was good to change things up a bit. Not to mention, when the man he was going to marry made a request for a date, Brantley damn sure wasn't going to pass up the opportunity.

Granted, Brantley hadn't realized it would be a group outing, but that didn't bother him either. When Kaleb had mentioned needing to get out of the house, they'd invited him to come along. Kaleb had then passed the word on to his brothers, which was how Sawyer had come to join them. From there, word traveled like wildfire, and the next thing he knew, two of Brantley's brothers, Cal and Griffin, as well as their brother-in-law Killian, were signed up. And to balance things out, Luca Switzer had jumped on the bandwagon.

And here they were, taking up space in one of the lanes, surrounded by others who were out to have a good time. The place smelled like talcum powder, chicken wings, and cheap beer, the air thick with laughter and conversation and the occasional *thunk* of a bowling ball hitting the pins. It was what Brantley considered a perfect night out.

"Sawyer, you're up," Kaleb announced.

"Might as well call the game now," Sawyer grumbled. "That or let me use the gutter bumpers. This shit's startin' to get embarrassing."

"And a grown-ass man usin' the bumpers *wouldn't* be?" Brantley retorted with a snort.

"Did he do it again?" Cal, Brantley's youngest brother, asked when he returned from the snack bar carrying a plate of nachos, his eyes on the screen overhead.

"He did," Kaleb answered.

"Son of a bitch."

Brantley noticed Reese's crooked grin, and he was damn tempted to drag the man to a storage room so he could kiss that smirk clean off his handsome face.

"Next time, he's on my team," Luca stated as he moved toward the steps. "Anyone else need another beer?"

"I'll take one if you're offerin'," Brantley told him, his gaze never leaving Reese.

"Me, too," Sawyer hollered.

"Me, three," Killian said.

"I'll go with you," Kaleb offered.

When the crowd had thinned and Reese approached, Brantley crooked his finger to urge him closer. "Tell the truth. You were on your high school bowlin' team, weren't you?"

Reese chuckled softly. "I'm from the same small town you are, Navy boy. Coyote Ridge doesn't have a bowlin' team."

"Good point." He leaned in close to Reese's ear, lowered his voice. "Just fair warnin'. You bowl seven in a row, I'm gonna blow you in the parkin' lot."

Reese's surprised swallow was loud in his ear.

Brantley pulled back, met that whiskey-brown gaze, speaking just loud enough for only Reese to hear. "Your cock in my mouth with you pinned against the truck."

He loved that Reese's cheeks turned crimson. The man blushed more than a virgin schoolgirl, and Brantley happened to find that trait highly appealing. More so now that Reese would happily oblige him whenever he made an offer like that. In the beginning, Reese would've turned beet red and then found a way to hide out until the night was over. They'd come a long way since then.

"For fudge sakes," Sawyer exclaimed, throwing his hands in the air as the ball bounced down the lane.

"Did you just say fudge?" Brantley asked, laughing when the ball managed to topple two pins and made a third one wobble.

His cousin spun around. "Hey, some of us have kids. My wife'd kick my ass if I came home usin' the f-bomb again. The last time I did, Matthew used it to refer to his little brother."

Brantley smiled, waiting for Sawyer to elaborate.

Sawyer sighed. "He called him a fuckapotomous for a week."

"Oh, shit," Reese said with a huff of amusement.

Brantley couldn't help it, he nearly fell over with laughter. He could only imagine five-year-old Matthew singing the word as he shouted at his three-year-old brother.

Sawyer pointed at Brantley. "Your turn."

Brantley passed his beer to Reese so he could take his turn. He didn't put too much effort into it, which he figured was the reason he split the pins.

"That all you got?" Griffin called out from behind him. "What kinda shit-roll is that?"

He ignored his brother and waited patiently until the ball returned, smiling to himself. He knew without a doubt Reese was going to roll another strike. The man was on fire tonight, and Brantley was seeing a whole new side to him he hadn't realized existed. Then again, Reese had been different since his return from Dallas a month and a half ago. Ever since they patched things up between them, overcoming some of the obstacles they'd put in their own way, things had been good. Really good, in fact.

Brantley put some extra spin on the ball and took down one of the two pins left standing. When he turned, he found Reese smiling back at him. That grin made him feel like he'd just knocked down every pin in every lane in one fell swoop.

"Good thing you've got the pro on your team," Sawyer said.

Yeah, damn good thing.

"All right, bro," Sawyer said to Kaleb. "Knock 'em all down, or next time I'm invitin' Braydon and leavin' your ass at home."

"I'm pretty sure *I* invited *you*."

"Don't matter," Sawyer countered. "Roll a strike or you're out, Braydon's in."

Brantley chuckled, as did the others.

For the next ten minutes, the others took their turns. A few spares were added to the scorecard, but no more strikes.

Not until Reese took his next turn, anyway. No sooner did every pin fall than Reese pivoted on his heel and met Brantley's gaze. There was a mischievous gleam in the man's eyes, one that told Brantley he was looking forward to that promise.

Brantley glanced at his watch, his grin widening. Yeah, win or lose at bowling, he was still a winner overall.

After all, he was going to blow Reese's mind, as well as other parts of his body, and he wouldn't have to wait too much longer to do it.

A COUPLE OF HOURS LATER, AFTER THEY'D finished their games and given each other shit for their lack of bowling skills, Reese pushed open the door to lead the way into the muggy April night. The parking lot had thinned as the hours passed until only a handful of vehicles were left in the main lot. With Brantley at his side, they ventured around to the side of the building where they'd managed to snag one of the last remaining spots.

Reese was riding an adrenaline high, having been deemed the game winner, although technically, he'd been teamed up with Brantley, so they had both earned the title. He wouldn't lie; it felt good to be a winner. More so to have spent a night out with friends, enjoying the company of others.

"Any reason you stopped at seven?" Brantley prompted as they moved along the sidewalk leading to Brantley's truck.

Reese cut his eyes to the sexy man strolling beside him, attempting to read his expression in the shadows cast by the single light behind them. "You said I had to do seven in a row. There was nothin' 'bout more than that."

"We both know you had more in you."

"Maybe, but I didn't wanna make Sawyer cry."

Brantley's chuckle was soft and sexy. "There for a minute, I thought he might."

Reese grinned, drawing air deep into his lungs when Brantley's hand brushed his. As they walked, he could feel the heat beginning to churn in his veins, warming his blood and making his head spin with anticipation. He knew what was coming, and he could honestly say he was so fucking ready. Quite the opposite of what would've happened a year ago if he'd been in this same situation. But now, with Brantley back in it, his world had righted itself. Learning to accept who he was and what he wanted had taken time, but he'd managed to get to a good place.

Clearly taking his silence for concern, Brantley asked, "You sure you're up for this?"

Reaching over, Reese took Brantley's hand and moved it to the front of his jeans, letting the man feel just how *up for this* he really was. Hell, he'd been sporting a hard-on since Brantley made the offer. Not an easy thing to deal with when bowling, which was likely the real reason he hadn't gotten another strike after the seventh despite Brantley's unwavering faith that he could have.

Brantley stopped in front of the truck and turned to face him. With practiced ease, he had Reese backed against the grill in an instant. The streetlamp that shone on the cars at the front of the lot cast just enough glow to let Reese see Brantley's blue-gray eyes and the glitter of promise in them.

They flashed even hotter when Brantley said, "Do you know how fuckin' bad I want you right now?"

"I've got some idea," Reese countered, gripping Brantley's hips and pulling him forward, letting him feel the evidence of his arousal.

"I like that the feelin's mutual," Brantley growled softly, leaning into him.

So did Reese. Hell, he felt like a randy teenager. He couldn't remember a time when anyone had turned him on the way Brantley did. Didn't matter that they were in a public place or that anyone could come around the corner of the building and see them. The only thing he wanted was to feel Brantley's mouth on him. Every-damn-where.

Reese hissed when Brantley gripped his hair and tugged his head back.

"You're lucky we're in public right now," Brantley mumbled against his neck.

"You call this lucky?" he teased, grinding his hips to Brantley's so their denim-covered erections were trapped between them. "Because it feels more like need than luck to me."

The man's smirk was sinful.

"I won't lie," Brantley said, his voice low. "I like this side of you."

The side Brantley was referring to was the one that had come out of its shell in recent months. Since returning to Coyote Ridge, back to the man he'd hurt with his actions, Reese had felt like a new man. Gone was the hesitance that had come with learning that he was gay. Reese no longer cared what others thought because their opinions didn't matter. The only person whose opinion he cared about was standing just a few inches in front of him. That in itself was a blessing considering Reese had damn near fucked up the best thing that had ever happened to him. Thankfully, Brantley had forgiven him and the past was now behind them.

Feeling bold, Reese leaned in and nipped Brantley's jaw, speaking close to his ear. "You gonna keep talkin'? Or maybe you could put that mouth to good use."

Brantley huffed a laugh, but then he leaned in and crushed his lips to Reese's.

And just like that, the world fell away. The only thing in Reese's orbit was the man he loved and that devilish tongue that swept right into his mouth. He groaned, letting Brantley know just how good it felt to be kissed. It didn't hurt that Brantley's hands were rough, his motions jerky, signifying just how much he wanted this. The chemistry between them was intensifying the longer they were together, growing more potent by the second. It was a heady feeling to know someone wanted you as much as you wanted them. Especially someone like Brantley, the man who was always in control. Reese fucking loved that he could strip that control from him so easily.

They remained like that, standing in the shadows at the side of the building, making out, hands groping, tongues dueling. It took tremendous restraint to remember that they were still in public, and there was a very good chance the bowling alley had security cameras.

When Brantley pulled back, they were both breathing hard.

"Get in the truck, Tavoularis."

Chuckling, Reese managed to make his way to the truck's passenger side, his cock so hard it hurt. His jeans had gotten significantly tighter since they'd come outside, and he wasn't sure he'd be able to sit down. At least not until some of the blood that had pooled between his legs dispersed to other parts of his body.

When he opened the passenger door, he realized Brantley was behind him, adjusting himself as he gripped the door with one hand. The grimace on his face told Reese he was feeling the same discomfort. Reese was on the verge of telling Brantley to hightail it home so they could pick up where they'd left off but bit back the words at the last second. Brantley had admitted he liked this side of him, and Reese did not want to let him think he'd lost his nerve.

Instead, he unbuttoned his jeans and lowered the zipper before turning to face him. When he met Brantley's gaze, he noticed he was watching him intently, those steel-blue eyes dark as the night that enveloped them.

"We're not leavin' until you fulfill that promise you made," Reese said smoothly, sliding his hand into his boxers and gripping his cock firmly.

Brantley's gaze followed the movement of his hand even as he stepped forward, shielding Reese's body from anyone who might be in the parking lot.

"I've been lookin' forward to it all damn night," Brantley whispered, grinning before he squatted down before him. "You might wanna keep an eye out for security."

Reese managed to grip the door at the same time Brantley fisted his cock.

"Oh, Jesus," he rasped when that warm, wet tongue laved the swollen head of his dick.

And then there he was, his cock tunneling into Brantley's mouth while they stood outside the truck. Anyone who might come by wouldn't be able to see anything because of the angle of the truck and the door blocking their view, but the fact that someone might made it all the more intense.

Reese palmed Brantley's head, guiding him forward, his cock tunneling to the back of his throat. He gasped, overwhelmed by pleasure.

Standing watch wasn't easy to do, but he managed to keep one eye on their surroundings while his brain went offline, focused solely on the warm drag of Brantley's tongue along his shaft. He knew there would be more to come when they got home, but he wanted to savor this moment for as long as possible.

"Fuck," Reese whispered roughly. "Oh, fuck, Brantley."

As though that was his cue, Brantley deep-throated him, taking him to the root, the muscles of his throat working the sensitive head. Reese gripped Brantley's head with both hands, holding him there for long seconds as he fought the urge to come. He lost the battle long before he was ready, but he couldn't find it in himself to care as he grunted and came right down Brantley's throat.

"Mmm," Brantley said, standing tall. "When we get home, I'm gonna do that again just so I can hear you say my name when you come."

Reese grinned, tucking his spent cock away. "I'm gonna hold you to that."

CHAPTER TWO

Saturday, April 30, 2022

THE DARK GROWL OF THUNDER ROLLING ACROSS the sky brought Brantley out of a deep sleep. He took stock of his surroundings—the gentle turn of the ceiling fan above him, the soft pillow beneath his head, the cool sheet covering him. He stretched his legs and back as he shifted on the bed. It took him a moment to get his bearings, but it was easier than it usually was. He figured that had something to do with the familiar warmth and scent of the man sleeping beside him.

The bed jerked, causing Brantley to rouse a little more. It was then he realized Reese was thrashing in the bed, trapped in the throes of another nightmare. He'd been having them more frequently, and Brantley wasn't sure what to make of that. While Reese seemed far more at ease when he was awake, his subconscious was clearly attempting to process something.

Brantley shifted, lightly sliding his hand over Reese's arm, his shoulder, then across his chest. He let his palm rest heavily in the center. "You're safe, Reese. You're home."

Reese's big, hard body went stone-still, his heart pounding rapidly beneath Brantley's palm.

"You're safe," he repeated, inching closer now that the danger of being punched had passed.

Another rumble of thunder rolled through, strong enough to rattle the windows. He considered checking the weather radar to see if they were under any warnings but decided against it. His only concern at the moment was for the man beside him.

Brantley pressed up against Reese's side, touching every inch he could. "You okay?"

"Mmm-hmm," was Reese's only response, and it didn't sound certain.

He propped his head on his hand, then pressed his lips to Reese's shoulder, letting his arm relax over his chest, and brushed his thumb along Reese's jaw. "You wanna talk about it?"

Reese's grunt was a definite negative, and Brantley had expected no less. Neither of them preferred to talk about the traumas of their pasts. For Reese, he could've been reliving the time he'd spent in captivity or the night he'd taken a bullet to the chest. Both incidents kept Reese from sleeping soundly, but for the life of him, Brantley didn't know how to help.

Well, that wasn't entirely true.

"How about a distraction?" he offered, kissing Reese's shoulder.

"Always," Reese mumbled, his muscles relaxing.

Brantley kissed Reese's shoulder again, lingering there as he shifted, moving over him, the warmth of Reese's hard body seeping into him, skin to skin. Reese accepted his full weight, one arm banding around his back as the other hand cupped Brantley's jaw and turned his head so their mouths came together.

Yes, this was Reese's way of saying he didn't care to talk, and Brantley respected that. They would. One day. Until then, he would show Reese without words that he was here for him, that he could and would always be exactly what he needed.

The kiss was sinfully sweet, brought on by the connection they shared. The usual urgency was absent, in its place, a yearning so deep Brantley could feel it in his chest.

"Make love to me," Reese whispered against his lips.

Brantley lifted his head and met Reese's gaze in the dark room. No other man from his past had ever made that request, and truthfully, he'd never expected to hear it. Coming from Reese, those were the sexiest words that'd ever been spoken.

He settled his hips squarely between Reese's splayed thighs, their cocks rubbing together. Sheer pleasure burst in his bloodstream the same way it always did when they came together like this.

He swiped his thumb along Reese's jaw. "Tell me you love me."

A faint smile formed on that beautiful mouth. "You know I do."

"Say it."

A glimmer of light returned to Reese's eyes, telling Brantley he was fully present, no longer trapped in his own personal hell.

"I love you."

Brantley smirked. "I know."

A soft chuckle rumbled in Reese's chest, then he was pulling Brantley's head down, their lips colliding once more. Brantley was aware of Reese reaching for the lube on the nightstand. Their lips never separated although Brantley lifted his hips, giving Reese room to slide his hand between them. He groaned softly as Reese slicked his cock, preparing him. Aside from the leisurely stroke of that big, strong hand along his shaft, there was no foreplay. And when Reese drew his knees up, shifting his pelvis, Brantley guided his cock home. He slid in slowly, loving the way the muscles in Reese's arms and chest tensed as he filled him, the way his body gripped him tightly in invitation.

They remained like that, their tongues swirling together, their bodies rocking in unison as Brantley fucked him slow and deep.

"Brantley … that feels so good."

Brantley lifted his head, peered down, and held Reese's stare as he claimed his body in a way no other man had ever done before him. Every time he acknowledged that fact, it gave him a sense of intense power. Knowing that Reese had never been with another man made him feel invincible. Like a god among men. To know that this man trusted him with his body and his heart was something he would never take for granted.

"Stroke yourself," Brantley whispered, still holding Reese's gaze.

He felt Reese's hand move between them, pumping his cock in a rhythm that matched the gentle rocking of Brantley's hips. It wasn't long before they were both panting, the pleasure building to a crescendo. They continued to stare at one another as they took that final leap over the edge and into the abyss, the two of them coming at the same time.

Two hours later, right before the sun broke over the horizon, Brantley roused once again. He was alone in the bed, but he could hear Reese moving around the room.

"The rain stopped," Reese said softly.

Brantley grunted an acknowledgment, opening his eyes and letting his gaze linger on Reese's naked back as he pulled a shirt over his head. He was getting ready for their morning run, something they were back to doing every day without fail.

"She's not gonna wait for long," Reese said, turning around and looking at Tesha, who was now on the bed.

Brantley peered over to see the dog staring down at him, her tail wagging insistently, causing her entire body to quake. He reached up and rubbed her head, smiling. "Good morning to you, too, girl."

Her tongue lolled out of her mouth in that way that made her look like she was smiling.

"All right. I'm gettin' up," he assured her, throwing the blankets off.

Ten minutes later, they were out the door, feet pounding the soft earth beneath them as Tesha led the way. Neither of them said a word, but that was the norm. Since Reese's return, Brantley had started taking his cues from him. They hadn't yet made it back to their full ten miles each day, but with every week that passed, they were getting closer as Reese's body got stronger. He figured it wouldn't be long before he was the one trying to keep up, but he didn't care to rush it.

Once they made their way back to the house, their morning routine set in. While Reese headed for the shower, Brantley started the coffee. Then they traded, Brantley going to clean up while Reese started breakfast. When he returned, fully dressed and ready to start the day, Reese was standing at the kitchen island, his phone to his ear.

Reese's tone was placating when he said, "I hear you, Z."

Brantley headed for the cabinet, retrieved a coffee mug, and poured himself a cup. He took a sip, stepping back to give Reese room to move to the stove where bacon was frying in a pan.

"Hold on a minute," Reese said, pulling the phone away and setting it on the counter before tapping the screen. "You're on speaker. Brantley's here."

"Mornin', Z," Brantley greeted when Reese set the phone on the counter.

"Mornin'," Z responded, his voice chipper, a direct contradiction to the look on Reese's face. "Hopefully, you'll be more amenable to my request than my brother."

Brantley glanced at Reese to see he was shaking his head as he turned the bacon in the skillet.

"I wasn't under the impression you made requests," Brantley said, keeping his tone upbeat despite the tension he could feel coming from Reese.

"Everyone has an off day," Z teased.

"This certainly qualifies," Reese muttered as he kept his attention on the bacon frying in the pan.

Z's laugh came through the phone's speaker. "I told RT you'd hate the idea."

"Understatement of the fuckin' century," Reese grumbled.

"What idea's that?" Brantley inquired, curious as to what was at play here.

"Let me preface this by sayin', I get that your task force was designed for one specific thing, but we've got a request. It might sound a little … unusual."

"You think?" Reese grunted.

"All right, Tavoularis," Brantley said firmly, addressing them both at the same time. "One of you better spill it now."

From the phone came a gruff chuckle. "We need you to find a guy."

Brantley took a sip of his coffee. "Is this guy missin'?"

"You could say that."

"Oh, for fuck's sake," Reese hissed, spinning around and waving the spatula. "He wants us to play bounty hunters."

Brantley frowned, the words processing. "Wait. He wants … *what?*"

Reese's eyebrows rose. "You heard me."

He glanced at the phone, then back to Reese. "Bounty hunters?"

"Surely you've heard of the concept," Z said, his voice ringing with amusement. "You know. Like Dog the Bounty Hunter."

"You … *huh?*" Brantley glanced down at the phone. "I don't know what that means."

"You know Dog," Z said, disbelief replacing his amusement. "Duane Chapman? Only the most famous bounty hunter in the history of bounty hunters. Long blond hair. Sunglasses. On TV."

"I still don't know what you're talkin' about," he reiterated. "And I thought Boba Fett was the most famous bounty hunter."

Z huffed. "You do find missin' people, don't you?"

Figuring it was rhetorical, Brantley didn't respond.

Another huff from the phone, this one more frustrated. "Jesus. Y'all can be such pains in my ass, you know that?"

Another rhetorical, so Brantley took a sip of his coffee.

"Well, technically, this guy is missin'," Z said calmly. "He missed his court date yesterday afternoon, and a bench warrant was issued for his arrest."

"That's not the type of missing people we look for, Z," Brantley informed him, a tad curious as to what had brought this on.

"I told you my request was unusual."

"I'll say," Reese muttered.

Still eager to know, Brantley asked, "What did he get arrested for?"

"Drug possession," Z answered simply.

"And you want us to step in why?"

"Well…" There was a soft grunt on the other end. "Possession was just one of the charges. He was also tagged for auto theft."

Brantley stared at Reese, no longer wondering why his partner was frustrated with this situation.

"I don't—" he tried to say but was quickly cut off.

"And assaultin' a police officer," Z tacked on. "With his car. Well, technically, not *his* car, but *a* car."

Brantley set his coffee mug down. "What the fuck, Z?"

"It sounds worse than it is."

"I'm not sure that's even possible," Brantley retorted. "You've got a drug dealer who stole somethin' and hit a cop with his car, and you want us to find him?"

"Not *his* car," Z clarified. "The car is the somethin' he stole. And technically, the drugs weren't his—"

"Z!" Brantley hissed.

"Fine." Z laughed. "It was all a misunderstanding. A series of misfortunate events, if you will."

"Was it?" Reese bit out, his tone just shy of hysterical.

Brantley stared at the man, realizing then that he was definitely missing a huge piece of the puzzle.

REESE COULD FEEL BRANTLEY'S GAZE ON HIM, knew he was wondering why he was … well, he didn't want to admit he was freaking out, but yeah, he might be. Just a little bit.

Why wouldn't he though? His brother was asking them to play bounty hunters for a day. Or a week. Or however long it took to find a man who'd clearly gone and lost his ever-loving mind. And there was no doubt, the guy had crashed through the crazy forest and hit a few too many trees along the way. And that was *before* he'd gone and gotten himself in a world of trouble.

"I take it you know who Z's talkin' about?" Brantley asked.

"Oh, he knows him, all right," Z answered for him, a smile in his voice. "Uncle Toby used to be a big part of our lives."

"You have an uncle?" Brantley's incredulity caused his voice to pitch higher than usual.

"Technically, no." Reese rolled his eyes and moved the pan away from the heat. "He just liked to refer to himself that way."

Brantley's forehead creased, concern lighting his eyes.

"Nothin' creepy, I assure you," Reese clarified.

"So, you'll do it?" Z asked, clearly not keen on listening to Reese relay the details to Brantley.

"Depends," Brantley stated. "I have no desire to make another trip to Dallas right now."

"Good. Because he's in Austin. Or rather, that's where his last known address is." Z exhaled, sounding relieved. "I'll have the info sent over. Keep me in the loop?"

"You're gonna owe us for this," Reese told his brother.

The sound of Z's laughter grated on his last nerve before the call ended.

"All right, spill, Tavoularis."

"We really should've told him no," Reese said, grabbing another skillet so he could cook the eggs.

"That bad, huh?"

"Let's just say Toby's not the kinda guy you wanna be chasin' all over town."

Brantley refilled his coffee mug. "Since it sounds to me like we *will be*, maybe you could fill me in on the basics."

"I don't even know where to start."

"First, clarify for me whether you're related to the guy or not."

"Definitely not." Reese focused on cooking the eggs. "He was a friend of my father's. Back in high school. They drifted apart when they went off to college, then reconnected after my dad married my mom. He hung around after that. I don't remember how old I was when he disappeared again. Probably eight or nine, I guess."

"He was close to your folks?"

This was the part Reese really didn't know how to explain. Wasn't sure he even wanted to if he could.

"It's like pullin' teeth here, Reese. At least feed me while you're mullin' it over."

Reese tossed some bread into the toaster, pulled the butter out of the fridge. He remained silent while he plated the eggs and bacon, then buttered the toast when it popped up. The entire time, he could feel Brantley's full attention heavy on his back, but he refrained from speaking, buying as much time as he could before he tackled the most difficult subject in the history of difficult subjects.

When he turned around to pass Brantley his plate, he could see the concern in Brantley's steel-blue eyes, knew he had to get this out if for no other reason than to ease Brantley's mind.

"Tobias Land, a.k.a. Toby, was my father's best friend growin' up," he explained, pouring himself a cup of coffee while Brantley started chowing down. "Based on the stories I heard, he spent a lot of time at our house after he met my mother. He … uh … I think he was in love with her."

Brantley stopped chewing, his eyebrows slowly rising toward his hairline.

Reese hurried to clarify. "It wasn't exactly mutual. She was in love with my father, but she had a fondness for Toby. And yes, my father knew. He…" *Ah, Jesus.* He swallowed hard and continued with, "Well, he kinda approved of their relationship."

"What *relationship* did they have exactly?"

Reese took a gulp of coffee, let it sear his throat before answering. "It was a … um … a threesome-type deal."

God, just saying it out loud made his skin crawl and his ears heat.

Not that he had anything against those sorts of relationships. To each his own and all that shit. However, thinking about his parents in that manner … he would rather eat razor blades dipped in cyanide.

"So your mother and Toby were intimate? And your dad knew about it?"

Reese cringed. "Yeah."

Brantley processed for a minute, devouring a piece of toast before saying, "I've met your mother. She seems like a good judge of character, so I'm gonna assume Toby's not a bad guy."

Exhaling heavily, Reese set his mug down. "He's not. A little out there, maybe, but he's not a bad guy. Or he wasn't back then. People change, so who knows." He met Brantley's gaze. "I believe Z when he says what happened to Toby was a misunderstanding."

"So he's not a drug-pushin' thief who mowed down a cop on purpose?"

Reese laughed, some of the tension easing. "No. God, no. Knowin' him, he was in the wrong place at the wrong time."

"Hittin' a cop with a car … not sure that's happenstance."

"It wasn't like that."

"So you *do* know what happened?"

He nodded, leaned back against the counter, and crossed his arms over his chest. "Toby has a thing for strip clubs. More specifically, fully nude cabarets."

"Cabaret?" Brantley's smile was slow and wicked. "As in singin' and dancin'?"

"Exactly." Reese forged ahead. "It's my understanding he frequents one specific club. Got himself in a bit of hot water when he borrowed some money from a guy he met there."

"Borrowed money?" Brantley picked up another slice of bacon. "For?"

Reese shrugged. "No idea. But we're talkin' the kind of loan with interest that defies calculations. To hear Z tell it, Toby went to work out a deal 'cause he couldn't repay the entire amount. I figure they didn't agree to his terms since he ended up makin' a fast getaway. In doin' so, he stole a car. Turns out, the car belonged to the guy he got the loan from. Found himself in a high-speed chase. Some crazy voice in his head told him to ram a police car to save himself. The cops weren't in the car, thank God. However, they were nearby. When they searched the car he stole, there were drugs in it."

Brantley's eyes were wide, a grin splitting his face. "He stole a car filled with drugs and rammed a police car to escape the bad guys?"

"In a nutshell, yeah."

"So why didn't hc just go to court yesterday?"

"Probably has somethin' to do with the fact the loan shark/drug dealer's got a bounty on his head."

"And now he has two."

That he did.

"You know where he might be?"

Reese shook his head. "Haven't got a fuckin' clue. Toby's a nice guy. He's got good intentions. At least I think he does. But he's what you'd call flaky."

Brantley chuckled. "Sounds like it." His expression turned serious. "You think he's in trouble?"

"I do. Yeah. And I think my do-gooder brother wants to help the guy out."

"By takin' him in?"

Oh, if it could only be that easy. "More like findin' him before the bad guys do. I'm sure this'll turn into babysittin' duty before it's all over."

"Does your mom know what's goin' on?" Brantley smirked again. "I mean, are they still—"

"Don't say it," Reese choked. "Don't go there. Don't put that image in my head."

Brantley laughed, the sound both sexy and annoying. "I think it's too late for that, don't you?"

Reese closed his eyes and grimaced as he fought the images that tried to imprint on his brain.

CHAPTER THREE

Brantley figured he shouldn't find the entire situation amusing, but he couldn't help it. It sounded like something right out of a Ryan Reynolds movie. Seriously. Who steals a car to run from a loan shark and decides it's a good idea to ram a police car as a cry for help only to learn that you've got drugs in the trunk?

Well, that would be a guy who used to share Reese's mom with Reese's dad. That in itself was amusing because Brantley knew Reese's mother, and the absolute last thing he would've ever guessed was that Cindy Tavoularis was into stuff like that. Not that he was knocking it. To each his (or her) own. But Cindy? He just couldn't see it.

He chuckled, finishing off his extra-crispy bacon. Not that he was going to mention that Reese had overcooked it. He figured that was the least of their worries at the moment. Plus, Brantley wasn't picky when it came to bacon. As long as it wasn't plants disguised as bacon, he was golden.

Clearing his throat, he looked at Reese. "If it's all the same to you, I say we find Uncle Toby—"

"*Please* don't call him that."

Brantley tried to hide his smile, but he failed. "Fine. We'll find Toby, and when we do, we can deliver him safely to police custody so they can get him to the courthouse where he belongs."

Reese's brown eyes narrowed. "You make it sound like this'll be simple."

Clearly, Reese knew something Brantley didn't, but that didn't change anything. He was actually looking forward to taking a case that didn't come with ridiculous amounts of stress. When he'd originally agreed to create a task force dedicated to finding missing people, he hadn't exactly thought it through. In fact, it wasn't until a couple of weeks ago, when Trey opted to go a different route, that he realized just how stressful a job they had. From the moment they took a case, they were working against the clock. Because someone's life hung in the balance, it meant eating and sleeping took a back seat to finding that person.

Now that he thought about it, it wasn't much different than when he'd been in the Teams. Most of their missions were at a critical level, but life had been different back then. Brantley's entire existence had orbited around his job, his career in the Navy. He'd welcomed the danger and the adrenaline rush that'd come with it. But that was then. His path had changed. No longer was he on the hunt for terrorists or searching for weapons of mass destruction. He had a life now. Family, friends. And most importantly, a man he wanted to dedicate his time to rather than be out there trying to save the world every minute of every day.

So, yeah, Brantley couldn't say he didn't welcome a change of pace.

He got to his feet and grabbed his plate, carrying it around to the sink and setting it aside before stepping up to Reese, who was still leaning against the counter, arms crossed over his chest. He gently took Reese's wrists and urged his arms down to his sides before moving closer.

"If you give me one solid reason why we shouldn't do this, I'll call Z and tell him it's not an option."

Reese's eyes locked with his. "I have a dozen excuses but no valid reasons."

He loved this man's honesty.

Smiling, he leaned in and pressed a kiss to his lips. "Then we're doin' this."

Reese relaxed a little, his hands resting on Brantley's hips. "Just as long as we don't bring in the rest of the team."

"No? I figure JJ might be impressed that Cindy's—"

"Jesus *God*, don't say it," Reese rumbled, his face pinched.

Brantley laughed. "Fine. We'll leave the team out of it." Brantley kissed him again. "If another case comes up, they can handle it while we look for Unc—Toby."

Reese's head tilted slightly. "You're gonna enjoy this, aren't you?"

"Meetin' a man who had a threesome with your mom…"

"Eww." Reese pulled away. "That's just— God. I think I need to bleach my brain now."

Brantley laughed, then turned to the sink to take care of the dishes.

An hour later, after he'd run Tesha through some of her training exercises, Brantley went in search of Reese. He found him upstairs in his office, his laptop open in front of him. He was looking at it, but the way he was rubbing his temples told Brantley he wasn't seeing much of the screen.

Sympathetic to the situation, Brantley strolled around to stand behind him. He took over massaging his temples while Reese leaned back in the chair.

"You do that and I won't be able to focus."

Taking that as a challenge, Brantley continued until Reese had relaxed fully against the chair, his shoulders loosening, his hands falling into his lap.

What he wanted to do was strip the man down and ravish him with his tongue. It was hell honing his patience, especially these past few weeks when the only thing he cared about was making up for lost time. Resisting the urge to take him on every available surface was a true test of his control. Didn't matter that they'd made love early this morning, Brantley still ached for Reese in ways that defied logic.

However, he hadn't made it through BUD/s because of his looks. He was a Navy SEAL, and the one thing he could count on was his dedication to the mission. Even if it was finding a cooky old man prone to doing stupid shit.

"Tell me about Toby," Brantley prompted. "You said he was your dad's best friend in high school."

"That's the stories I remember," Reese said, his words accompanied by a soft moan when Brantley shifted to massaging his scalp.

"So he's from here?"

"Born and raised right here in Coyote Ridge."

"Does he have any family we can talk to? Maybe they've seen him."

"No family and no friends that I can find."

"Did you call your mom?"

Reese tilted his head to the side and peered up at Brantley, one eyebrow raised.

"Would you prefer *I* call her?" Brantley offered.

Leaning forward, Reese dropped his head in his hands, shaking it emphatically. "I'd prefer neither of us did."

"Scared she's gonna give you the dirty deets of her torrid fling with him?"

When Reese looked up, his eyes were wide, his mouth hanging open, his expression horrified.

Brantley barked a laugh. "Sorry."

"No, you're not."

He laughed again. "No, I'm not. When did you learn about…?" He waved a hand. "You know."

"If you're thinkin' I walked in on them or some shit, you're wrong. Not the way you're thinkin', anyway."

Brantley turned toward the window, smiling as he stared out. "Could you imagine?"

"No," Reese snapped. "No, I definitely can't. And don't try to put images in my head."

"I wouldn't dare." He glanced back over his shoulder. "Seriously. When did you find out?"

"Not until years after he stopped coming around. At least I thought he had." Reese exhaled. "I was in the air force, home on leave. When I got to my parents', Toby was there with my mom. Dad had run to the store, I think."

Brantley turned around, leaned against the wall, and watched Reese as he processed the memory.

"Toby had apparently spent the night." Reese's face pinched in a grimace. "He was walkin' around in his boxer shorts, and my mom…" He shook his head again.

"So you *did* catch them?"

Reese grunted as he flopped back against the chair. "They were kissin'. I lost my shit when I saw them. It wasn't until my dad came home a couple minutes into my tirade that I calmed down. He tried to explain, but I didn't stick around to hear it."

Brantley tried to imagine what that would've been like. His parents hadn't been into that sort of thing, but they had been very intimate throughout his youth. Hell, Frank and Iris had seven kids, so it only made sense, but that hadn't made it any easier. Avoiding walking in on them had become an art form in itself. And yes, thinking about it still made him cringe. The thought of coming home to find his mom making out with a man who wasn't his dad … yeah, he couldn't do it. He *wouldn't* do it.

"Eventually, I heard my dad out, forcing him to gloss over the details," Reese continued. "I didn't understand it, but I didn't hold it against them. According to my dad, it wasn't serious. I mean, they weren't lookin' to make it a permanent thing between them."

"And after the accident?" Brantley prompted, hoping to delicately navigate the sensitive subject of Thomas Tavoualaris's car accident that had ultimately left him in a coma for his remaining years. "Did Toby come around?"

"He did, yeah. He was there for my mom." Reese's eyes slammed into his face. "As a friend."

"Understood."

"She would've seen it as a betrayal," Reese said. "Hell, my dad was in a coma for years before she ever even considered datin' anyone else. Then Hugh came along."

Brantley knew that Cindy and Hugh had been friends first. Cindy had remained faithful to Thomas for the many years he spent in a coma, being cared for by others in a long-term care facility. She probably would still be single if it weren't for Hugh.

"You should talk to your mom," Brantley suggested. "Maybe she's talked to Toby recently. It's possible she'll know where he is."

Reese sighed. "You're right." He closed his eyes. "But I'm gonna need a minute."

Smirking, Brantley slipped out of Reese's office and headed toward his own. While he found Reese's pain amusing, at least regarding his mother's youthful exploits, he did have some sympathy.

Not to mention, he expected to get laid in the near future. The last thing he wanted was to really piss Reese off.

REESE DIDN'T KNOW HOW MUCH TIME HAD passed before he finally worked up the nerve to call his mother. Fifteen minutes? Forty?

Not that it mattered. Ten years could've passed and he still wouldn't have been prepared for the conversation currently taking place.

"I haven't seen Toby in … well, I guess it's been about a year now."

"A year?" Reese's tone was a bit harsher than he'd anticipated. "Does Hugh know about Toby?"

A soft chuckle sounded on the other end of the phone and he was grateful he hadn't opted to make a FaceTime call. If he had, his mother would've seen his face, and right now, he figured it was about the color of a beet because, try as he might, he couldn't get those images of Toby kissing his mother all those years ago out of his head.

"Of course he does," Cindy said smoothly. "I've told him everything."

"*Every*thing?"

"Yes," she said more insistently. "Hugh's well aware of the fact I had a sexual relationship with Toby while I was married to your father."

"Oh, God, Mom!" Reese covered his eyes as though that would block out what she'd just said.

"Reese Jacob Tavoularis, you're a grown man, and I happen to know you're not a prude, so don't pretend that you don't understand."

"Understanding's *not* the problem, Mom. *Hearin'* about it is the problem."

His mother laughed. "Well, it doesn't change the fact that it's true."

Unfortunately. "So you haven't heard from him lately?"

"No. Like I said, it's been about a year."

"Did you know he was arrested a few months ago?"

"Arrested?" She sounded sincerely shocked. "Why? What happened?"

Well, that told Reese exactly how much effort Z had put into this. If he had to guess, his brother wanted to look like he was doing a good deed, but he didn't want to be the one to have to get up close and personal with the guy who'd banged their mom at one point in her life.

He put his hand on his stomach, wishing his churning gut would settle. This was not exactly how he'd wanted to spend a Saturday. Or any day, for that matter.

Reese gave his mother the high-level details based on the police report he'd managed to wrangle up. If he hadn't known the man, he would've thought it was a plot for some action-comedy based on the description from the police officer whose car had been hit.

"No one's that unlucky," Cindy said with a hint of amusement in her tone.

"Toby is." Reese sighed. "Do you happen to have a way to get in touch with him? I've got a phone number, but it's disconnected."

"Toby's the type who drops by when he's in the mood. I've never called him."

Reese groaned.

Another soft laugh sounded in his ear, but then thankfully, his mother changed the subject. "How're you feeling?"

"Physically, I'm fine," he assured her. "Mentally, I'll be screwed up for the rest of my life."

"So dramatic. I guess it's a good thing you're not in charge of the wedding. How's Brantley?"

"He's good." Reese's gaze drifted across the open space to Brantley's office. "Really good."

His mother sighed. "I'm glad to hear it. I'm glad things are workin' out for you boys."

Yeah, he was, too. Nearly losing the man he loved had been a life lesson he never wanted to relive. Now that he had a second chance, he knew there was nothing and no one who would stand in the way of him doing everything in his power to make that man happy.

"Anything else you want to interrogate me about?" Cindy asked, her tone light. "Perhaps you'd like me to forewarn you about Hugh's friend Mark."

"Mom!"

Cindy giggled uncontrollably. "Fine. I won't tell you. But if he's ever in trouble, I'll make sure Hugh knows you don't want the details."

Reese groaned so hard it made his throat raw, and that seemed to entertain his mother even more.

"Any more questions about Toby?" she prompted when her laughter faded.

"Not at this time, but I reserve the right to change that in the future."

His mother laughed, and it made Reese relax a little. Although he didn't care to think about her sex life, he was glad his mother was happy. That was truly all that mattered in the long run.

"If you do find Toby, be nice to him, Reese. He's a very sweet man, even if he doesn't always make the soundest decisions."

Figuring his poor heart couldn't handle the details of what she might be referring to, he opted not to ask her to clarify. "I'll tell him you said hello."

"All right. Remember, we'll be coming down in a couple of weeks. I'm meeting with Iris to finalize some of the details for the wedding. And I fully intend to be there when you go for your tuxedo fitting."

"I'm pretty sure I can do that on my own. I've been dressin' myself for years now."

"You could, yes. But why would you? My baby boy's getting married. I intend to be part of every step."

"I appreciate it, Mom." And that much was true. While he would've been completely content to elope, he knew Cindy and Iris were looking forward to a big wedding. And he suspected deep down Brantley was, too. For that reason alone, Reese was willing to jump through whatever hoops they put in front of him.

"I'll call you later, Mom. Tell Hugh I said hello."

"I will. I love you."

"Love you, too."

When the call disconnected, Reese set the phone on the desk. As he was getting to his feet, Brantley was doing the same.

Before he could tell Brantley about the conversation with his mother, the man was smiling.

"How do you feel about full nude cabaret?"

Reese stopped walking. "Unless you'll be the naked one singin' show tunes, I'd say it's a hard pass for me."

Brantley smirked. "You want me to sing? Because I will."

Reese chuckled. "Only if you're naked."

"That can be arranged. You just hafta say please."

Knowing this was about to go down a rabbit hole, Reese redirected. "Did you find somethin'?"

"I found out where Toby likes to spend his time. Thought maybe we could swing by there. Talk to the manager."

"I was thinkin' we'd start with his house first."

"We could do that, too." Brantley frowned. "I'm sure the police have been by there already, though."

"True. Doesn't mean he's not hidin' out in a makeshift bomb shelter hidden in a secret compartment in his alien spaceship in the backyard."

Brantley smirked. "He has one?"

Reese shrugged. "Wouldn't surprise me if he did."

They could swing by Toby's, and if they were lucky, he'd be there, and their assignment would be complete. And if not, they could head over to the cabaret. At least it was early in the day. With any luck, everyone in the place would have their clothes on. And if not … well, it couldn't be any worse than the mental image of his mother with…

"Oh, Jesus," he muttered as he followed Brantley toward the stairs.

"Still thinkin' about it, huh?"

"Just kill me now."

Brantley's laugh echoed all the way down the stairs.

CHAPTER FOUR

JESSICA JAMES STARED OUT THE TRUCK WINDOW, willing her stomach to stop churning.

"I think I'm gonna be sick," she muttered.

Baz's head turned so fast it was a wonder she didn't hear his neck crack. "Do I need to pull over?"

JJ sighed heavily, wishing it could've been that simple. "No. It's not mornin' sickness."

Thankfully, she hadn't been plagued with the type of pregnancy illness she'd read horror stories about. At fourteen weeks along, she'd figured it would've presented itself by now, so she considered herself lucky in that regard. Every now and then she'd get a little queasy, and admittedly, there were foods that the mere thought of turned her stomach, but no endless bouts of toilet hugging for her. Not yet and hopefully not ever.

Nope. This wasn't a pregnancy-related issue. It was a meet-the-parents issue. And the closer they got to Baz's dad's house, the worse it got.

"I promise, they don't bite," he said, his tone reassuring.

"What if they ask me questions? What am I supposed to say?"

"Will it help if I demand they remain silent the entire time?"

She glanced over at Baz. "Would you?"

He grinned, his eyes on the road. "Of course."

"Would they do it?"

"Not in a million years."

When Baz reached for her hand, she linked her fingers with his. His touch soothed something inside her, even if it didn't help ease her anxiety. She'd never met the parents before. Not in the traditional, let's-take-the-next-step-in-our-relationship sorta way, at least.

Well, that wasn't exactly true. She'd met Dante's parents, but that was back when she was a clueless, naive teenager who'd thought her high school boyfriend hung the moon, so it didn't count. Since he'd been the only semi-serious relationship she'd ever had, that had been an exception. As far as the rest, JJ wasn't sure whether half the guys she'd dated even *had* parents.

"I don't know how to do this," she admitted, trying to take deep, steady breaths.

Baz squeezed her hand. "Sure you do."

She huffed. "I don't even talk to my *own* parents, Baz."

His eyes flashed with sympathy when he peered over. He didn't say anything, and she was grateful. The last thing JJ wanted was to get into a conversation about how she was estranged from her mother and her father, and they were estranged from each other. Their lives had been torn apart when her brother, Jeremy, ended his own life all those years ago, and JJ had never really put forth the effort to fix things. Even now, with a baby on the way, she had no desire to talk to them.

However, she knew Baz had a good relationship with both his parents. And oddly enough, they had a good relationship with each other despite the fact they were divorced. If she was being honest, that was one of the motivations for actually doing this. JJ was curious because she'd never met anyone who had a good relationship with their ex.

"They're gonna love you, JJ. Just like I do."

She seriously doubted that, but she appreciated the sentiment.

Half an hour later, Baz was pulling the truck into the vast estate that belonged to his wealthy father. JJ had been here before because Baz had utilized his father's guest house as a safe space for her after her attack when Dante had staged his own kidnapping. Funny how whenever she thought about the thirty-seven-hundred-square-foot architectural marvel, she imagined air quotes around *guest house*. And while she didn't know what Baz's father's house looked like because they had never ventured over to the main residence, she figured it was going to be impressive. Based on the accommodations he afforded those who were merely visiting, this was going to be an experience she wouldn't soon forget.

No sooner did she think about it than the house appeared in all its wondrous glory. Like the guest house, it was an architectural eye-gasm. Two stories chock full of clean lines, white walls, and acres of glass had JJ's breath lodging in her chest. If she could've designed a dream house, this would've been it.

Baz circled the enormous pond in front of the house and pulled the truck to a stop.

She peered over. "Are there fish in there?"

"It's a koi pond," he said as though that simplified things.

"Seriously?"

"My father has an affinity for beautiful things."

Yeah, she'd heard he'd had numerous wives, so that seemed a given.

"Welcome to my father's house," he said, motioning out her window at the front door. Nope. Scratch that. Doors *plural* because there were two enormous solid wood panels that kept people out. They had that burned wood design, darker in certain spots, with a high-gloss shine. If she had to guess, the doors were nine, maybe ten feet tall and about as wide.

"JJ?"

"Hmm?"

"Breathe, baby."

"Easier said than done," she mumbled, not taking her eyes off the house. "No valet?"

Baz chuckled, then got out of the truck. She waited for him to come around to her side, but only because her hands were trembling so much she didn't think she could get the door open on her own.

Why was this so freaking hard? It wasn't like they were aliens from another planet, and she was going to be asked to join their race and move to Mars. And it wasn't like she was a social hermit. She could talk to people when she had to. Plus, she was strong and intelligent, and… Baz opened her door, cutting off her internal motivational speech. Before she could step out, he moved in close. He cupped her cheek, turning her head toward him as he leaned in and pressed his lips to hers.

"Do you need a safe word?"

She laughed, pulling back to meet his gaze. "You joke, but maybe."

He grinned, and his handsome face relaxed one of the knots in her chest. She was tempted to tousle his silky blond hair and thank him for being so protective. But if she did that, she would probably try to seduce him into taking her back home, and the last thing she wanted was for Baz to realize she was a coward.

She could do this. She could. It wouldn't be easy, and she doubted it would be fun, but she knew Baz's parents were important to him. The fact that she hadn't met them yet was her fault. JJ was a chickenshit, there was no doubt about that, and she'd broken things off with him because of a suggested outing very similar to this one. But that was eons ago. Back before she'd thought the only man she had ever truly loved was going to have a baby with another woman. And if there was one thing she'd learned from the events of the past year, it was that she did not want to spend the rest of her life without this man. Which meant she had to put on her big-girl panties and do grown-up things like meet the parents.

"You ready?"

No. She nodded, then took Baz's hand when he offered it.

He led her along the decorative concrete path, allowing her time to admire the clean, white stucco house that was offset by the dark wood that lined the underside of the overhang protecting them from the Texas sun.

He was almost to the front doors when she jerked on his hand, pulling him to a stop.

With endless patience glittering in his teal-blue eyes, Baz looked down into her face.

"What's your dad's name?"

His smile was slow and so sexy, it was a good thing she wasn't moving, or she would've tripped over her own feet.

"Wesley. His wife's name is Aretha."

JJ frowned. "I thought it was Anna."

"No. Anna was my nanny when I was a kid."

"Right."

Wesley and Aretha. She hoped she could remember that.

"And my mother's name is Julie. My dad calls her Jules; everyone else calls her Julie."

Oh, jeez. She was never going to get that one right.

Baz leaned down and kissed her sweetly. "You've got this. They're gonna love you."

Yeah, well, she was about to find out whether or not that was true.

BAZ USED HIS THUMB TO OPEN THE biometric lock that granted him access to his father's house.

He heard JJ's sigh, figured she was likely impressed by the man's security. If she only knew all that this modern monstrosity entailed. Biometric locks were just the first of many things to protect his father's modern-day fortress and those who inhabited it.

"Ready?" he prompted with his hand on the steel handle.

"Not really, but let's do this."

Smiling, he opened the door of his father's house, JJ's hand gripping his like he was leading her to the gallows, not into a ten-thousand-square-foot mansion where her future-in-laws lived.

His grin widened, but he kept it hidden. The last thing he wanted was for her to know he was already thinking about marriage. If she knew, she would likely turn and run for the hills as fast as her sexy little feet would take her. He had every intention of marrying JJ, but taking things slow with her was the only way to move forward. Hell, it was a wonder she'd even agreed to meet his parents, and he figured the *only* reason she had was because she was having his baby, and she knew this would be something his parents wouldn't want to miss out on.

Just thinking about JJ carrying his child made his chest swell with love and pride. He remembered the visit to the doctor when they'd gotten the official confirmation and seen the first images of their future son or daughter. Despite having a name that reminded him of a dating app, Baz had liked the doctor who would be along for the journey. Dr. Tinder had assured them that the baby's heartbeat was strong, and he saw no complications thus far, sending them off with a sense of relief so potent Baz still didn't remember the drive home.

"Welcome, welcome. Y'all come on in," his father's voice sounded from deeper in the house. The man's thick Texas drawl was a direct contradiction to the modernness that was his lifestyle.

JJ's hand tightened on his.

Baz grinned, leading the way through the large open foyer with its dual staircases—complete with floating steps and glass railings—that led to the second floor. JJ was looking around, her eyes wide as she took in the decor. In the center of the circle was an enormous bonsai tree that his father cared for like his own child. The thing was fed by a rainwater delivery system, for fuck's sake.

But he figured JJ hadn't noticed the indoor topiary because her attention had been ensnared by the bookshelves that lined the outer walls, two stories high and filled to overflowing with vintage and antique books. There was no pretentious library for Wesley Buchanan. Nope. The man's love for reading superseded any desire to keep his prized possessions hidden away.

"Is that what you expected?" Baz asked.

"No." Her voice lowered. "Dead animals, maybe, but not books."

Before he could explain his father's love for the written word, Wesley appeared before them, his expressive face shifting into a wide grin. "There's my boy."

As expected, JJ's eyes widened as she took him in, and he knew without asking that she noticed the resemblance. Baz was the spitting image of his father, always had been. They shared the same thick blond hair and teal-blue eyes, along with the square jaw and thick eyebrows. The only thing Baz hadn't gotten from his father was his height. At six one, Baz was a few inches shorter. Since his mother topped out at five two, he considered himself lucky.

Baz smiled at his father. "Dad, I'd like you to meet Jessica James. JJ, meet the old man."

Wesley's bright blue eyes settled on JJ, and Baz saw the insta-love that glittered in them. That was Wesley Buchanan for you. The man did love a beautiful woman, and in Baz's humble opinion, there wasn't a more beautiful one on the planet than JJ.

"It's a pleasure to meet you, ladybug," Wesley said, his deep voice rich with awe. "Tell me I can hug you, girl."

JJ giggled nervously. "Sure."

As though he was handling a fragile package, Wesley put his arms around JJ and pulled her into his big body, hugging her warmly. His father was a big man, but it wasn't just his above-average height and those broad shoulders that made him larger than life. His personality was just as big, and Baz figured JJ would fall in love with his irresistible charm the same way all women did. Well, not *exactly* the same way, but he had no doubt she would find him fascinating.

Over JJ's head, Wesley's eyebrows rose, his approval evident as he smiled at Baz.

Releasing her, Wesley turned his arm, draping it over JJ's shoulders as he steered her away from the entry and deeper into the house. Baz followed behind them, grateful JJ couldn't see his smile.

"You have a beautiful home, Mr. Buchanan," JJ told him.

Baz relaxed a little, pleased that she was making an effort. He'd been waiting for this day. The day he would introduce the people who meant the most to him to the woman he loved more than life. From the moment he'd met JJ, Baz had known one day she would be embraced by his family, and now that the day had arrived, it would forever be imprinted on his brain.

"Call me Wes, darlin'. And thank you. It's my sanctuary."

They walked down the wide hall that bracketed the courtyard and one of two swimming pools that his father utilized often. The house had been designed around the courtyard, forming a C and lined with glass to let the outdoors in as much as possible.

"What can I get ya to drink?" Wesley asked, guiding JJ through the living room and toward the kitchen, which had always been the heart of this home.

"Iced tea would be good, Dad," Baz answered for her.

"With lemon or without?"

"Without," JJ said, her tone relaxed.

Expecting to find stepmother number six waiting for them in the kitchen but finding it empty, Baz asked, "Where's Aretha?"

"Your mama dragged her off to the store with her. Somethin' about a cake." He shrugged his broad shoulders. "I don't know about them girls."

JJ grinned up at him when Baz moved to stand at her side.

"You good?" he whispered.

When she nodded, he put his arm around her shoulder and pulled her close, pressing a kiss to the top of her head. She sighed, relaxing against him.

"They should be back soon." Wesley peered over, pulling a glass pitcher out of the fridge, his eyes filling with affection when he saw Baz with his arm around JJ. "Y'all go on and get comfortable. Can I get you somethin' to eat? We've got a big spread all ready to go. Aretha's all about brunch."

Baz looked at JJ. She shook her head, so he relayed the answer to his father, then led her over to the thick slab of sealed granite that created the table in the breakfast nook. Of course, *nook* was a term he used loosely since the table seated ten and took up more space than Baz's entire kitchen at his apartment.

"Thank you," JJ said kindly when Wesley delivered the glasses of iced tea along with a full pitcher in the event they needed refills.

No sooner did his father take a seat than they heard voices and laughter coming from the hallway leading to the garage. A second later, Aretha and Julie stepped into the kitchen, their gazes slamming directly into JJ as though they'd been magnetized to do so.

"She's here," Baz's mother said with a beaming smile. "I can't believe she's here."

JJ's hand landed on Baz's thigh beneath the table, squeezing gently.

Baz settled his over it and said, "Mom, I'd like you to meet Jessica James. JJ, this is my mother, Julie."

"Oh, my. It's a pleasure to finally meet you," Julie said, stepping back and motioning for Aretha to come over. "This is Aretha, the much younger, much prettier version."

Aretha lightly slapped Julie on the arm. "That is not true." She giggled. "Well, maybe the younger part."

Yes, the younger part was most definitely true. While Baz had grown up with a variety of stepmothers over the years, Aretha was by far the youngest in relation to his age. At thirty-nine, Aretha was only six years older than him, making her thirteen years younger than his mother and twenty-seven years younger than his father.

He wasn't going to mention that Aretha was only one year older than JJ. He knew age was a point of contention for her, but his father didn't have a problem with it, clearly.

"I'm sorry," Julie said as she moved around the table. "I'm gonna hug you."

JJ laughed but managed to turn in her chair as Baz's mother approached. She stood to return the hug, smiling widely when Julie held on to her hands as she stepped back, staring with both awe and pride on her pretty face.

"God, she's beautiful, Baz."

He'd known this would happen. His parents had been waiting for the day he would bring a woman home. While he hadn't had the chance to introduce them, he had told his parents everything about JJ. All the good things, anyway. He'd purposely left off the rocky state of their relationship, but only because he didn't want to sway their opinion of her. They were a protective lot. But they still would've loved JJ even if he had told them how things had fallen apart for a while. As far as they were concerned, this was a long time coming, and he couldn't say they were wrong.

"We got a cake," Aretha announced, gesturing toward the enormous white box sitting on the counter.

"What's the occasion?" he asked, glancing between them.

"We don't need a reason for cake," Julie said, releasing JJ and moving over to the center island.

"Well, that's too bad because we've got somethin' to celebrate," he said softly, waiting until all eyes moved to him.

His mother's eyes widened in anticipation.

Baz glanced between his mother and father, unable to stop the smile from splitting his entire face.

"Well, come on now, boy. What're we celebratin'?"

Baz peered at JJ, ensuring she saw all the love he felt for her.

"Are y'all getting married?" Aretha asked hopefully.

JJ snorted.

Baz smirked. "We are." He quickly looked at his parents. "But not yet."

Julie's smile faltered.

"First, we're gonna have a baby."

The squeal that split the air was loud enough to damage his hearing.

What made it even better … it came from his father.

CHAPTER FIVE

"ALL THINGS CONSIDERED, IT DOESN'T LOOK AS bad as I expected it to," Brantley told Reese as they stood in Tobias Land's once modernly decorated living room, surveying the damage.

Toby wasn't home, but Brantley hadn't figured he would be. When no one came to the door, it'd been the work of a moment to pick the lock and enter, but as Brantley took in the scene before him, it was a wonder the front door hadn't been standing wide open already. Evidently, someone else had come looking for Toby already, and he seriously doubted the police had done this.

From the looks of it, the entire house had been ransacked, at least if the living room was any indication. The furniture was overturned, pictures and knickknacks knocked off the walls and shelves. Books had been shredded, pillows turned into ribbons, white fluff bleeding onto the floor around them.

In all fairness, Brantley was merely assuming someone had gone through the place. He didn't know Toby Land, and Reese had said he was a little out there, so perhaps this was a unique decorating style, but he didn't think so.

"I'm startin' to think this isn't retaliation for stealin' a car," Reese mused, his gaze skimming the space.

Brantley would have to agree. "They were lookin' for somethin'."

"Question is, did they find it?"

Yes, that was *one* question. Another was what exactly had Toby taken that would require someone to go through this much effort to get it back? Or had they been looking for a clue as to where Toby had gone? The latter seemed a stretch, considering how they'd gone so far as to take apart the remote control and dismantle all the artwork that had been on the walls and shelves.

"Let's clear the house first," Brantley told Reese, feeling an itch on the back of his neck because they'd yet to move past the living room.

Ten minutes later, after they'd cleared every possible hiding spot in the house, Brantley returned to the living room. He picked up a picture from the floor, turned it over in his hand.

"I think you might've been right when you said he was in love with her," he told Reese when the man joined him.

"What?"

Brantley passed over the picture. It was one of Toby and Cindy, obviously taken many years ago. The photo depicted a handsome young man pressing a kiss to Cindy Tavoularis's cheek, his arm hooked around her neck as she smiled lovingly at the camera. They were leaning into one another in an embrace that spoke of their familiarity and affection for one another. If he had to guess, Reese's father had been the one on the other side of the camera.

"He doesn't look like a kookie old man," Brantley noted, referring to the handsome, dark-haired guy in the photo. Based on that image alone, Brantley couldn't blame Reese's mom for having a thing for him.

Reese's gaze snapped to his, and his nostrils flared.

It took effort, but Brantley managed not to smirk. Instead, he grabbed several other photographs that had been peeled from their frames, giving them a quick once-over as he set them down on the highboy behind the couch. There was one more picture of Cindy, this one of her by herself. It appeared to have been taken more recently. Another was of a couple with a little boy and a little girl, all four smiling.

"Those are his parents," Reese informed him, peering at the picture over Brantley's shoulder.

"That his sister?"

Reese nodded, his expression solemn.

Since Reese had already said Toby had no family in the area, Brantley could only assume there was a story behind it.

Rather than ask for details, Brantley strolled through the house, looking for clues as to where Toby might be. Overlooking the damage that had been done, it appeared Toby hadn't been home in a while. Nor had he taken anything with him when he left. The bathroom held all the necessities, and there was a suitcase lying on the closet floor, open but empty.

Based on the decor, the guy had both taste and money. While the house wasn't elaborate, someone had put some thought into the interior design. High-end fabrics, expensive Swarovski crystal knickknacks, and artist-signed paintings no longer held any monetary value due to their current state, but it had likely once been a comforting place to come home to.

After fifteen minutes of snooping, Brantley returned to the living room to find Reese with his phone to his ear and the picture of Cindy and Toby in his hand.

"I'd feel better if you put someone on her, Z," Reese said firmly. "I don't know who's lookin' for him, but they seem desperate to find him."

Brantley moved closer. When he did, Reese held up the photo so Brantley could see the back of it. Cindy's full name was scribbled on the back, circled by a heart.

"Thanks," Reese said. "I'll let you know what else we find."

A second later, he disconnected the call.

"I don't want them usin' her to find him," Reese said, as though he needed to explain anything.

"You don't think he'd head that way, do you?"

Reese met his gaze and shook his head. "He's a little flaky, but he'd want to protect her at all costs. Going up there would only put her in danger."

Brantley considered that. "Since we're here, we should look around. See if there's anyone else he might want to protect."

Reese nodded.

When he didn't move from the spot, Brantley smiled and said, "We should start in the office."

Reese was still staring at the picture of his mother and Toby when he responded to Brantley with an unenthusiastic, "Yeah."

He wasn't sure what they expected to find here, but he doubted it would net them much. He got the feeling there was a lot more to this situation than Z was letting on. That or his brother didn't know the entire story, and he was expecting Reese to do the heavy lifting. Now that he'd seen the picture of Toby and his mother, he knew he had no choice but to see it through. If there were even a remote chance his mother was in danger because of something Toby had done, he would get to the bottom of it.

With a resigned sigh, he set the picture down and headed in the direction Brantley had disappeared.

Toby's office looked much the same as the rest of the house. In a word, it had been destroyed. The bookshelves were empty; everything that had once been on them was on the floor. If it was glass, it was shattered. If it was paper, it was tossed about, most of it torn in two. There was a four-drawer filing cabinet that was no longer intact. The frame had been toppled, and the drawers were on the floor, everything in them dumped in a pile. Reese squatted down to sort through the folders lying haphazardly in the rubble.

"Looks like he had a computer," Brantley said from behind him. "Either he took it or whoever tossed the place did."

Reese glanced over, saw he was holding up miscellaneous cords with nothing connected to them. "Not a laptop, then."

"Not in here, anyway," Brantley noted. "What does the guy do for a living?"

"Some kinda high-paid sales rep."

"What does he sell?"

Reese shrugged. He figured he should probably know that little detail, but he didn't. Truth was, he hadn't given Toby much thought in years. The man had been a part of his life as a child, but not much after that. And once he'd discovered the relationship between him and his mother, he'd forced the man out of his thoughts entirely. Hard not to considering whenever he'd thought about the man, Reese remembered Toby kissing his mother that day.

A shiver ran down his spine, and he shoved the thought from his mind, picking up one of the folders and skimming what was left of the papers inside. It appeared he kept only essential things like tax documents and whatnot. Nothing related to a business.

"You might call your mother," Brantley suggested. "See if she can give you some insight into his job. Not sure it's related, but it could be."

Yeah, at this point, he figured anything was possible.

Reese spent a few more minutes rummaging through the remnants of the file cabinet. He was about to give up when he felt the edge of something bump his finger as he reached in to pull out a sheet of paper. Taped to the side wall was a large manilla envelope. Inside, he found a passport and social security card, bank statements, the deed to the house showing it was paid for, as well as finalized tax filings. You wouldn't know it now, but the guy appeared to have been organized.

While Brantley continued to root around at the desk, Reese ventured into the other rooms. A guest room held nothing personal, so he moved on from there. The guest bath resulted in the same.

He headed to the master bedroom but didn't linger too long. The dresser was empty, all the contents on the floor. Among the shredded clothes, he found a watch case. It was one of the big ones that people bought to store expensive watches that required movement to keep them functioning. It was empty. Had Toby taken the watches, or had the intruder stolen them? Considering the circumstances, he figured it was the latter. Although, now that he thought about it, there were plenty of expensive art pieces that had been destroyed rather than stolen, so who knows.

He peeked in the bathroom before moving through it to the closet. Again, nothing of value and nothing that would tell them what Toby had been up to recently.

With a sigh, Reese returned to the living room. He hadn't expected to find anything that would lead them to where Toby was hiding, but he wouldn't deny he'd been hoping. Maybe a deed to a cabin in the woods or a lake house. Somewhere Toby could go to hide out. Then again, there could've been something and whoever got here first had it, but he would never know.

He heard Brantley in the kitchen, so he headed that way, again hoping the man had better luck. When their eyes met, he saw the disappointment instantly and knew they wouldn't be finding Toby the easy way.

"Call your mom," Brantley urged, turning to face him. "Maybe if we can check out his place of business, we'll find something that'll help."

Reese nodded, pulling out his phone. He dialed, then moved to the back door and peeked out the blinds covering the small window.

"Hey, honey," she greeted kindly. "Two calls in one day. I'm starting to feel special."

"Where does Toby work?" he asked, forgoing the pleasantries.

She cleared her throat, then said, "Last I talked to him, he'd started his own travel agency."

Reese frowned. "I thought he was a sales rep."

"At one point in his life, sure. Toby's never been … what's the word? Loyal, I guess, to any one profession. Your father called him a wandering entrepreneur. As long as he could work for himself, he was willing to give it a try."

"Did he rent office space?"

"Honestly, I don't know. Why? What's wrong?"

He proceeded to give her the rundown of the state of his house.

"That's terrible," she said with exasperation. "God, I hope he's all right."

Yeah, Reese did, too.

"He's got a picture of you and him, Mom," Reese said, heading back to the picture lying on the table where he'd left it. "He wrote your name on the back, so Z's gonna post some bodyguards with you for a little while."

"What? Why?"

"We don't know who's after Toby, but whoever it is went to a lot of trouble lookin' for somethin'. It's better to be safe than sorry. If you hear from him, I need you to call me."

"I won't," she said, and if he wasn't mistaken, there was a hint of disappointment in that statement. "Hear from him, I mean. Of course I'd call you."

"Did somethin' happen?"

"After your father died," she said softly, "Toby came around a little. I think he was hoping to pick up where we left off."

Another shiver slithered down his spine.

"But I'd met Hugh by then and…"

Reese didn't need her to finish that statement. He knew how his mother felt about Hugh, knew they were happy together. And if she hadn't been joking about Mark—*God, he hoped she'd been joking*—then he figured there was no room in her life for Toby anymore.

"Watch your back, Mom," he said with a heavy sigh. "We're gonna keep lookin'. I'll let you know when we find him."

"Be careful, Reese."

"Always."

He disconnected the call and turned to find Brantley standing there, staring at him expectantly.

"From what I gathered, he doesn't have stable employment. She said last she talked to him, he was starting a travel agency."

Brantley frowned, standing tall. "I saw a brochure in his desk." He started toward the office. "I didn't think anything of it, but maybe it's his."

Reese followed him down the narrow hall and into the office. When Brantley passed over the glossy, trifold brochure, Reese skimmed it.

"Land Ho!" he read aloud.

Brantley chuckled. "Creative if he specializes in cruises."

Based on the pictures in the brochure, it looked like he did.

"There's a phone number," he noted, pulling his phone from his pocket and dialing. "Damn it. It's disconnected."

"We could get JJ to trace it? If it's a cell, maybe it'll give us somethin' to go on."

Reese glared at him.

Brantley put his hands up in surrender. "Okay. What if we ask Luca? I'll be discreet about it."

Blowing out a puff of air, Reese considered his options. Based on what they'd found so far, there was nothing that would help them find Toby or whoever was looking for him. He figured this was a dead end, but unfortunately, it was the only lead they had.

"Fine," he said. "But don't you dare tell him the guy had a thing with my mom."

Brantley laughed. "I promise."

Shaking off the disturbing thoughts, Reese thrust the brochure back at Brantley and turned and left the room. He didn't stop until he was back in the truck.

CHAPTER SIX

HALF AN HOUR LATER, BRANTLEY PULLED THE truck into the empty parking lot of the Red Room Revue. He hadn't bothered sharing the name of the cabaret club with Reese, figuring he would let it be a surprise. Not that the guy needed any more surprises today, but he hoped this one might lighten the mood.

"Oh, Jesus," Reese grumbled. "Are you fuckin' serious?"

Brantley chuckled. "I thought it was kinda catchy."

He put the truck in park and got out, scanning the area, noting what was around them. It wasn't Sixth Street or anything, but it wasn't as rundown as he'd thought it would be. Across the pot-hole-riddled road, there was a taqueria, and next to it, a donut shop. Beyond that, more little retail shops, many of them specializing in adult pleasure.

"It fits right in," he noted when he joined Reese as they walked toward the door.

Reese's eyebrows shot into his hairline. "You ever been to a strip club before?"

Brantley held the door open so Reese could enter, smiling at the question. "Many times."

He wasn't surprised to see Reese's forehead creased in confusion.

"I was a SEAL, remember? One of my guys had a life goal of visiting every strip club in the world."

"Seriously?"

"Oh, yeah. And I wasn't into makin' things awkward for my teammates." He huffed a laugh when Reese's confusion still didn't clear. "It didn't do anything for me if that's what you're wonderin'."

"What about a male strip club?"

Brantley chuckled. "Can't say I've been to one of those. You?"

Reese rolled his eyes, then turned his attention to the woman strolling toward them. "We need to speak to the manager."

"My name's Janeese. I'm the manager." She was a soft-spoken black woman with glossy straight hair that cascaded down her back and somehow accentuated her hourglass figure. He wasn't sure whether she'd been an entertainer at some point, but he could imagine how she would strike someone's fancy. "How can I help you?"

Brantley peered around the space while Reese pulled out his phone and flashed a picture of Toby.

When Reese asked, "Have you seen this man lately?" Brantley watched the woman's expression, looking for the truth.

"Not in a while, no."

"But you know who he is," Brantley said, not bothering to phrase it as a question because he'd seen the recognition in her eyes.

"I do. Toby Land. He's one of our frequent flyers. He used to date one of our girls. He hasn't been coming around lately."

"Is she here?" Reese inquired. "The girl he dated?"

"Serendipity? No."

Well, if they had any hopes of singling out a woman for more info, Brantley figured Serendipity would be an easy name to track down. Of course, he wasn't sure it was her *real* name, but still.

"Does she work tonight?"

Janeese's gaze slid toward the back, but she thought she was being discreet. "She does. Should be here around eight."

Brantley caught movement at the back, saw a man coming through a door marked EMPLOYEES ONLY. He was a burly guy with a bald head, a wrinkled forehead, and no discernible neck, the kind who pretended those extra layers of fat were actually muscle. With his chest inflated and his chin tipped back, he moved toward them, his hand shifting his cheap suit jacket back to reveal the weapon holstered at his hip.

Feeling ornery, Brantley put his hand on the butt of his gun, smiled. "Your hired muscle gonna have a problem?"

Janeese glanced back over her shoulder. She forced a smile, but her tone held a hint of discomfiture when she said, "That's Ronny. He's a big teddy bear."

Sure he was.

"Well, you might wanna tell Quick Draw McGraw we're not here to cause problems." Brantley met Janeese's gaze. "I'd hate to shoot him."

Her eyes narrowed, but she masked her expression quickly before forcing another smile. "As I said, we haven't seen Toby around lately. Is there anything else I can help you with?"

"Do you have a way to get in touch with him?" Reese inquired, his attention moving between Ronny and Janeese.

"No, but if you see him, you can let him know his loan's come due, and the big boss wants to talk to him," Ronny said, a slight whine in his voice.

Brantley fought the urge to smile. "Where might the big boss be now?"

"Takin' care of business."

"So he owns the place?" Reese asked, stepping past Janeese to speak directly to No Neck Twitchy Fingers.

Brantley noticed the way Reese's shoulders squared, as though he was gearing up for a fight. If he wasn't mistaken, there was a sheen of sweat on his brow, too. Actually, now that he was looking, he noticed Reese's hand was trembling, his eyes darting to the gun on the big guy's hip frequently.

"Why don't we just leave a card," Brantley suggested, stepping in front of Reese and pulling a card from his pocket to pass over to Janeese.

When she took it and glanced down, Brantley nudged Reese's arm, lowered his voice, and said, "They don't have a beef with us."

Reese's eyes lifted to Brantley's face, and for a second, he saw the wild, unfettered fear in them.

Hoping to distract Reese from what he clearly perceived as a threat, Brantley put his hand on his shoulder, squeezed lightly. "Let's go see if we can find Uncle Toby. I'd like to hear some of his stories."

That seemed to shake Reese out of his funk because his eyebrows danced upward, and his eyes cleared. A groan rumbled in his chest, and he knew the man was thinking about Toby and Cindy and their … history.

Disaster averted.

At least for now.

REESE WALKED OUT OF THE CABARET CLUB, doing his best not to notice that his hands were still trembling. He was the only one pretending if the empathetic look Brantley was shooting his way was any indication.

"I think our best option's to talk to Serendipity," Brantley said as they got into the truck. "Who names their kid Serendipity, anyway? Or you think that's a stage name?"

"I'm fine," Reese said, acknowledging that Brantley was trying to create a diversion.

"Are you?"

Reese appreciated that there was no accusation in Brantley's tone. He sounded sincere and, yes, a little worried. Reese couldn't blame him. There for a minute, he'd thought he was having a panic attack. Okay, fine. He probably had been having one, but acknowledging it wasn't going to make anything better. Then again, denying it would only make it worse.

Fuck.

He exhaled heavily and nodded. "Yeah. I'm sure. I'm good."

The silence that lingered told Reese that Brantley didn't believe him. He wasn't sure how to prove otherwise since it technically was a little white lie.

Brantley hit the button to start the truck. "How about this? Since it's obvious the big boss doesn't know where Toby is either, I say we head to the range for a couple of hours and waste some time until Serendipity's at work. This evenin', we'll come back, see if we can chat with Toby's ex, and figure out where he might be. In the meantime, I've got Luca lookin' into the phone. If he finds somethin', we'll check it out first. What'd'ya say?"

"Sure."

Brantley turned toward him.

The next thing Reese knew, a hard hand was on the back of his neck, and he was being pulled forward until his mouth was almost touching Brantley's.

His voice was low and husky when he said, "It's either that or I take you home and fuck you because right now, that's the only thing I can think about. I figured the range would be a good distraction for both of us."

Reese relaxed a little, letting the warmth of Brantley's hand on his neck settle him. He leaned in, took that kiss Brantley was offering. He let it linger for longer than he'd intended, and when he came up for air, he was ready for the second option.

Brantley's hand lightly massaged the back of his neck as he pressed his forehead to Reese's.

"How about this? We'll go to the range, then grab some lunch. After, we'll head back to the house. I'll fuck you, then we'll do some more research on who this guy is that Toby owes money to."

"Okay," Reese said softly, running his hand over Brantley's arm. He couldn't pretend he wasn't affected by the fact Brantley wanted to take care of him, even if it was by providing a way to get his mind off the aftereffects that still lingered in his brain from having been shot point-blank. Since that day, he'd had a different outlook on guns than before. More specifically, on being on the bullet end of one.

"I'd kiss you a little longer, but I think we're drawin' an audience," Brantley whispered.

If he'd said it to get a reaction out of him, he failed because Reese responded with, "Let 'em watch," before he kissed Brantley again, lingering a little longer this time.

When they pulled apart, Brantley groaned, adjusting himself as he sat back. Reese glanced out the window, noticing Brantley hadn't been lying. They did have an audience. It was the guy from the club—Ronny, he believed his name was—and two more goons. They were standing near the wall, glaring daggers in their direction.

"Maybe Matt'll let us shoot the AKs," Brantley mused.

Reese couldn't stop the grin as the last of his trepidation faded away.

At least for the time being.

Three hours later, they were walking into the diner, and Reese was feeling like himself again.

A nudge on his arm had him glancing over to see Brantley silently gesturing for him to look at something. He followed his gaze and found Luca Switzer sitting in a booth with Honor Anderson, one of Brantley's many cousins. They appeared to be in a heated conversation, neither looking pleased to be in the other's company.

"Are they seein' each other?" Reese asked, following the hostess who was leading them to their table.

"No idea. But it damn sure doesn't look like he's workin'. I gave him somethin' to do. He should be doin' it."

Wanting to avoid a scene, Reese urged Brantley to keep moving. "It's Saturday. Everyone deserves a day off. I'm sure he'll get to it when he's finished here."

Because he could feel Brantley's curiosity, he took a seat, leaving the other side of the booth available for Brantley so he could keep an eye on things from afar. He probably shouldn't be enabling him, but he could tell there was more than curiosity burning in Brantley's gaze. Reese didn't know Honor well, but he did know that she and her three sisters—Whitney, Violet, and Amanda—were kinda like the Rapunzels of the Walker clan. Rather than let the witch get her hands on them, though, the Walkers had formed a metaphorical protective wall around the women to keep their magical powers protected from evil almost from birth.

Granted, they didn't really have magical powers, nor did they appreciate the overprotectiveness of the bunch, but it didn't change anything.

"He's a good guy," Reese reminded Brantley before grabbing one of the menus from the slot on the table and shoving it toward Brantley. "And you're starin'."

Brantley cleared his throat, his gaze swinging over to Reese. He at least had the decency to appear sheepish.

"They're both adults," Reese said when Brantley's gaze swung over to the table again. "She's not a fairy princess in need of savin'."

"According to my family she is," Brantley grumbled.

Although he was curious as to the reason behind the family's protectiveness of the women, Reese wasn't sure he was in the right mindset to hear it at the moment. Every time he tried to think about something else, his thoughts drifted back to Toby and his mother and whatever convoluted relationship they'd had going on back in the day.

"What can I get you?" the waitress asked as she stepped up to their table.

Grateful for the interruption, Reese glanced at Brantley. He grinned when the man acted as though he wasn't sure where he was or what the waitress was offering.

"Two sweet teas, and I'll have the chef salad," Reese told her when Brantley didn't speak up. "Ranch dressin' on the side."

Brantley's eyes slid toward him, and amusement replaced the confusion. "And I'll have real food. Double bacon cheeseburger, well done. Double order of fries."

With a smile, the waitress jotted it down and then sauntered off.

"Rabbit food?" Brantley asked, settling into his seat.

"I think I've put back on all the weight I need to," he admitted. He'd been working on adding back the pounds he'd lost after he'd gotten shot. Being back with Brantley had made it easier than it would've been otherwise. Not only because Brantley's diet was the equivalent of a teenage sports player but also because he'd found peace in being home.

But now that he was healed and healthy, he figured it was time to stop acting like he was a growing teenage boy. Brantley got away with it because he had the metabolism of a hummingbird. Reese wasn't so lucky.

"You won't hear me complainin'," Brantley retorted, his eyes flashing with heat.

Warmth filled Reese's chest, and the dregs of the earlier incident faded away completely.

CHAPTER SEVEN

IT TOOK EFFORT, BUT BRANTLEY MANAGED TO make it through lunch without confronting Luca and Honor. It really was none of his business who his cousin dated. Not to mention, Reese was right; Luca was a nice guy. He likely had nothing to worry about where his cousin was concerned.

Not that Brantley was going to give him a stamp of approval. He'd let someone else in his overprotective family have that duty.

"I think I recall you offerin' a distraction," Reese said as Brantley was pulling the truck into their driveway.

All thought of Luca on a date with his cousin vanished from his head, replaced with mental images of Reese naked on the bed.

"I recall that, too," he replied, turning off the truck's engine. "Can't very well do that out here, now, can we?"

He could tell Reese was trying to determine where his head was at. He figured that was a good thing. Brantley hated seeing that faraway look in Reese's gaze, the one that spoke of the traumatic event that was disrupting his sleep and making it difficult to function. Brantley'd been there. Hell, he was still there, but his demons were at bay momentarily. He figured that had something to do with the fact he wanted to take care of Reese. And not just sexually. However, he wanted that more than his next fucking breath.

When they got inside, Tesha loped their way, tongue lolling out of her mouth.

"You miss us, girl?" Reese asked, giving her head a rub. "How 'bout a treat?"

Her hind end started wagging excitedly as she trotted along beside him into the kitchen.

Brantley detoured toward the sofa, dropping down onto it with a sigh. The normality of this moment sent a surge of relief through his entire body and had him wondering if this was what it would be like after they were married.

His thoughts drifted to the last conversation he'd had with JJ. She'd gone through a list of about four million things she was working on with Iris and Cindy for their big day. He wasn't sure giving them carte blanche was the right way to go, but since JJ had assured him he would have to do nothing aside from getting fitted for his tux and showing up for the wedding, he couldn't very well complain. As long as he didn't have to pick out patterns or food, he was willing to take the risk.

"What's on your mind?" Reese asked when he joined him in the living room.

"Thinkin' about marryin' you," he said, smiling.

"We're still on for that?" Reese teased.

"Countin' down the days." Brantley peered up at him, relief morphing into heat that penetrated his bloodstream and made his fingers itch with the need to touch this man. "Come here," he urged, patting his thighs.

Reese's eyebrows shot skyward. "You want me to sit on your lap?"

"I want you to straddle me, yeah," he corrected, relaxing back into the cushion.

To his surprise, Reese wasted no time kneeling on the sofa. As soon as he did, Brantley pushed his hands beneath Reese's T-shirt, seeking smooth, warm skin. He would never tire of touching him, that much he knew for certain.

"Take off the shirt."

Reese was watching him intently, but he did, pulling his shirt over his head and tossing it beside them.

Brantley's gaze slid to the scar on Reese's chest, the one made by the bullet that had nearly claimed his life. A knot formed in his throat when he remembered Reese telling him he'd been in ICU for several days after Brantley had returned to Coyote Ridge. He'd left Dallas after learning Reese was stable, and no one had told him otherwise. Not Z, not RT, not Cindy. He wasn't sure why that was, and he was scared to find out, which was the only reason he hadn't brought up the subject, despite how hard it was to even talk to Z, knowing the man had kept it from him.

Then again, Brantley was the one who'd run away. He'd let Reese's betrayal send him careening in a different direction. He'd thought the man was recovering, which was the only reason he'd left, but little did he know, he could've lost him.

Firm fingers pressed the middle of his brow, pulling Brantley from his thoughts.

"What's botherin' you?" Reese asked, smoothing away the frown line.

He ran his hands over the smooth planes of Reese's chest and smiled. "Nothin' at all."

As he explored Reese's upper body, Brantley watched the way his expression evened out. The more he touched him, the more Reese relaxed, their eyes locked for long minutes as though they were sharing a silent story between them.

Sitting forward, Brantley brought their mouths together. He kissed Reese as he shifted him down onto his back, reversing their positions until Brantley was looming over him. He got lost in the throaty moans that escaped Reese as he began kissing down his neck, his shoulders, his chest. He kept going, taking his time, his hands and mouth wandering over smooth, warm flesh.

When his lips trailed along the fine hair that dipped into Reese's waistband, all those sleek muscles in Reese's abdomen tightened. Brantley sat on his haunches, straddling Reese's thighs, and watched his face as he began unbuttoning Reese's jeans.

"I could do anything I want to you right now," Brantley mused.

"Anything," Reese echoed, smiling. "And not just right now."

Yeah, he suspected that was the truth. There was so much trust in Reese's gaze, it humbled him beyond measure.

Once Reese's jeans were unbuttoned and unzipped, Brantley dipped his fingertips into the waistband of Reese's boxers, brushing the swollen head of his cock.

Reese sighed, his eyes closing.

He teased him for long minutes, grateful some of Reese's stress from earlier had vanished. Once Reese was completely relaxed, Brantley took his thick, heavy cock in his mouth, licking, laving, sucking until he was tense and trembling, but this time for an entirely different reason. Only when he was drawn tight as a bow did Brantley send him careening over the edge and into the abyss.

"WHERE ARE YOU GOIN'?" REESE ASKED WHEN Brantley got to his feet, leaving him in a boneless, sated heap on the couch.

"I've got some research to do."

Reese twisted his body, attempting to follow Brantley with his gaze. The task was impossible when Brantley headed for the stairs.

"That's not fair!" Reese shouted after him, yanking his jeans up. "I didn't get to return the favor."

"I'm ready whenever you are, Tavoularis," Brantley called back.

Chuckling, Reese managed to right his clothes while his labored breaths evened out. He'd been hoping to get in on the action, but it appeared Brantley had other things to do. That or he was fucking with him. Reese knew it was entirely possible he could go upstairs and find Brantley naked in his office, cock in hand. He loved that about him, the spontaneity. It kept him on his toes.

Unfortunately, Brantley wasn't naked, and he wasn't teasing himself while waiting for Reese to join him.

"One second, my dick is in your mouth; the next, your face is buried in your computer screen," he mumbled, stopping in the doorway and leaning against the jamb.

"What can I say? I'm an enigma."

Reese laughed, realizing the tension in his shoulders was gone entirely. But that tension had been replaced by an overwhelming need to get his hands on Brantley, to bring the man to orgasm with his mouth and hands. He felt he'd been on the receiving end a little too much as of late. He needed to find a way to turn the tables and get Brantley beneath him for a change.

"I wish like fuck Luca would get me that information," Brantley said, fingers moving swiftly over the keyboard. He huffed. "I hate to say this, but we might need JJ's help on this."

"Not an option," Reese said quickly.

"If you're worried that she'll judge you, you—"

"She's meetin' Baz's parents today," Reese inserted, effectively cutting him off.

Brantley's gaze shifted from the computer to him, his eyebrows lifting. "That's right. She is."

"Which means gettin' her help isn't an option. JJ and Baz need this time together."

Brantley's smirk was slow and sexy, his amusement not so much.

"And not *only* because I'd prefer to keep the hunt for my mother's former lover a secret," Reese tacked on. "We're on our own for this one."

One of Brantley's eyebrows arched. "What about Luca? I could call him. Tell him it's urgent."

"We're not draggin' his ass over here on a Saturday so you can disrupt his date with your cousin. He'll get to it when he gets to it."

Brantley rolled his eyes.

Reese grinned. "We might not be computer geniuses, but I think we can handle findin' one man."

"And how do you propose we do that?"

"Well, I think it might help if we check out the last known address for that travel agency. There's a good chance he had neighbors. Might've even kept in touch with them."

Brantley leaned back in his chair, angled his head as though studying him. "So, what you're sayin' is I just needed to suck your dick to kickstart your brain?"

Reese barked a laugh, completely shocked by that statement, although he wasn't sure why.

Brantley's answering smile said it had hit the mark, and Reese realized the man was still handling him, doing whatever it took to keep his mind off of what had happened earlier.

One of the many, *many* reasons he loved this man.

Reese pushed off the doorjamb, moving into Brantley's office. When he moved to the side of the desk, Brantley followed his movements by turning his chair.

Reese held out his hand, waited for Brantley to take it. When he did, he tugged, urging him to his feet.

"Where're we goin'?"

"*You* are gonna sit down on this couch," Reese told him, leading him to the black leather sofa.

Before Brantley could flop down, Reese grabbed the waistband of his jeans, fumbled with the button, freeing it.

"Whatcha doin', Tavoularis?"

"Takin' what belongs to me," he said, looking down as he freed Brantley's cock from the confines of his jeans.

He shoved the denim down Brantley's lean hips until it was around his thighs. Reese looked up, smiled at Brantley, then pushed on his chest, sending him down to the couch with a grunt.

"You think puttin' *my* dick in *your* mouth'll kickstart *my* brain?"

Reese chuckled. "It's worth a try, don't you think?"

Brantley appeared to consider that, tilting his head to the side before finally saying, "Eh. Worth a shot."

"Challenge accepted."

The moment Reese took Brantley's cock in his mouth, that devil-may-care attitude faded away. Reese hummed and sucked, worshiping the man the same way Brantley did him. He took his time, ensuring not to send Brantley over the edge too quickly, wanting it to be as good for him.

"Fuck," Brantley whispered, palming Reese's head, holding him still as he rocked his hips. "Your mouth … I fuckin' love your mouth."

Reese bobbed his head, taking him to the root, sucking more insistently.

"Reese…" Brantley's palms tightened on his head, effectively stilling him. "Lemme fuck your face."

Heat zinged down Reese's spine at the crudeness of the comment, but he remained still as Brantley began driving his hips up, fucking Reese's mouth while mumbling his name again and again.

"Oh, fuck ... too good." Brantley fisted Reese's hair hard enough to send a pain so sharp it bordered on pleasure shooting through his scalp. "Oh, God!" Brantley drove deep into Reese's throat and growled. "Oh, fuck ... swallow."

The instant Reese did, Brantley bellowed, shooting right down his throat.

"I'm not sure ... about bringin' ... mental clarity," Brantley huffed and panted, sliding his hands over Reese's head as he sat up. "But fuck me ... that was ... fuckin' incredible."

Reese couldn't agree more.

CHAPTER EIGHT

"I HAVE TO ADMIT, I'M A LITTLE surprised by you."

JJ glanced over at Baz, who was looking all kinds of sexy behind the wheel of his truck. She couldn't explain why she found him so hot, regardless of what he was doing, but she did. Perhaps it sounded a little creepy, but now that she'd met Baz's father, she found him even hotter. If he aged as well as Wes had, he would only get more handsome in the coming years.

"Why? What did I do?" She stared at him, trying to decipher his words. "I was on my best behavior."

Baz chuckled softly, a delectable sound that always warmed her from the inside out. "Better than best, I agree."

"Then how did I surprise you?"

His gaze cut over briefly before returning to the road as he drove them home. "Well, for starters, you agreed to have lunch with my mother next week."

JJ felt her face warm. She wasn't sure why she was embarrassed to be called out on that. She had accepted Julie's invitation to lunch, just the two of them, without hesitation. There was something about the woman that made JJ feel comfortable.

Granted, she'd taken into consideration Julie Buchanan could very well be setting her up for an interrogation. Baz was her only child, and there had been indisputable proof that he was a household favorite. From what JJ had surmised, Baz was loved, and his happiness was his parents' primary motivation.

"Why did your mom keep your dad's last name?" she inquired, giving voice to her burning curiosity.

"Because of me."

Ah. Well, that made a lot of sense. She kept the same name as her only child.

"Where's her husband? I thought he'd be here?"

For the first time all day, she noticed Baz's expression shutter.

"Is somethin' wrong between them?"

He sighed, then fiddled with the air conditioner vent. "Dad told me she's gettin' a divorce." He cut his eyes to her for a second, then turned them back to the road. "She hasn't told me yet, and I don't know why."

"Oh, shit. I'm sorry." JJ peered out the passenger-side window. "Maybe she's worried you'll be upset with her. Do you like the husband?"

"For starters, don't feel bad for her. I'm sure it was her idea. My mother's not quite the wanderer my father is, but she's not an easy woman to pin down. She hasn't had as many weddings, but she's had just as many … *others* as my father."

"So you're sayin' it's their natural progression? It's time to move on? Or are they not gettin' along?"

Baz shrugged. "He's been traveling to Japan a lot. It bothers her that he's been there more than he's been home in the past year."

JJ could understand that. She could understand being with someone who traveled, but not if it meant they spent more time away than home. What would be the point in staying with someone when you couldn't spend time with them?

"Which means there's likely an expiration date for Aretha," Baz added, his tone somber.

She could tell there was a story there, and she wanted to hear it more than anything, but JJ didn't know how to phrase the question, so she remained quiet, hoping he would continue. When he didn't, she made an assumption. "Your dad's still in love with your mom, huh?"

He chuckled. "Very much so. Always has been, and I suspect he always will be." He glanced over. "She's the love of his life."

"Is the feelin' mutual?"

"I think so, but my mother doesn't think he's the type who can commit for the long haul. His track record proves it."

"Because he's been married six times?"

Baz's focus remained on the road. "Yeah. Twice before my mother."

"Has she always been friends with his wives?"

"Every single one."

JJ had picked up on the fact that Wes and Julie were friends. Real friends. And she'd sensed the same between Julie and Aretha. It was obvious they were all fond of one another, which had made the visit easier to deal with. At first, it had seemed odd, but the longer they'd stayed, the more comfortable she'd gotten being around them. Probably had something to do with the fact that her own parents couldn't be in the same room with each other if there were sharp objects. Hate wasn't a strong enough word to describe what her parents felt for each other. And that was before Jeremy's death. They simply used her brother's suicide as an excuse for everything that had gone wrong in their lives.

"Have they ever tried to work things out? You know, since the divorce?"

Baz shook his head. "My mom swears they're better as friends."

Yeah, JJ wasn't so sure that was a fair assessment. She'd seen the way Wes looked at Julie. The man's eyes heated in much the same way his son's did. Granted, he was careful to mask it, but JJ had noticed.

"As they say, the heart wants what it wants," she mused, staring out the window.

Baz chuckled. "I think this pregnancy has turned you into a romantic."

JJ grinned. She didn't know about that, but she wouldn't deny she had a better outlook on things now than she had. That likely had something to do with Baz and the way he'd steamrolled right into her life and into her heart before she was prepared. Now that she knew firsthand what it felt like to be left loving someone who wasn't available, her internal wiring had been reset.

And because she'd been given a second chance—something that had never happened before—she wasn't going to question it.

When JJ got quiet, Baz worried that he'd ruined the lightness of the day by discussing his parents' imploding relationships, so he opted for a different tack. The last thing he wanted was to leave JJ with a bad feeling about his parents. They weren't the sort to conform to society's rules where love and relationships were concerned, but they had a way of making things work out for themselves, and he loved them for it.

"You want to go check on the house?" he suggested, glancing over at JJ. "See if they've made any progress?"

"Yes!" Her response was instant and ringing with excitement, her eyes glittering when she looked his way. "Is it wrong of me to want them to hurry it up?"

He chuckled. That was the same question she asked every time he brought up the house they'd recently purchased. They had officially closed on the property Bristol Walker had so kindly sold them, and they were well into the renovation stages. It helped that Bristol had allowed them to start getting things in order before it became theirs. It had saved them significant time because they'd been able to get the plans and the permits for the addition to the back. It had taken some compromise on both their parts, but they finally decided on a master suite and an office space for the new construction while making a few minor adjustments to the existing structure. They'd focused a majority of their money on updating the kitchen and existing bathroom and removing some of the walls to open up the space.

The general contractor they'd hired had told them three months for completion, including the planning and permitting phase. That meant they still had a couple of months to go, but Baz was as eager as JJ to get moved into the house. He was ready to start this new phase of his life with the woman he loved, and this seemed like the perfect first step.

"They're workin' today," JJ announced when they pulled up to the house a short time later.

"And that means I need to go in first," he informed her, anticipating JJ's exasperated sigh that came a moment later.

"Fine," she huffed. "But I'm comin' in, so don't you dare tell me it's too dangerous."

Baz was actually surprised that JJ had conceded this argument when it had first come up. While she didn't look pregnant physically—not quite yet—he wasn't taking any chances with her safety. Granted, it hadn't been a fun conversation when he'd first brought it up, insisting that she not go traipsing into a construction zone unprepared.

"I'll hurry," he assured her before getting out of the truck and heading to the front door.

A few minutes later, after he'd ensured there were no gaping holes in floors that she might fall into, he went back to the front porch. As he'd expected, JJ was pacing the small walkway that led to the driveway. When she heard the door open, her eyes snapped up to him.

He pushed the screen door open wide, holding it for her. "Come on."

A smile pulled at her full mouth as she bounded up the stairs, her excitement palpable.

Sometimes it was difficult to tie this new JJ to the one he'd fallen in love with all those months ago. She'd been through a lot in the past year, but you wouldn't know it by looking at her. Of course, sleeping beside her was a different story. The nightmares that jarred her awake at night were ever present, a glaring reminder of the hell she'd lived through after the ordeal with Dante. He knew she was trying to work through it on her own, but there were still signs that she was suffering from PTSD. The fact that she didn't want to be left alone was the most prominent. She didn't stay at the apartment without him, preferring to go to HQ since she insisted Brantley's converted barn with all its security was a much safer place for her.

Truth was, Baz wanted her to feel safe here, too. That was the reason he'd made a few minor adjustments to the plans after JJ had signed off on them. Nothing significant, but he was putting some safety measures in place, including a top-notch security system that even a world-class hacker like her wouldn't be able to breach.

"What are they workin' on to—?" JJ's words cut off when she stepped into the house, her gaze on the man installing the panel beside the door.

"JJ, this is—"

"Leif Walker," JJ said with a grin.

Looked like introductions weren't necessary.

Leif turned to look at JJ, his smile slow as recognition set in. "Well, I'll be damned."

Baz watched the interaction between the two. "I take it you know each other?"

"We went to school together," JJ explained, her gaze sliding to Baz. "Kinda. They were a couple of years behind me, but there's not a person in Coyote Ridge who's not familiar with the twins who put a pig in Principal Tucker's office."

He raised his hands, palms up, in a sign of innocence. "In my defense, it wasn't feral."

"That didn't stop it from eatin' a good chunk of his desk."

Leif laughed. "We're never gonna live that one down."

"It was pretty impressive." JJ grinned. "And more than a little destructive."

"Just a little," Leif agreed, using his fingers to demonstrate a small amount.

"I thought you and your brother owned a security system company," JJ noted, glancing for the first time at the panel on the wall.

"We do." He gestured toward the panel. "And you, my friend, are gettin' the top-of-the-line package."

JJ's gaze shifted back to Baz, and he could see the questions burning in her gaze. He smiled. "Surprise."

He watched as it registered and felt a hint of relief when her expression relaxed. Of course, that relief was short-lived when, a moment later, tears formed.

Oh, hell. He knew he should've talked to her first. Now he'd gone and made her cry.

His heart squeezed tight in his chest as he stepped toward her. "What's wrong? Did I screw up?"

"Nothin'." She shook her head dramatically and looked away. "And no, you didn't."

Baz frowned, glancing over at Leif, who was staring at her like she'd grown a third eyeball.

JJ waved them off. "Hey, I'm pregnant. That's the *only* reason I'm cryin'."

Baz laughed, relaxing once more as he pulled her against him and let her bury her face in his chest.

These were good tears, he realized.

When she went up on her toes and put her mouth close to his ear, Baz's entire body heated.

"You're gettin' laid when we get home, Detective," she whispered, her words spoken so softly he hardly heard them.

Then again, his cock heard them loud and clear.

CHAPTER NINE

TURNED OUT THAT THE RETAIL SPACE WHERE Toby had set up shop for his travel agency netted them nothing, but Brantley hadn't expected that it would. Well, nothing more than confirming he had been in business at one point. The space had already been rented out again, this time to a real estate broker taking advantage of the hot market.

The neighbors on either side had nothing to contribute to finding Toby. However, the consensus was that Toby was a nice guy, and they had hated to see him go. Friendly and chatty seemed to be the theme when describing Tobias Land.

"Two down, one to go," Brantley told Reese as they walked to the fourth and final shop in the small commercial space.

Reese swung the door open, triggering a bell to ring above it. When they stepped inside, Brantley was instantly assaulted by a thousand different smells that merged into one rather unflattering scent. He instantly felt sorry for Tesha and her keen sense of smell. If he'd known they were coming here, he would've left her at the house again despite the fact he knew Reese preferred her with them at all times.

"Maybe they should light only one candle at a time. Or one *scent* even," he murmured as he led the way toward the counter at the side of the long, narrow space.

Reese's response was a choked agreement.

"Good afternoon, gentlemen," a lively bald man said, a beaming grin splitting his long, narrow face. He had enormous brown eyes set in sockets as wide as saucers. "How may I assist you today?"

Brantley stepped aside and let Reese do the talking. He inquired about Toby, flashing the picture he had on his phone.

"Oh, yes," the man said in an effeminate croon, his gaze sliding from the phone to Reese, then traveling very slowly up and down.

Brantley fought the urge to grin. There was no mistaking this man's interest in Reese.

"And you would be?" he inquired, cocking a hip and smiling up at Reese.

"Reese Tavoularis." Reese pulled out his credentials as he tilted his head toward Brantley. "This is my partner, Brantley Walker. We're with Sniper 1 Security."

Based on the man's expression, Reese had told him he preferred long walks on the beach and quiet dinners by firelight, not the name of the company he worked for.

He held up his hand, tilting it the way a royal lady would when she was expecting to be greeted by a gentleman. "Carl Woods," he introduced, fluttering his fingers before dropping his hand when Reese didn't take it. "And who would this be?" he asked, glancing down at Tesha.

As soon as he started to reach for her, Reese said, "She's working. Please don't touch."

Carl's eyes shot up to Reese face, but even that didn't deter his interest.

"Do you know Toby?" Brantley asked, trying to ease the awkwardness filling the space faster than the overpowering floral scent of the candles.

Carl glanced his way briefly, then fluttered his lashes at Reese. "Sure. I know Toby."

Looked like the uncomfortable situations were going to continue coming Reese's way today. Brantley couldn't keep from grinning, enjoying the fact Reese was getting hit on.

"Can you tell us the last time he was around here?" Reese inquired, oblivious to the fact this man was all but drooling.

Carl cocked a hip and drummed a finger on his lower lip. "It's been a while. Six months, maybe. Why do you ask?"

"We think he might be in trouble," Reese said simply.

"I'll say." Carl waved a hand dramatically. "Those goons came by two days ago looking for him."

The way he referred to them as *those goons* told Brantley this wasn't the first time he'd seen them around. "You recognize the men who came lookin' for him?"

"*Do I?*" he retorted dramatically as he fluttered a hand. "They came by at least twice a week when Toby was at work."

"He knew them?" Reese questioned.

"If I had to guess, he did business with them. Or with their boss, anyway."

Brantley glanced at Reese. He wasn't sure he liked the way that sounded.

Carl was watching them closely, but his gaze continued to slide over Reese as though he was caressing him with his mind. "I tried asking him about them once, but he shrugged it off. Said they were potential clients."

Clients? Were they simply coming to collect the money Toby owed? Or was there more to this story than they knew?

Carl's expression shifted to pleasant, and Brantley saw the salesman morph into place. "Could I interest you in something?" he offered Reese, and Brantley knew it wasn't an accident that he waved his hand down the front of his body as though offering himself up.

He considered letting Reese handle this one, but there was a good chance this man would never stop calling if Reese gave him his card, so Brantley produced one of his.

"If you happen to see or hear from Toby, would you mind givin' me a call?" he said as he passed it over.

Carl took the card and skimmed it momentarily before looking up at Reese expectantly. "And you, handsome? You happen to have a card you're willing to give out?"

Brantley chuckled softly.

Reese, finally recognizing what was going on, cleared his throat. "I don't."

"Well, that's too bad. I happen to have a fragrance here that's guaranteed to put you in the mood."

Brantley was turning toward the door when he heard Reese say, "I happen to have someone who handles that rather easily, but thanks."

"Lucky woman."

Reese laughed. "Definitely not a woman."

The smile that formed on Brantley's mouth was likely going to be planted there for the foreseeable future.

REESE HAD NEVER BEEN MORE DESPERATE FOR fresh air than he was as they strolled out of the small candle shop. He didn't dare look back, feeling Carl's eyes boring holes into him as he walked away.

"Sorry about that, girl," he told Tesha, helping her into the truck.

He climbed into the passenger side and buckled his seat belt.

"You enjoyed that a little too much," he told Brantley as they were pulling out of the parking lot of the retail center.

"What? That he was flirtin' with you?"

Reese rolled his eyes and looked out the window, but his smile came easily.

"I'm curious about one thing, though."

Reese peered back at him. "What's that?"

"Just *how* easily do I put you in the mood?"

"It only takes a look, Navy boy."

The sound of Brantley's laughter rolled through him. "My wickedly skilled mouth doesn't hurt either, huh?"

"It's not bad."

Brantley's head snapped over, eyes narrowed. "Not bad?"

Reese laughed, content he'd managed to get that parting shot in there. "You might just need a little more practice."

"Yeah?"

Reese's thoughts drifted back to the earlier encounter on the couch when Brantley had blown his mind with minimal effort. Any witty retort he'd intended came out as a groan as his body hardened just from the memory.

He managed to keep himself under control, not wanting this to get out of hand since they still had work left to do.

Brantley's cell phone rang.

"Walker," he answered curtly.

"Hey, boss." Luca's voice came through the speakers in the truck.

"Tell me you found somethin'," Brantley said in lieu of a pleasantry.

"Not much, but I was able to get you the last location that phone pinged from. It's a pretty rural area about an hour from here. I checked out satellite images, and it looks like a lake dotted with a few cabins. I can't pinpoint which one."

"Send me the coordinates," Brantley instructed. "We're gonna go check it out."

"Will do. Anything else you need?"

Reese watched Brantley, waiting for him to bring up that Luca had been out with Honor earlier. He could tell it was hovering on the tip of his tongue, but to Reese's surprise, he didn't mention it.

"No. We should be good. I'll hit you up if I need anything else."

"Sure thing, boss."

The call disconnected.

"I have to say, I'm impressed," Reese told him.

"Don't be."

"Oh, come on, now. Luca's a good guy. I'm sure your cousin's in good hands."

Brantley's head snapped over. "Please don't mention Luca's hands and my cousin in the same sentence."

Laughing, Reese relaxed against the seat and stared out the window. "Wait. Where're we goin'? I thought we were headin' to the cabaret."

"Nope. I've got Slade and Evan doin' that."

Reese sat up straight. "What?"

He noticed Brantley's Adam's apple bob slowly in his throat before he said, "I doubt we'll get through the door of the club, much less get a chance to talk to anyone."

That made a ridiculous amount of sense, but Reese didn't think that was the reason Brantley had opted to send them in their place.

"I'm good, Brantley," he said smoothly. "I swear it."

Brantley peered over briefly before turning his attention back to the road.

"You don't believe me."

There was no response.

Reese considered getting pissed at that, but he refrained. For one, he still recalled the panic that had flooded his system when he'd seen the guy at the club earlier. Even now, the bullet wound in his chest throbbed whenever he thought about what had happened that night.

"Thank you," he said simply, reaching over and putting his hand on Brantley's.

To his surprise, Brantley turned his hand over and linked their fingers. "It takes time."

He knew that. As much as he wanted to believe he was back to his old self, he knew better. He was still screwed up in the head. The good news was, there had been a time when he hadn't been sure he'd ever be able to overcome the trauma of what happened that night. However, being home, being with Brantley … he felt himself getting stronger both mentally and physically.

"What do you say we take a drive," Brantley said, giving Reese's hand a squeeze. "See if maybe Toby's hidin' out at the lake."

"Sounds like a plan." After all, it sounded like a much better idea than going to an all-nude cabaret.

SLADE ELLIOTT GOT OUT OF THE CAR and closed the door as he stood staring at the mural painted on the brick wall that held the entrance to the Red Room Revue.

"You ever been here?"

He glanced over at Evan Vaughn and raised an eyebrow. "Do I look like a guy who frequents this type of place?"

"You want an honest answer?"

Slade chuckled, then smiled unabashedly. "Fine, but no, I haven't been to this particular establishment."

Didn't mean he wasn't a fan of strip clubs. Not his usual haunt on a night out, but he'd gone a time or twenty in his thirty-one years. Mostly before he'd fallen in love, gotten married, and settled into a life that he'd thought would be rainbows and unicorns. He should've known better. When the marriage imploded, Slade hadn't found much interest in anything worthwhile, and places like this weren't high on his list of things to do these days.

"I prefer dance clubs," he admitted to his partner as they started toward the building.

"Let me guess, the ones that focus on line dancing."

"Don't knock it till you've tried it."

Evan grinned as he pulled the door open, and they stepped inside.

The place was just as he'd thought it would be. Dark and loud, with the main focus on a center stage currently occupied by three statuesque blonds lifting their top hats—the only article of clothing on their bodies—as they performed a choreographed number.

All eyes were on the trio, with the exception of a couple of bouncers hovering in the background.

"I say we blend in," Evan noted as he moved toward a table closer to the stage.

Slade grinned, wondering if his partner was more interested than he would willingly admit.

He wouldn't lie, it was good to see some spark of interest from Evan, even if it was for bouncing tits and long legs. Aside from an intense focus on work, Evan didn't seem like the type to take an interest in anything other than his daughter. They'd been partnered for months, and trying to get the guy to open up about anything was like herding cats—an impossible task that made you tired just thinking about it.

Slade pulled a chair out beside Evan and took a seat. He kept his head directed at the stage even as his gaze scanned the interior of the space. He wasn't sure whether or not this Serendipity was a performer or a waitress, and since they had no idea what she looked like, they had their work cut out for them.

When a waitress finally came around, they ordered two beers. She flashed a smile when Evan glanced over at him and said, "I wonder if Serendipity'll be here tonight."

Slade only hoped the stacked brunette wearing sequined pasties on her nipples and a matching thong wasn't Serendipity. If she was, the ruse was over.

"Oh, she's here," the waitress crooned in a voice that was most certainly not her everyday one. "Her first number's not until eight, though."

Great. That meant they would be here for at least an hour.

"She around?" Evan asked, glancing past the waitress, his expression that of an eager admirer. "I just wanna say hi."

All right. So the guy was a better actor than Slade would've given him credit for. The laid-back drawl was a nice touch, considering Evan usually spoke in a dry monotone that gave the impression he cared about absolutely nothing.

"I'll see if I can find her while I get your drinks." The waitress winked. "I'm Sasha, by the way."

"Nice to meet you, darlin'," Evan greeted, taking her hand and pressing a kiss to her knuckles as a refined southern gentleman would've done.

Slade smirked as he peered up at Sasha. When she looked at Evan, she likely saw dollar signs. Then again, when Evan looked at her, he probably saw a means to an end.

Huh. Slade had to wonder when he'd become so cynical. Probably had everything to do with his ex-wife. She'd turned his world upside down and sideways when he met her, then she'd exited the same way, taking what little he had to his name despite her new boyfriend—a man nearly twice Slade's age—was going to give her the world. Her words.

Oh, well. Life went on.

"Nice drawl, by the way," Slade told Evan when Sasha sashayed away.

"Thanks," he said, the dry monotone back in place. "I've been working on it."

"Yeah?"

"Got to fit in around here. The lack of *g*'s at the end of your words is disconcerting."

"Is it?" Slade grinned. "It's disconcertin'?"

"Yup."

"Admit it, it's catchy."

"It's something, all right."

Slade caught sight of Sasha talking to another woman. When she pointed in their direction, Slade nudged Evan's arm. "I think we found Serendipity."

Evan's head slowly turned as he took in the room, a move that was far more natural than it should've been, considering he was looking at only one thing. Slade admired the way the man blended in so easily.

"Hey, guys," the woman Slade assumed was Serendipity said as she strolled toward them.

She wore a jewel-red robe, her hair pinned up high on her head, and a pair of stilettos on her feet. He figured beneath she was wearing little to nothing, and surprisingly, Slade found he didn't care one way or the other.

Not only was he cynical, it was possible he was now dead inside. He wasn't sure he liked where this reflection was headed.

"Serendipity," Evan greeted as though he'd known the woman forever.

She smiled, and Slade could tell she was trying to figure out whether she knew them.

When recognition never dawned, Slade broke the awkward silence. "You don't know us," he said smoothly, keeping his expression pleasant for the bouncers who were keeping an eye on all the girls. "We're here to ask you about Toby Land."

"No, don't look back," Evan said, chuckling softly as though he found something amusing. A second later, he pulled out his wallet and a wad of cash. "We just want to know if you've seen him lately."

Her big blue eyes, ringed by lashes coated with too much mascara, glanced from Evan's face to the money in his hand and then back up. "Not in a while." There was disappointment in her tone.

"You two close?" Slade asked.

"We were. We dated for a while." She added a smile for anyone watching. "He's not allowed in here anymore."

"Can you tell us what business he had with your boss?" Evan made a show of peeling off what appeared to be ten-dollar bills.

Although she was pretending she wasn't interested in the money, Serendipity's gaze darted back to the cash in his hand before meeting his eyes again. "It had something to do with his travel agency. That's all I know."

Evan nodded, passed over two bills.

"Do you know where else he might go if he's not home?"

She shook her head. "You're gonna have to buy a dance."

Slade's gaze shifted, and that was when he noticed one of the bouncers moving toward them.

"How much?"

"Twenty for a lap dance, or fifty for a private dance."

Slade figured they didn't have time for more than a quickie, for lack of a better term. Evan must've thought so, too, because he peeled off two more tens and passed them over.

Serendipity stood tall and made a show of untying the sash on her robe. A moment later, the silk was sliding down her arms, revealing her trim, toned body and the matching red thong she wore beneath.

Eh. There was a hint of stirring in his loins, so maybe he wasn't quite as dead as he'd thought.

"The last time I saw him was the night he left here and got arrested," she said smoothly as she began gyrating her hips, going through the motions.

Evan rested his hands on the arms of his chair and stared up at her, smiling as though he was enjoying the show.

As she moved, Serendipity continued to tell them absolutely nothing. Yes, she had dated Toby for a little while. No, it wasn't anything serious. He was doing something on the side, and it pertained to the travel agency, but she didn't know what and didn't want to know.

By the time the song was finished and Serendipity was putting her robe back on, they'd learned little more than they already knew.

"Thank you," Evan said, passing over two more tens before she sauntered off.

They made it through one more song before heading out.

"Did you at least enjoy the show?" Slade joked as they were getting into the SUV.

"Not really my thing."

Slade frowned. "You into guys?"

Evan's head snapped over, and he frowned. "No. Why?"

Slade chuckled. "Just checkin'."

CHAPTER TEN

"HE'S OUT THERE SOMEWHERE," BRANTLEY TOLD REESE, hoping he sounded reassuring.

It had been a gamble following the last cell phone tower ping to a remote area. They hadn't found anything or anyone to confirm whether Toby had been out there at any point. The cabins Luca had mentioned were deserted, many of them crumbling in on themselves.

"Toby's a grown man," Reese said, his tone smooth and even. "I'm sure he's figured out how to hide from both the law and this guy."

By *this guy*, Brantley knew he was referring to the owner of the Red Room Revue. Thanks to Reese doing some research during the drive there, they'd learned his name was Johnathan Hartwood. His record was a mile long and likely growing by the second based on his history. Not only was he in the drug-selling business, he'd also dabbled in human and arms trafficking as well as protection rackets. From all accounts, he was your run-of-the-mill, wanna-be mafioso, only without the clout and backing.

Brantley's phone rang, so he hit the button to take the call.

"Walker," he greeted.

"Hey, boss." Slade's voice came through the speaker, the sound drawing Tesha's attention, her head appearing between the front seats.

"What's up?"

"So we just left the club," he said with that laid-back drawl that made Brantley believe the guy didn't have a care in the world.

"Did you talk to the girlfriend?"

"Serendipity. Yeah. Not much help on that front. She hasn't seen him since everything went down with her boss. The night he got arrested. She did say that Toby had somethin' goin' with her boss. She didn't know much about it. Said it had to do with the travel agency Toby owned."

Frowning, Brantley glanced over at Reese. He did not like the sound of that. Based on Reese's pinched expression, he didn't either.

"You need us to do anything else?" Slade offered.

"Nah. Thanks for that. We appreciate the help."

"Anytime. Just holler."

"Will do. See y'all on Monday and tell Evan thanks."

"Sure thing."

The call disconnected, and Brantley glanced over at Reese again. His expression had evened out, but he looked as though he was lost in thought.

"What's on your mind?"

Reese's eyebrow cocked. "What?"

"Where'd you go there, Tavoularis?"

"Just wonderin' what the hell he was doin' workin' with Hartwood. Why the fuck would he get himself mixed up in that?"

"Maybe he didn't have a choice," Brantley suggested.

"Yeah. Maybe."

Again, Reese seemed to slip away in his head, so Brantley drove the rest of the way home in silence. It wasn't until he reached the Coyote Ridge town limits that he spoke up again.

"You wanna grab a bite to eat?"

"Unless you're cravin' somethin' specific, I've got a coupla steaks thawin' at the house."

"I'm always cravin' somethin' specific," Brantley told him, sliding his hand along Reese's arm, which was draped over the center console.

Reese chuckled softly. "You're insatiable, you know that?"

"Damn right I am," he replied, his eyes on the road, his thoughts already on getting Reese naked. "Are you complainin'?"

Reese's fingers brushed Brantley's thigh. "Not even a little."

With a smile on his face and anticipation burning in his veins, Brantley pushed his foot to the floor. He needed to get this man home. ASAP.

A short time later, the three of them were back at the house. Brantley had his feet propped up on one of the chairs on the deck, a beer in his hand. Tesha was sniffing around the backyard, patiently waiting for Reese to finish checking the steaks on the grill so he'd throw the ball for her again. She didn't seem to care that they were quickly being swallowed by night.

He probably should've been thinking about Toby and where the man might've slipped off to, but he wasn't. Not for the first time, the case he was working on was taking a backseat to his personal life. He wouldn't lie, he'd grown accustomed to the normality of it. It was a far cry from his days as a SEAL, always on the go, eagerly anticipating the next mission. When he'd received his medical discharge from the navy, Brantley had figured his life would be chock full of nothing for the remainder of his days. He hadn't been able to imagine a world that didn't involve him being a Navy SEAL, wasn't sure he'd even wanted to.

His gaze slid to Reese as the man closed the grill and reached for the tennis ball he'd set on the deck railing. He picked it up, then whistled in the direction of the yard. Tesha spun around, her attention instantly on Reese. A second later, Reese lobbed the ball in her direction, sending her scurrying to get it. That simple action made Brantley smile.

No, he wasn't in the navy anymore. He wasn't out saving the world, but he had to admit, while this new path he was on was a far cry from the action-packed days of old, it was worth everything he'd been through to get here.

"ARE YOU WATCHIN' THE NEWS?" REESE ASKED when he joined Brantley in the bedroom a couple of hours later.

They'd had dinner, cleaned up, then continued to sit outside enjoying the peace and quiet of country life until the consistent chirp of crickets and the cool breeze had lulled them into a relaxed state. Worried he'd fall asleep in the chair, Reese had suggested they get some sleep so they could start again early tomorrow. He wasn't surprised when Brantley had readily agreed.

"I was actually lookin' for porn," Brantley quipped.

Reese pulled the blankets back and crawled into the bed. "Yeah?"

"Mmm-hmm. Thought I'd get in the mood."

"Now I know you're lyin'."

Brantley glanced over. "Why's that?"

"'Cause you're always in the mood."

"You know me too well." Brantley smirked, then pushed the blankets down, drawing Reese's attention to his lap. More specifically, to the thick, hard shaft currently gliding through Brantley's fist.

Heat coiled deep inside him, then slowly spread out to all his limbs as he watched Brantley stroke himself slowly. Up, down. The man wasn't in a rush, and if Reese had to guess, he knew precisely how his actions affected him.

Reese unabashedly stared, wanting Brantley to see the heat that consumed him, the anticipation that fizzed in his bloodstream at the thought of being with him. His heart thumped in his chest, his hands clenching into fists as he fought the urge to make the first move. He was waiting for Brantley because he knew the man would start to unravel slowly if he did.

"You like watchin' me," Brantley said, his tone gruffer than usual.

It wasn't a question, but Reese answered anyway, nodding his head.

Brantley's thumb caressed the swollen head, gliding through the precum pooling there. Reese was captivated by the sight, unable to look away although his mouth watered to taste him.

"I love watchin' your eyes glaze over," Brantley crooned, his voice low. "The way your mouth opens when you think about suckin' me."

Yeah, this was what Reese was hoping for. When he honed his patience, it tended to pay off because Brantley became more verbal, urging Reese with seductive words and that deep, guttural growl.

"I want you to put that fuckin' mouth on me, Reese," Brantley said, his cock moving through his fist, the head darkening as more blood filled it.

Reese's eyes slid to Brantley's face. He was watching him intently, as though trying to predict his next move. Reese managed to hold himself back, although he knew it was futile. He would give in because his desire for this man was potent. In the beginning, he hadn't understood this overwhelming, powerful yearning, but as time passed, he realized there was nothing to understand. It was a simple, primal instinct, an ingrained, baser need that sparked to life and grew hotter because he'd met the one person he was meant to spend his life with.

A soft growl sounded from Brantley's throat. It was sexy as hell and made Reese's cock thicken as it throbbed in time with his heartbeat.

It wasn't long before his control snapped, and Reese was moving. When he did, Brantley's hand paused, causing Reese to say, "Don't stop. Keep strokin'."

Brantley's stomach muscles tightened as his fist resumed the slow, leisurely pump up and down that told Reese they weren't going to rush tonight.

Reese shoved the blankets to the end of the bed before settling himself between Brantley's spread legs. He laid on his stomach, feet dangling off the end while propping his upper body on his arms. He was close enough to Brantley's impressive cock that he would feel the warmth of Reese's breath along his shaft, but that was all he offered, wanting to take his time working them both up to that inevitable high they would reach when they eventually climaxed together.

"Fuck," Brantley rasped, his eyes hooded as he angled his cock toward Reese's mouth. "Lick the head."

Reese's cock, currently trapped beneath him, throbbed painfully as he leaned forward, dragging his tongue along the wide crest.

"Oh, yeah." Brantley sighed, his body relaxing, knees falling wide. "A little more."

Reese followed his instruction, licking, teasing, refraining from offering anything more until Brantley requested it.

"Lick the shaft," Brantley insisted as he angled his cock toward his stomach, revealing the thick vein that ran along the underside.

Meeting Brantley's gaze, Reese glided his tongue along that vein, loving the way Brantley shivered when he did. He canted his head, dragging the flat of his tongue up the length of him, then back down. On the third pass, he continued lower, licking over Brantley's balls and earning a hiss of approval.

Reese remembered the first time Brantley had done this to him. The man had worshipped his cock for what felt like hours, driving Reese insane from the pleasure of it. He was merely returning the favor.

"More, baby," Brantley groaned.

Reese's chest swelled at the endearment. Brantley had started referring to him that way only recently, but Reese secretly loved that he did.

Granting Brantley his wish, Reese focused his full attention on sucking and licking Brantley's balls. He drew each gently into his mouth, then both simultaneously. Every time he did, Brantley would grunt his approval, his hand brushing Reese's arm in encouragement.

"Fuck, that feels good."

Minutes passed while Reese worshipped Brantley, deep guttural growls and harsh words rasping from Brantley's throat.

When Brantley became silent, only soft moans escaping him, Reese paused and lifted his head. He slid his palm beneath Brantley's right leg, flattening it against his thigh before pushing his leg back toward him. Brantley's blue-gray eyes flashed with passion and heat when he realized what Reese intended to do.

Brantley curled his fingers around his cock, angling it toward Reese's mouth once more. He sucked him deep into his mouth while pushing Brantley's other leg back, exposing his hole. Reese slowly glided his tongue down Brantley's rigid shaft, grazing his balls as he moved lower. Pressing Brantley's legs back, exposing him even more, Reese teased Brantley's taint briefly before rimming him.

"Son of a bitch," Brantley hissed, sinking into the pillow so he was flat on his back. "Fuck me with your tongue."

Reese gave Brantley exactly what he asked for, tonguing his hole while Brantley began to writhe against the bed. He took his time, savoring the grunts and groans Brantley emitted, proof of the pleasure Reese was bringing him.

"I need your cock inside me, Reese. Now."

Reese pretended not to hear him, continuing to rim him, his movements more aggressive. When Brantley's verbal litany turned vulgar, Reese pushed his thumb inside his hole, fucking into him while Brantley gripped his cock tightly.

"Please, baby," Brantley begged.

Those words had Reese's cock jerking, his entire body flashing hot.

Unable to resist the temptation of sinking into Brantley's hot, tight ass, Reese shot up to his knees. As he got into position, Brantley twisted his upper body, reaching for the lube sitting on the nightstand. A minute later, Reese's cock was slick and so fucking hard he hurt. He aligned their bodies and pushed the head inside while Brantley rested his calves on Reese's shoulders. The position allowed him to lean forward, bending Brantley's body in half while he sank deeper.

"God, yes," Brantley rasped. "Fuck me."

Reese fought the urge to drill into him hard and fast. He made love to him, their eyes locked as he pushed in, retreated. The heated friction along his cock had him gritting his teeth. Pleasure assaulted him when Brantley clamped down on him, his ass gripping Reese's cock like a velvet fist.

"Fuck. Me."

Again, Reese resisted the overwhelming desire to do as Brantley requested. He held out longer and longer, his body coiling tightly as his release threatened. Still, he didn't give in. Minutes passed as he rode Brantley, driving them to the pinnacle.

"Fuck me, baby," Brantley growled softly. "Please."

That was all it took: that sweet endearment and the rare plea for more.

Reese drove into him hard, retreated. Slammed in again. His hips pistoned as he lost control, the sound of their moans echoing in the space.

"Oh, fuck, yes." Brantley fisted his cock, began jerking it roughly. "Oh, fuck, baby."

"Come for me," Reese demanded, his gaze sliding to Brantley's cock tunneling through his fist. "Come for me so I can come in your ass."

Brantley's garbled shout was followed by streams of cum that shot over his bare chest. Reese was focused on the sight when he reached the point of no return. He drove deep inside Brantley and let go with Brantley's name falling from his lips.

CHAPTER ELEVEN

Tuesday, May 3, 2022

"Mornin'."

Brantley peered up from his phone to see JJ walking in through the sliding glass door, a smile on her face despite the raindrops splattered on her hair. Two steps behind her was Baz, looking just as chipper as he swept a hand over his hair to shake off the water.

"Hey, there, girl," JJ greeted Tesha when she ambled over to sniff out their company. "I know. The weather sucks, huh?"

According to the meteorologist, the rain should be letting up sometime in the near future, but it probably wasn't going to be today. As it was, the storm that had rolled through had put a damper on his morning run. Then again, he'd gotten his exercise in another form, one involving water from a showerhead and a sinfully sexy man who'd bent over and let Brantley take him in the shower.

All in all, Brantley figured the rain wasn't necessarily a bad thing.

He set his phone on the counter and smiled back. "Mornin'. Coffee?"

JJ peered over her shoulder at Baz briefly before giving a reluctant shake of her head. "I'm not allowed."

Baz rolled his eyes. "Then why'd you have one cup already this mornin'?"

JJ smiled sheepishly, winking at Brantley conspiratorially.

Brantley chuckled, then offered coffee to Baz.

"Nah. I'm abstaining to show solidarity for the pregnant gal."

"More for me then," he said, taking a sip of his own coffee. He found it amusing how JJ's eyes caressed the mug like it was a long-lost lover.

The yearning look disappeared from JJ's face as she skimmed the room. "Where's Reese?"

"Shower."

She popped her eyebrows dramatically. "Really? He's naked, huh?"

"Settle down there," Baz grumbled good-naturedly.

"Have a seat," Brantley motioned to the stools at the island. "What brings y'all over here?"

"Nosy Nelly said we had to."

"Hey, now." JJ shot him a look over her shoulder. "I am *not* nosy. Just … curious."

"Same difference."

Brantley took another sip of his coffee and watched the pair. Despite their bickering, or maybe because of it, they looked genuinely happy. It wasn't something he was used to seeing when it came to JJ and her personal life. The woman did not make things easy on herself for whatever reason.

"Y'all are workin' a case," JJ accused, at the same time thunder rolled across the sky.

Brantley paused before taking another sip, the comment catching him off guard.

"I *knew* it." JJ's eyes narrowed on his face, then rapid-fired more questions. "What is it? Who're you lookin' for? And why'm I not helpin'?"

"You mean *we*," Baz corrected.

"Right," she said, sitting up straight. "Why aren't *we* helpin'?"

Feeling cornered, Brantley glanced toward the hall that led to his bedroom. When Reese didn't miraculously appear, he glanced back at JJ.

"Brantley Walker, you're hidin' somethin' from me," she declared, her gaze skimming his face as though she was trying to read his pores to get the whole story. "And the only reason you'd do that is if it's a juicy backstory. Spill."

"There's no story."

There was no heat in her tone when she said, "Liar."

"Okay, then it's not my story to tell."

Her green eyes narrowed into slits. "Spill it, B."

She clearly wasn't going to let this go.

"Fine," he said, setting his coffee mug on the counter. "We're workin' on somethin'. We didn't ask for your help because it's not our usual case."

JJ settled on the stool, squaring her shoulders and resting her forearms on the counter.

Oh, boy.

Her chin tipped up as she gave him her full attention. She reminded him of his fifth-grade teacher, Mrs. Galloway. The mean old bat had loved to give Brantley shit whenever he'd had an excuse as to why he didn't turn in his homework. The only thing missing was a pair of Coke-bottle glasses resting on her nose, a shock of gray hair on her head, and a cardigan keeping the chill at bay. Oh, and about thirty years.

"But it's okay to bring in Luca, Slade, and Evan?"

Ah, hell. Why'd they have to go and open their big fucking mouths?

"Those hens cluck more than anyone I know," he grumbled, shaking his head and picking up his mug again.

"So you *did* include them on the mission?"

"It's not a mission," he countered.

"But you asked them for their help."

"I didn't exactly ask."

JJ's eyes narrowed, and he could tell she wasn't pleased with how this was going.

Brantley frowned, then peered at Baz, who was standing behind her shaking his head slowly and mouthing, "Abort."

"I didn't bring them in," Brantley said defensively, although it was a bit of a lie. Yes, he'd asked for their help with a couple of things, but he hadn't given them any of the pertinent information.

Thankfully, Brantley heard footsteps behind him. Without looking back, he pointed in Reese's direction and said, "It's his fault. Ask him about it."

Reese stopped at the end of the kitchen island, looking at each of them in turn. "Ask me what?"

JJ made a show of shifting on her stool to turn her body toward Reese. Her eyebrows rose slowly, scrunching her forehead. "Why was I not asked to help with the case you're workin' on?"

Brantley hid his smile behind his coffee mug as he took a step back and leaned his hip against the counter. He had told Reese this would happen. They'd continued to search for Tobias Land since Saturday but had been coming up empty at every turn. Just last night, Brantley told him they should probably loop JJ in and see if she could find him. The woman could work miracles, ones not even Luca was capable of producing.

Reese waved a dismissive hand as he moved toward the coffee pot. "You were busy on Saturday. Plus, it's not a case."

"I wasn't bus—okay, wait. Yes, I was busy on Saturday," JJ conceded. "But not Sunday." Her eyes narrowed. "Or yesterday."

Brantley watched from the sidelines, grateful to be out of the line of fire.

"And if it's not a case, why'd you have Slade and Evan go to a strip club?"

Reese cut his eyes to Brantley and pinned him with a glare.

He couldn't help it, he chuckled. "Hey, I didn't tell her."

"Thank God for that," Reese muttered under his breath, returning his attention to his coffee mug.

Brantley saw the way JJ was glancing between them as though she could read the secret of what they were relaying in the air between them.

"Oh, for fuck's sake," she said on a rough exhale. "Just tell me what's goin' on. It'll save us all time. You know how this works. Now that I suspect somethin', I'm not gonna let up until you tell me. That's gonna irritate *you*"—she pointed a finger at Reese—"which in turn is gonna piss *you*"—she pointed a finger at Brantley—"off. Might as well get it over with now."

Brantley looked at Baz, noticed the man was smirking, his expression saying, "She does make a good point."

Reese sighed. "Fine."

Brantley added more coffee to his mug while Reese proceeded to fill JJ in on the hunt for Tobias Land. He gave her the details of his fleeing from bad guys and crashing into a police car, the drugs found in the trunk. He explained how the guy had skipped bail and how Reese's brother had asked him to help out.

At a high level, it sounded relatively simple, Brantley figured, which explained the confusion that contorted JJ's pretty face.

"So who is he to you?" she asked when Reese was finished with the basics.

Reese busied himself sipping coffee, and Brantley knew he was trying to avoid going down a rabbit hole. He probably could've helped the man out and given her some bullshit explanation, but he was enjoying this a bit too much, so he kept his trap shut.

"We're just doin' my brother a favor," Reese said, unable to look directly at JJ when he said it.

Brantley smiled, but he didn't bother hiding it behind his cup this time, which earned him another glare from Reese.

This was turning out to be a damn fine morning, weather notwithstanding.

REESE HAD HOPED HE WOULDN'T BE HAVING this conversation with anyone else. It was bad enough he'd had to tell Brantley about the relationship Toby'd had with his mother.

Unfortunately, three days of searching had proved futile, and he was growing genuinely concerned for Toby's safety. Not to mention his mother's. The one thing he had done was dig deeper into Johnathan Hartwood, the owner of the Red Room Revue and the guy Toby was evidently running from. Although Reese would classify him as a wanna-be gangster and not the real deal, he was bad news. He was also determined, which meant, based on the laws of motion—for every action, there is an equal and opposite reaction—Hartwood would eventually find Toby as long as he continued to look and would do so for as long as Toby continued to evade him. It was inevitable that their paths would cross again, and Reese wanted to intercede if at all possible.

"So I take it you know this guy personally?" JJ asked.

"Would you like some orange juice?" he offered.

"You can change the subject all day long; I'm still not gonna give up," she countered, then plastered a beaming smile on her face. "But yes, orange juice would be lovely. Thanks."

Reese busied himself with getting the orange juice from the fridge and a cup from the cabinet. He purposely stepped into Brantley's space as he did, forcing the man to move each time. Although Reese was motivated by irritation, he got the impression Brantley found this amusing.

"He was friends with my parents," Reese said when he turned around and found JJ staring at him expectantly.

"Good ol' Uncle Toby," Brantley chimed in. "Long-time friend, part-time criminal."

"What am I missing?" JJ asked, glancing between them.

Reese grabbed his coffee and leaned back against the counter. "Toby was a"—he cut his gaze to Brantley—"*good* friend of my parents."

"Good?" JJ's expression turned to one of intrigue. "That sounds juicy. Why does it sound juicy?"

As he sipped his coffee, Reese reminded himself that she was likely his best option in finding Toby quickly. He'd tried things his way and had failed, which meant he had no choice but to go this route. He only hoped he could make it through this without bursting into flame.

"He had a … relationship of sorts … with my parents."

JJ's eyes danced over his face, and Reese knew she was translating that into a million different meanings.

"You mean somethin' like what Kaden, Keegan, and Bristol have."

She didn't phrase it as a question, and Reese hated himself all the more at that moment.

"Yes."

"Are you sure? Or was it like Travis, Gage, and Kylie…"

JJ trailed off, her expression reflecting sadness at the thought. Although it had been a year since Kylie Walker's death, the memory still caused a dark cloud to descend.

"Sorry."

"Kaden and them," he clarified.

Her smile returned, her eyes glittering with interest. "Was it serious?"

"No."

JJ nodded her head and took a sip of her orange juice. Reese could practically hear the wheels turning, knew she was about to say something that was going to make his ears burn with embarrassment.

"Cindy likes to mix it up with two guys at the same time, huh?" she mused, sounding both impressed and, yes, curious. "Lucky girl."

Reese knew his face was beet red, but he refrained from gagging.

"Rein it in there, woman," Baz inserted, smiling at JJ. "I'm more than enough for you."

She laughed, then patted his hand. "Of course you are."

Some of the tension eased from Reese's shoulders as he watched the pair, but it didn't last long.

"So this is more of a favor to your mom," JJ noted.

"Not a favor," Reese corrected, then went on to explain how they'd gone to Toby's house and found it ransacked. He told her about the picture he'd seen of his mother and the fact that her name had been scribbled on the back of it.

JJ's expression turned serious. "Do you think she's in danger?"

"Z's got a couple of guys keepin' an eye on her around the clock," Brantley told her. "Just in case."

A fact Reese knew Cindy found fascinating, something he had learned during the conversation they'd had last night when his mother decided to overshare the details of her weekend with Hugh. And Mark.

He could've gone his entire life without knowing that his mother had a fascination for threesomes, thanks to the fact his father had introduced her to them.

Ah, hell. He really wished someone made brain bleach.

"Why'd you send Slade and Evan to the strip club?" JJ took a sip of her juice. "And did they find anything?"

"We were hopin' Toby's former girlfriend might be able to provide some insight into where he is," Brantley explained while Reese took a gulp of coffee and let the scalding hot liquid burn off some of his mortification. It didn't help.

"And did she?" Baz asked, now sitting beside JJ and looking equally as enthralled by the story.

"Not on his whereabouts, no," Brantley answered. "She did tell us that Toby and Hartwood were in business together."

JJ's eyebrows lowered. "I thought you said he borrowed money."

"That's what Z told us," Reese noted. "But I'm not sure it's the case."

He proceeded to tell her about the travel agency and how he believed it was somehow tied into it. He opened the junk drawer and pulled out the brochure he'd snagged from Toby's house, passing it to JJ.

While she glanced at it, Baz's eyes went hard. "I don't want to go down a dark road here, but you're talkin' about a guy who manages a club that exploits women, and based on what I know of the place he runs, he's also into other nefarious activities. Have you considered…?"

Reese was grateful he'd trailed off because, yes, he'd already given some thought to human trafficking, which no doubt Baz was referring to, and it made him sick to his stomach to think about.

"Considered what?" JJ asked, glancing between the three of them.

Before anyone could respond, her eyes widened. "Oh."

"Right now, there's no evidence to support Toby bein' involved in trafficking of anything at all," Brantley said defensively. "It's all speculation. Until we find him, we won't know what he's into."

"But you think it's a possibility?" JJ directed the question at Reese.

"Personally, no," he said honestly. "Not Toby."

"I got the impression you don't know him well," she countered.

"I don't. But I know my parents, and if they suspected Toby was even capable of something like that…" Reese honestly couldn't see his parents ever associating with someone who could do something so heinous.

"Circling back to what you said," Brantley said to Baz. "You have a run-in with this guy before?"

"His name was whispered at the precinct, yeah," Baz said. "It came up anytime we dealt with a matter near his club."

As a former Austin Police Department detective, that made sense. Reese figured there were quite a few criminals who'd become infamous within the department, people they looked at regularly in hopes of solving a crime.

Baz's gaze locked on Reese's face. "If it's any consolation, there were rumors of trafficking, but never humans."

"Arms?"

Baz nodded.

That made more sense, but still, Reese didn't see Toby willingly getting involved in that. However, he would've been able to provide a certain level of protection for moving weapons back and forth into Mexico under the guise of his travel agency. Which meant he might've been the perfect patsy for Hartwood to exploit.

Brantley cleared his throat, drawing Reese's attention.

"What?"

"Of all the names I never wanted to mention in this house again, there might be someone who could help us with this."

Reese frowned, not following.

"Max Adorite."

Reese's insides chilled, his gaze holding steady on Brantley's.

Brantley's eyebrow rose as though lending merit to his following statement. "He does have control over the movement of weapons through the state."

"He does?" JJ sounded sincerely concerned.

Brantley glanced at her briefly. "Among other things." He turned his attention back to Reese. "And word is, he's recently made some significant organizational changes."

Yeah, Reese had heard that, too. Maximillian Adorite, the boss of the Southern Boy Mafia, as the media referred to his organization, had restructured after his sister's attempted kidnapping. From what Reese had heard from Z, Max had hit pause on his legit business dealings and was focusing more on establishing a hard line for control against the Moroso family. According to speculation, they were on the verge of a gang war, and Max was hell-bent on coming out on top.

"It might be worth pursuing," Baz suggested.

Reese held Brantley's gaze. He knew Brantley held Max responsible for what had happened to Reese because the thugs who'd shot him had been working for Sabrina Moroso, the head of the Moroso crime syndicate.

"I agree," Brantley said, his steel-blue gaze glittering with conviction.

Reese swallowed hard, hating that it was definitely something they needed to consider.

CHAPTER TWELVE

JJ COULD FEEL THE SHIFT IN THE air. The tension that radiated from Reese was palpable, as was the regret that flashed in his eyes.

She kept her mouth shut while the staring contest between Brantley and Reese continued, but she had a million more questions. The first being: who was going to volunteer to have a conversation with the Mob boss because, yes, she agreed Max Adorite could possibly provide some insightful information, especially if he considered this sleazeball Hartwood to be some kind of rival. Would he? Did mobsters think like that? Did he even care?

Oh, just a few of the many questions she'd like to find answers for.

"It's an avenue we should check out," Brantley finally said. JJ wasn't sure if he was attempting to convince Reese or himself.

JJ exhaled, not realizing she'd been holding her breath. "Does that mean we're goin' to Dallas?"

Once more, no one spoke, but Brantley and Reese shared a silent conversation with their eyes. If only she'd been born with the ability to read minds. It would've made life so much easier.

"It means I'll make a call first," Brantley said, breaking eye contact with Reese and glancing her way. "In the meantime, I need you to see what information you can dig up. Start from the top."

She frowned as her brain instantly hit rewind, returning to the first thing she knew about this guy they were looking for. A name wasn't much to go on, and they'd already managed to nail a few details, so why the top? And where did she start? His residence? The more she thought about it, the more confused she became.

With a sigh, she decided to see if they could help her along. "And how do you propose I do that?"

"You've got skills; I'm sure you'll think of somethin'."

Skills, yes. A workable starting point, no. JJ didn't have anything to go on other than a name, which meant her skills were moot, but she didn't tell Brantley that. She doubted he wanted to hear her complaining right now.

"He has a computer," Reese noted, his shoulders near his ears as his tension seemed to escalate.

That was good news. "Did you get it?"

Reese shook his head. "Either he's got it, or someone else took it from his house."

The answer was precisely what she'd expected. It would've been too easy if they had whipped out Uncle Toby's laptop.

However, just because they didn't have the computer didn't mean she wouldn't find something. People logged into sites every day; they stored information in the cloud. There were log-ins and passwords, sites they liked to frequent. She simply needed to do a little research, find out what he was interested in, and tug on the strings until she found something that might lead them to where Toby was hiding.

"Maybe we can work this from two angles since we're scheduled for our monthly training at the end of the week," Baz said, his hand gently squeezing JJ's shoulder as he spoke to Brantley and Reese. "We could go up to Dallas early, see what we can find."

"Maybe one of us should talk to Cindy," JJ offered, glancing at Reese. When she saw him blanch, she added, "And no, I don't mean that in a creepy, perverted way. It's just that you're her son. I doubt she wants to regale you with her love life."

"No, no," Reese said, his nostrils flaring. "She didn't have a problem with that."

JJ grinned. "So you think. I bet there's a lot she's holdin' back from you. It's possible she has some information about Toby that she doesn't realize might help."

Reese's expression smoothed out as Brantley said, "That's a good point."

"I don't mind talkin' to her," she added. She didn't have to mention that she'd developed a quick friendship with Reese's mother in the past couple of weeks. JJ was working with Cindy and Iris on the preparations for Reese and Brantley's wedding, so it had been easy to do so.

Granted, she wasn't sure it would be appropriate to broach a subject that seemed so sensitive for her son, but JJ was up for the challenge. If it meant they might find this man who was obviously important to Reese in some way, she'd make the sacrifice.

Oh, who was she kidding? JJ was mentally rubbing her hands together with anticipation.

"Why don't we give y'all some time to figure out your next steps," Baz said, getting to his feet. "We'll head over to the barn, get set up for the day."

"Fine." JJ sighed in resignation, letting them hear her disappointment. It earned her the exact reaction she'd hoped for, settling Reese a little and getting Brantley's shoulders to unknot.

She allowed Baz to lead her out of the house and onto the back porch. He grabbed the umbrella he'd produced earlier and lifted it, shielding them from the downpour that was currently soaking the Austin area.

They made it to the barn without being swept away by a current, Tesha close on their heels, yipping gleefully at the colorful umbrella until Baz closed it before carrying it to the small kitchenette.

"You up to goin' to Dallas?" he called as she started up the stairs.

"Yep." She'd actually been looking forward to it. While most of the team spent their time at the training facility, JJ got to hang out at the Sniper 1 Security offices. More accurately, she got to use their fancy tools and see the cool new spy toys they were working with. She'd learned a few tips and tricks from those who worked in a similar position as she did as the "researcher" of the team. It had opened her eyes to new things, and she looked forward to seeing what they would teach her next.

Not that she cared to share that with anyone. She'd never hear the end of it if they learned of a way to get under her skin by teasing her relentlessly.

"You think that's the route they're gonna take?" she hollered down to Baz.

"If it'll accomplish the goal, yeah." Baz appeared at the top of the stairs. "Plus, if there's any chance Reese's mom'll get caught up in this, I know they'll put the past behind them."

The past being that Reese had dated Madison Adorite, one of Max's sisters. Not only had they dated, there'd been an impromptu proposal. And since Madison was the woman Reese had been with the night he was shot—because he'd been protecting her, of course—JJ knew there would be some friction between Reese and Brantley, no matter how hard they tried to pretend otherwise.

She just hoped they could avoid another epic meltdown.

"I THINK YOU SHOULD TAKE THE LEAD on this," Reese said when JJ and Baz slipped out the door and into the rain.

Brantley grabbed his mug and returned to the coffee maker, pouring what was left from the carafe. "And if I said I don't want to take the lead?"

He could feel Reese's tension, had since the moment he brought up the Adorites.

"Brantley…"

Putting his cup down, he turned to Reese. It was time to get serious for a minute.

He stepped up to Reese, closing the gap between them. They were nearly toe-to-toe, almost eye-to-eye.

"When I say that somethin's in the past, that's exactly what I mean," he said smoothly, keeping his tone cool and even. "What happened before has no bearing on the here and now."

"There's a good chance—"

Brantley cut Reese off, stepping forward and putting a hand on his chest. He slowly slid it higher, up and around to the back of his neck. He pulled Reese forward until their foreheads touched, then lowered his voice even more. "I love you. I trust you. Nothing that might happen is gonna cause friction between us."

"You can't promise that."

"I can promise you that we will be walkin' down the aisle one hundred thirty-seven days from now."

He could feel Reese's forehead crease. "You know how many days until we're gettin' married?"

"Damn right I do. It's what I'm lookin' forward to most in this world."

Reese's hands moved to his hips, pulling him in before his arms banded around him. "I love you."

"I love you, too."

"I just don't want to do anything that'll fuck this up."

Brantley chuckled. "I'm sure we're both gonna fuck shit up from time to time. That's the way it works. We do somethin' stupid, then we make up with hot, dirty sex."

Reese released a gruff chuckle as Brantley'd hoped he would.

Pulling back, he met Reese's stare. "We'll go to Dallas, see if we can get a sit-down with Max Adorite. We'll share the information we have and see if there's anything he might know. I doubt Hartwood's a big fish, but he could be workin' with someone. That would put him on the Adorites' radar."

Reese nodded. "All right."

"But we're gonna need to bring the entire team in for this."

Reese sighed, releasing Brantley and stepping back. "Fine. But if one single person makes a comment about my mother…" His face pinched as though he was in pain.

Brantley laughed. "Trust me when I tell you, the whole threesome thing's not new for these people. We live in Coyote Ridge, for fuck's sake."

Reese seemed to consider that. "True."

With things settled between them—for now—Brantley finished his coffee and led the way over to the barn.

Shortly after Reese and Brantley got to the barn, joining JJ, Baz, and Elana, who had graciously brought breakfast tacos for everyone, the rest of the team began to trickle in.

Slade arrived first, followed by Evan, then Charlie, Deck, Becs, Darius, Holly, and Luca. Jay was the last to arrive, still getting there before their official start time of oh-eight-hundred. Reese couldn't keep himself from wondering what Trey was doing at that moment. Ever since the guy had left the task force to pursue other interests, Reese had thought about him. His leaving was a definite loss for the team, but they were forging ahead without him.

"Mornin'," Brantley greeted once the team had settled in, grabbing tacos and coffee before taking their seats. "We've got a change of plans this week." His gaze swung to Evan, then Jay, and finally over to Becs. "If any of you need to stay behind because of kids or family obligations, no worries."

"What's going on?" Evan's light brown eyes sparked with curiosity.

"Does it have somethin' to do with Tobias Land?" Slade asked.

"Toby," Brantley corrected. "Yes, it does."

"Do we have a case?" Charlie inquired.

"Is this guy missin'?" Darius questioned.

"What do we know about him?" Holly asked.

"If you'll pipe down a minute, I'll tell you," Brantley said with a gruff laugh. "Shit."

The group laughed, and Reese got the sneaking suspicion they were learning how to push Brantley's buttons and making a unified effort to do so. If it was even possible, he liked this team more because of it.

"Over the weekend, we got a call from Reese's brother," Brantley began, then went on to explain the high-level details.

"Isn't this right in your wheelhouse?" Charlie asked Slade. "You were a bounty hunter, right?"

"I was." He smiled, looking proud that she'd brought it up.

"Technically, there is a bounty on his head," Brantley told them. "But we're more concerned with the danger he's in than deliverin' him straight to the police."

"What's the bounty?" Slade asked, glancing between Reese and Brantley.

"It's a sizable amount, but we're not worried about the money," Brantley stated.

Slade chuckled. "I agree. *We* might not be interested, but if it's high enough, others are gonna be lookin' for him, too."

Reese hadn't considered that, but it made sense. Which meant they would need to increase their urgency if they expected to keep Toby out of harm's way.

"Good point," Brantley said, then went on to explain to the others what they'd done so far in their search for him: the minimal research, checking out his house, his previous business, talking to the ex-girlfriend at the strip club, and the run-down tract of cabins that had netted them zilch.

"You think he's in Dallas?"

"It's a good possibility," Reese chimed in. "Based on some searches I did last night, he owned a few properties up that way. I don't think he'll be hidin' out at any of them, but I think he'll consider it a safe place to be."

"However, there's still a chance he'll be here," Brantley added, "which is why I need two people to volunteer to stay behind."

Charlie was the first to raise her hand. Because her mother's health was failing, she preferred to stay close to home, and Reese couldn't blame her.

No one else volunteered, so Brantley picked Jay. "You've got kids and a wife. I'm sure they'd prefer you to be close by."

Jay seemed pleased that he'd been chosen without having to draw attention to himself.

"What about y'all?" Brantley asked Evan and Becs, the only others with children. "Do you need to stay behind?"

"I don't," Evan stated. "My mother's with Sophia."

Sophia was Evan's seven-year-old daughter.

Brantley glanced at Becs again.

Her gaze swung to Evan, and Reese couldn't help but wonder if something was going on there.

"She can stay with Soph," Evan said easily, although he didn't look at Becs for long, and the same went for her.

Becs must've felt all the eyes on her because she finally spoke up, as though it warranted an explanation. "Carly and Sophia have become good friends since the party you threw. They've had a few sleepovers since."

Reese glanced between Evan and Becs, wondering if the parents had been having sleepovers as well.

Not that it was any of his business. There were obviously no rules about dating co-workers considering Reese and Brantley had been together since the inception of the task force.

But Becs and Evan? For some reason, Reese couldn't see it. Probably had something to do with the fact that Evan Vaughn was a hardened-by-life former homicide detective, and Becs … well, she was nine years younger than him and looked far too sweet for a guy with so many rough edges. She did, however, seem to have a fascination with Luca Switzer, although Reese didn't think it was reciprocated.

Shaking off his mental confusion, Reese focused back on the task at hand. What these people did on their own time wasn't any concern of his.

"All right then," Brantley said firmly. "If there aren't any questions or details you want hashed out, let's get on the road."

Reese felt that uncomfortable churn in his gut once again, but he shoved it away. He was determined to take a page from Brantley's playbook and not let the past dictate his future.

He only hoped that wasn't easier said than done.

CHAPTER THIRTEEN

"YOU MIND IF I RIDE UP WITH you?"

Evan disconnected the call to his mother to see Slade moving toward him. He didn't know why the guy was asking when Evan had already assumed he would be tagging along. They'd partnered up because they worked well together, and for the most part, Evan didn't mind Slade's company.

"Yeah," he told Slade. "You can ride with me."

"Did you have to *think* about that?" Slade said with a mischievous smirk.

Evan leaned back in his desk chair. "What? No."

"Are you sure?" Slade glanced over at Becs, then back to him. "'Cuz I don't wanna be the third wheel."

"Oh, shut up. There are no third wheels," he grumbled. Like he said, they worked well *for the most part.* It went without saying that he had to deal with Slade's constant ribbing.

"That's not entirely true." Slade nodded toward the upper floor. "If I asked to go with JJ and Baz"—he canted his head dramatically—"third wheel." He looked toward the door. "Or if I asked Brantley"—he mimicked the same head tilt—"third wheel." He smiled wickedly. "Now I'm startin' to wonder if you and—"

"Shut up," Evan hissed, glaring daggers at him. "No. Third. Wheel."

Slade chuckled, that good-ol'-boy sound causing Becs to look up from what she'd been doing on her computer. She smiled sweetly, as though wishing she knew what the joke was. Evan instantly looked away, feeling like a kid caught with his hand in a cookie jar.

He'd been expecting the harassment, he just hadn't been sure who would dish it out first. Based on the looks he'd garnered when Becs had asked him about her daughter staying at his house, everyone was thinking it. Of course, everyone was dead wrong in their assumptions. Regardless of what it looked like, Evan was not having some secretive affair with Rebecca Richter. They were friends, nothing more. Yes, her daughter, Carly, had come over to play with Sophia many times since he'd first started working for the task force, spent the night a few times even, but Evan was not mixing it up with Becs. She was a sweet, kind-hearted young woman, one he respected and genuinely liked, which meant she was completely off-limits.

"Nothin's up with you two?"

He should've known Slade was going to press the issue. The man was nothing if not nosy as fuck, a trait Evan didn't usually mind. And he wouldn't now if it weren't for the fact that Evan's charade was hinged on the fact that no one learned the truth: that Becs was the first woman who had caught his full, undivided attention since his wife, God rest her soul.

From the first day he laid eyes on the woman, he'd realized there was something about her that struck a nerve within him. A nerve he honestly hadn't expected to ever hear from again. For years, he'd been content to indulge in one-night stands to sate the biological urges that plagued him, but even those had been few and far between. Not to mention completely absent since meeting Becs.

"Don't you need to go home and pack?" Evan said, closing the lid on his laptop. "I'll swing by and pick you up after I get things settled with Sophia."

Slade exhaled as though he was put out by being denied his fact-finding quest. "Fine."

Shaking his head, he waited until Slade left, then grabbed his cell phone and pushed to his feet. He felt Luca's eyes follow him as he strolled toward Becs's desk.

"You need a ride to Dallas?" he offered, thrusting his hands in his pockets because he didn't know what else to do with them.

She peered up at him with eyes so blue they reminded him of the Caribbean, so clear and so vibrant it was mesmerizing. Her strawberry-blond hair was pulled back in a ponytail, a sweep of bangs brushing across her forehead, her flawless skin so pale he wanted to ask her if she wore sunscreen every day. In a word, she was beautiful, and for whatever reason, just looking at her did weird things to his insides.

Becs smiled sweetly. "I was gonna ride up with Elana and Holly, but thank you for offering."

He nodded. "Did you get things squared away with my mother?"

Another smile. "I did. She said she'd be happy to watch Carly. Thank you for that, by the way. I know the girls'll have a good time."

That they would. The last time Carly had stayed over, Sophia had informed him they were now best friends forever. At seven—almost eight, as she liked to remind him—he wasn't sure how his daughter could predict something like that, but he didn't question it. He happened to be quite fond of Carly Richter, the cute little nine-year-old who loved all the same things Sophia did.

And he didn't mind the fact that the little girls' friendship gave him the opportunity to spend time with Becs every now and then. In fact, he looked forward to it, although he would never admit that to anyone.

"All right then," he told her. "Be safe, and I'll see you when you get up there. I mean, *we*," he corrected quickly. "We'll see all of you." *Ah, Jesus Christ.* "We'll see *the three* of you."

Her smile widened, and her blue eyes sparkled. "Okay."

As he turned toward the door, Evan realized there was probably a reason he hadn't found an interest in another woman since his wife died: he was utterly clueless as to how to talk to one.

BECS PRETENDED TO STARE AT HER COMPUTER while she snuck a glance at Luca watching Evan walk toward the door. It was risky because everyone in the room had been so focused on the fact that her daughter and Evan's had become close friends.

She knew what they were thinking, but they were wrong. She wasn't having some torrid love affair with Evan, although she got the feeling he might like her. Then again, it could just be he was awkward around women—in a charming way, she doubted he even realized—and simply didn't know how to express himself.

It was cute, she had to admit. He was the sort of man who genuinely cared about someone's well-being, even if he made an effort to keep everyone at arm's length.

As she was thinking about him, her gaze shifted to him as he opened the door to leave. It was then she saw him glance back at her briefly, but the moment he noticed her watching him, he looked away.

Yeah, he was cute, although she doubted he'd be happy to hear her use such a juvenile adjective to describe him.

Evan Vaughn was such a sweet man, though you wouldn't know it by looking at him. There was a hint of insecurity beneath the smooth, clean top layer that he covered up with a gruffness that seemed second nature. If she was being honest, he was attractive, in a fierce, alpha male kind of way. But he didn't do it for her the way some men did. Men like Luca Switzer. She'd always been attracted to the rough-around-the-edges cowboy types, and Luca certainly fit the bill. With his backward ball cap and a body packed with muscle, he played a starring role in her darkest fantasies.

He wore T-shirts and jeans that showcased his hard body while Evan wore remnants of his former life—cheap suits that didn't quite fit him but did an excellent job of concealing the dad bod beneath. In fact, his wardrobe was so bland and unflattering, she wasn't even sure if he had any muscle whatsoever.

Unlike Luca, whose arms and shoulders drew a woman's eyes when the muscles bunched and flexed. For a computer geek who spent most of his time in a chair, he was getting his exercise somehow.

Becs knew her infatuation with Luca would never go anywhere, but she was okay with that. It was safer that way. Luca Switzer was far too much like her ex-husband—flirtatious, fun, and, yes, hot in a way that made her think of wickedly intense orgasms. However, like her ex-husband, she got the impression Luca wasn't the type who liked to stand by his commitments, especially to women, so she was keeping her distance, settling for fantasizing about him late at night when she was alone.

She fought the urge to fan herself and peered back down at her computer. She fired off the email she'd been working on, then got to her feet. She needed to run home, pack her things, and get Carly ready to go to Evan's. Her daughter was going to be over the moon with joy that she got to spend a couple of extra days with Sophia, but Becs had to admit, she was missing her already. It wasn't easy to be away from Carly, but she'd known when she took this job that there would be some travel involved, so she was learning to deal with it.

After all, she'd finally found a job she loved, something she was good at. And most importantly, something she actually looked forward to each day.

"You sure you wanna go up there?" Baz asked JJ when he finally managed to get her in the car so they could go home to pack their things for the trip. She'd already jumped right into searching for Toby Land despite her initial hesitations. Admittedly, he loved that about her. The fact that she had self-doubts but pushed through them regardless of the situation. However, once she set her mind to something, getting her to do anything else required effort and a significant amount of patience.

"Of course." She glanced over at him, her expression concerned. "Why wouldn't I?"

"I just wanna make sure you're comfortable. It's a three-hour drive."

"I'm pregnant, Baz, not an invalid."

His eyes widened. "I wasn't insinuating—"

JJ reached for his hand, curling her fingers over it. "I'm teasin' you, Detective."

He let out a breath and focused on the road. "Just promise you'll tell me if you wanna stop."

"I do wanna stop at Buckee's," she informed him. "It's my goal to stop there at least once every trip."

Now he was shaking his head, his worry vanishing. Something about this morning's conversation with Brantley and Reese had made his nerves riot. He figured it had to do with the last time they'd gone to Dallas with Reese. The man had gone and gotten himself shot, and they'd all returned to Coyote Ridge with one less team member. It hadn't sat well with Baz, and he wanted to avoid a repeat.

"You know they're fine, right?" JJ said softly, her hand gently squeezing his.

He frowned, glancing over at her quickly. "What?"

"Brantley and Reese," she clarified. "They're solid. You don't have to worry about them."

"Who said I was worried?"

She chuckled. "I'm pretty sure *worry* is your middle name."

"That is *not* true. Now, if you want to say *caring* or *compassionate*, I might not be offended."

She laughed, a gleeful sound that erased all his concerns instantly. "Whatever. Worrywart."

It was his turn to laugh as he turned his hand over and threaded his fingers with JJ's. He started a mental list of things he needed to do when they got back to the apartment, clothes he needed to pack, chargers he needed to grab.

"I think Evan's got a thing for Becs."

Shaking off his thoughts and focusing on what JJ had said, he cut a glance her way again. "What?"

She was staring out the front windshield, grinning. "Yep. I said it. I think Evan's got the hots for Becs."

"No way." He didn't see it.

"He does, but I think Becs has a thing for Luca."

His head snapped over this time. "Seriously?"

JJ glanced his way, her green eyes glittering with mischief. "How can you not notice this stuff? I see the way she looks at him when she doesn't think anyone's lookin'."

Baz focused on driving. "I think you're makin' shit up in that pretty little head of yours."

"What? Luca's hot. I can totally see why Becs would like lookin' at him."

Baz snorted. "I thought he was your nemesis. Now you're tellin' me he's hot?"

"He's a cowboy. What girl doesn't imagine fallin' in love with a cowboy?"

"Did you?"

"Of course," she answered with too much conviction in her tone. "Hell, I was in love with Brantley Walker for most of my early teenage years."

"Your gay best friend doesn't count."

JJ laughed. "Sure it does. My teenage heart didn't care that he was gay."

"Not only gay," Baz said firmly. "He was datin' your brother."

Another laugh, just as carefree and light. "He was. Which meant I got to see him all the time."

Curious, Baz looked over at her. "Did y'all become best friends because he was datin' your brother? Or did he date your brother because y'all were best friends?"

She pursed her lips, clearly thinking about it. "Good questions. I don't know."

"What was he like back then? Brantley?"

"A lot like he is now. Cool, confident. Just without the military strictness. That came later."

"And Reese?"

JJ shook her head. "I didn't know Reese, but I knew his brother, Z." She smiled. "Now that I think about it, I'm surprised my brother never had the hots for him."

"For Z?"

"Yep. He was one of those larger-than-life types. Smart, funny. Smokin' hot."

Baz knew she was now focusing on the word *hot* just to get a rise out of him. He appreciated the effort she was making to keep the mood light. The woman knew just what to say to shift his mindset, and he was grateful for that. The last thing he wanted was to dwell on the past and think about all the ways the future could go horribly wrong. Things were good right now. Really good. With everyone.

Which made him wonder why he couldn't shake the feeling that something was off.

CHAPTER FOURTEEN

Five hours later...
Dallas, Texas

"ARE YOU HUNGRY?"

Brantley dumped his duffel bag on the bed and glanced behind him. "I'm always hungry, so was that a trick question?"

He could feel the tension coming off Reese in waves. It had been there since they'd entered the city limits, and he figured Reese was spending far too much time thinking about the last time they'd been here together. This was their first time back since the shit hit the fan, and he'd known it was going to dredge up old feelings and new concerns. And perhaps trigger Reese's PTSD since the man had been shot at a restaurant not too far from where they were right now.

Whatever it was that had Reese tied up in knots, Brantley wanted to ease his mind, and he knew just the thing to help.

Reese was leaning over his bag to pull something out, so Brantley moved up behind him, sliding his hand over Reese's stomach, then venturing lower.

"It's still a little early for dinner," Reese continued, "but—"

"I'm not interested in food, Reese."

Reese stood tall, leaned into him. "No?"

"I don't have low blood sugar," Brantley reminded him, speaking gruffly in his ear. "And I'm not on a rigid schedule."

"No?"

"No." Brantley cupped Reese through his jeans, gliding the heel of his hand along what was quickly becoming a very impressive erection. "Not at all."

He continued to fondle him until Reese relaxed against him. Brantley easily counterbalanced his weight by leaning forward, sliding his palms beneath Reese's shirt to caress hot, smooth skin while inhaling his musky scent—a combination of the cologne Reese favored and his body wash. Brantley liked the combination, but more than that, he loved how intoxicated it made him feel.

"What're you doin', Navy boy?" There was a definite rough grind to Reese's voice.

"It was a long drive. I thought I'd relax for a minute."

"Yeah?"

"Mmm-hmm."

"And you think sex'll relax either of us?"

Brantley smiled, kissing the side of Reese's neck. "I don't know, but I intend to find out. Unbutton your jeans."

While he continued to grind his palm along the hard ridge of Reese's cock, Reese began to work loose the button on his jeans.

"I really want to be inside you right now," Brantley whispered, nipping Reese's shoulder. "I want to bend you over that desk and fuck you hard." His voice dropped an octave as he imagined it. "I want to hear you say my name when I'm deep inside you. To feel your ass grip me like a fist as you groan and beg for more."

A soft groan was Reese's response.

"Yeah." Brantley smiled against his neck. "That's the sound. You like that idea, my cock buried to the hilt in your tight, hot ass."

Reese's hands fumbled as he pushed his jeans down his lean hips, a sound resembling agreement coming from his throat.

Brantley gripped Reese's cock in his fist and lightly stroked him, maintaining a leisurely pace. While he wanted nothing more than to bend him over that desk or, better yet, throw Reese to the bed and fuck him like a wild animal, he knew the only way to keep Reese's mind in the present was to go slow. And since this was as much a distraction as it was to sate their baser urges, Brantley relied on his tight-leashed control to keep himself from doing just that.

"But I'm not goin' to. Not yet, anyway."

"Why not?" Reese rasped, his hips pumping gently as he rocked his cock into Brantley's fist.

"Because we've got some time to kill."

"Do we?"

Brantley chuckled, loving that Reese had been reduced to two-word sentences because of what Brantley was doing.

"Take off your shirt," he instructed.

Reese shifted in the circle of Brantley's arms, dragging his shirt up and over his head, tossing it aside.

Catching sight of the big mirror mounted to the wall over the dresser, Brantley managed to turn them so that they were facing it. He watched over Reese's shoulder, admiring the sexy man as he continued to rub him. Reese's handsome face was contorted by pleasure, his chest muscles flexing as his breathing deepened, stomach muscles clenching whenever Brantley tightened his fist on his cock.

"We should consider gettin' a mirror in the bedroom," Brantley mused.

Reese's gaze met his in the reflection. "We should."

Brantley pressed a kiss to Reese's bare shoulder, felt the muscle tense, then relax almost instantly. He licked the back of Reese's neck before kissing the other shoulder while continuing to watch them in the mirror.

Reese's eyes drooped shut, and a soft groan sounded again. "Brantley…"

"Tell me, baby," he encouraged. "Tell me what you want me to do to you."

"Everything."

God, he loved this man. He loved everything about him, especially the way he gave in so quickly.

"Don't move," he instructed, releasing Reese's cock and taking a step back. He made a brief detour to the bed and rummaged through his duffel bag until he found the lube.

When he turned around again, he was content to see Reese hadn't budged from where he stood, his sexy ass beckoning Brantley as he stood stone-still, his chest rising and falling with every breath.

It was the work of a moment to get Reese's jeans shoved down to his ankles.

"Spread your legs as wide as you can," Brantley told him, moving up behind him again.

Reese did.

Uncapping the lube, Brantley squirted a generous amount in his hand, then tossed the tube away. He greased both hands before reaching around Reese once more to fist his cock. A gruff sigh sounded when his slick hand glided along the thick shaft. Another when Brantley pressed two fingers between Reese's ass cheeks, teasing along the crack until he found his target.

He was watching their reflection in the mirror, focusing on Reese's face, the way his mouth opened slightly when Brantley dipped his middle finger inside him.

"Oh, fuck," Reese moaned.

Brantley worked Reese's cock with one hand and fingered his asshole with the other, taking pleasure from seeing Reese succumb to it. When he added a second finger, Reese groaned, widening his knees to give him better access.

He slowly penetrated him, scissoring his fingers open just a little to stretch his tight sphincter. As he did, he imagined sinking his cock into the blistering heat of Reese's body.

"More," Reese pleaded.

Brantley gave him more, curling his fingers, searching for his prostate. When he grazed it, Reese hissed, his body jerking and another groan escaping. He nipped Reese's shoulder, stroked his cock, and fingered his hole all at the same time. Before his eyes, Reese's entire body hardened, his cock pulsing in his hand as he neared that inevitable point of no return. Brantley never let up, but he didn't rush. He loved seeing Reese like this, completely at his mercy.

"Brantley … oh, fuck … you're gonna make me come."

Since that was the goal, he didn't falter, continuing to drive him higher and higher until Reese fell back against him, his cock pulsing, his ass clamping down on his fingers, his body shuddering as he came in his arms.

REESE KNEW A DISTRACTION WHEN HE SAW one.

While he appreciated the lengths Brantley would go to in order to get him to relax, Reese wanted to tell him it wasn't necessary, but he refrained from doing so. He wanted to savor the high for a bit longer, letting his mind remain clear even as he pulled his jeans up and buttoned and zipped them.

"My turn," Reese said when Brantley emerged from the bathroom a minute later.

He could see the outline of Brantley's erection straining against the black tactical pants he wore. The smirk that formed was ridiculously sexy. "Oh, yeah? And what did you have in mind?"

Rather than tell him, Reese took Brantley's hand and led him over to the small armchair in the corner. He turned Brantley around to face him, then proceeded to pull his shirt up over his head, tossing it behind him carelessly. He met Brantley's gaze, smiling as he leaned in and kissed him, working open his pants and freeing his cock.

The kiss blazed with passion, Brantley tilting his head, changing the angle, their tongues thrashing as adrenaline—fueled by lust—flooded Reese's bloodstream. He knew he would never get enough of this man.

When it was clear Brantley was about to take control, Reese forced himself to stop. He tore his mouth away, content that Brantley was breathing as hard as he was.

"Have a seat," he ordered, taking a step back.

Brantley's eyes remained locked on his face as he eased down into the chair, his knees spread wide, his cock standing up proudly. His pants shackled his ankles, but Brantley didn't seem to care as he got comfortable, a silent invitation burning in his blue-gray eyes.

Reese was pretty sure he'd never seen a more prime specimen in his entire life. Brantley's body was a masterpiece of hard angles and smooth planes. He loved looking at him when he was bare-chested, seeing how his abs clenched and relaxed, all that lean muscle shifting and bunching.

Without preamble, Reese lowered to his knees before him, positioning himself between Brantley's legs as best he could with his pants still wrapped around his ankles. He figured it was only fair since he'd been hindered the same way a few minutes ago.

"Ah, hell," Brantley groaned when Reese took him into his mouth, swirling his tongue around the wide crest, lapping at the precum pooling on the tip.

Reese hummed, knowing it would send vibrations along Brantley's shaft, earning him another garbled groan.

"You're so fuckin' good at that," Brantley growled, his voice a dark rumble. "Suck me."

He settled into the movements, bobbing his head up and down as he slowly worked Brantley higher and higher. Like Brantley had done, Reese kept his pace slow, not wanting to rush. He'd always known sex was a stress reliever, but he'd never realized he could get as much satisfaction from sucking Brantley's cock. There was something ridiculously hot about having a man like Brantley surrender to him like this.

A heavy hand curled over his head as Brantley began to thrust his hips upward, pushing his cock deep into Reese's throat.

"God, yes. That mouth … so fuckin' hot. Suck me, Reese. I wanna come down your throat."

And yes, he loved that Brantley had become so verbal during their encounters. He never held back, telling Reese exactly what he liked, what he wanted.

Minutes ticked by as Reese alternated between sucking and licking. Every so often, he would fondle Brantley's balls, teasing lightly, not wanting this to end too soon. He could feel the tension coiling in Brantley's body, his thigh muscles tightening as his balls drew up tight to his body, his abs more defined as he fought the inevitable.

"Take all of me," Brantley insisted, his hand pushing Reese's head down. "To the back of your throat."

Reese gave him what he wanted, taking the head of Brantley's cock into his throat. He gagged and pulled back, repeated the motion again and again. The man was too big—both long and thick—but he gave it his all, and it had the desired result because Brantley was panting and moaning, his hands fisting Reese's hair roughly as he began fucking his face, chasing his orgasm.

"I'm gonna come," Brantley warned. "I'm gonna come right down your throat."

A second later, he did, and it filled Reese with so much satisfaction he was almost positive the earth moved.

CHAPTER FIFTEEN

BRANTLEY STROLLED INTO THE RESTAURANT WITH REESE at his side. He followed the line to the cashier set up to take their money before they entered the all-you-can-eat buffet that the team had adopted as their go-to dinner place whenever they were in town.

He didn't see the appeal—the food was mediocre at best—but he understood the reasoning. It was a relatively inexpensive way to feed them all and cover all the various food bases while they were at it. With tonight's specials being prime rib *and* kung pao chicken, who could go wrong?

Brantley wasn't surprised that the cashier recognized him, offering a toothy grin as she rang them up and gave him the receipt.

Another half hour passed while everyone arrived, then made a pass around the multiple food stations and grabbed what they wanted to start with. It wasn't until they'd all taken their seats that Brantley skimmed the faces at the table, realizing they'd not only adopted a restaurant but a seating chart as well. He wondered if that was intentional or if they merely gravitated to their placements naturally.

Since the restaurant didn't have sections set up for large parties, they'd pulled four tables together, making a space large enough for the twelve of them to spread out comfortably. Brantley was at one end, positioned so he could see all the exits and everyone in the place. Reese was across from him, already making a dent in his enormous salad.

JJ was sitting next to Brantley, on his right, with an eclectic mix of food—a taquito, an egg roll, and chicken noodle soup—plus cherry cobbler for dessert in front of her. Across from JJ, Deck, with what appeared to be a vegetarian assortment—odd, but okay—was seated next to Reese, then Elana beside him, starting with soup and bread. Evan, with a porterhouse the size of Texas, was sitting beside Baz, who was the only other one acting like an adult besides Reese, starting with a salad.

Across from Evan was Slade digging into his standard double cheeseburger and fries. Next to him was Luca, who had yet to get food. Across from Luca was an empty chair where Becs would sit once she returned from the salad bar. Holly was next to her brother, Darius across from her, with a plate so full Brantley wasn't sure he'd eaten anytime in the past two weeks.

While Brantley ate his chicken fried chicken, he picked up on bits and pieces of the conversation taking place. Nothing overly heavy, primarily discussions about the drive up from Coyote Ridge, the traffic that was endured. As the minutes ticked by and the food was put away, the team lightened up, the mood shifting to friendly. Jokes and laughter ensued, and Brantley realized he'd come to enjoy these dinners. More accurately, he'd come to think of this team as a family in the time they'd been together.

"Baz and I are gonna meet up with your mother in the mornin'," JJ told Reese when a couple of the others went in search of a second helping or dessert.

Reese's eyes lifted to her face, and Brantley fought the urge to smile. It was true; he found the man's discomfort amusing. If the shoe had been on the other foot, he knew he'd be just as mortified by the idea of his mother mixing things up with not only his father but his father's friend as well, which he figured gave him the right to do so. Of course, he'd never imagine Frank Walker would share his wife with anyone, so it helped that there was no chance in hell it would ever be reversed.

"Whatever you learn … keep it to yourself," Reese grumbled, his gaze drifting back to his food.

"You mean you don't wanna know the details of her taboo romance with—"

Reese's gaze shot to JJ, effectively shutting her up and making her laugh at the same time.

She put her hands up in a sign of surrender. "I won't say a word. Promise."

"You can tell me. It'll give me ammunition to torment him with later," Brantley told her, his gaze on Reese, which was why he saw the man's eyes narrow. Brantley chuckled. "Kidding."

"Are y'all gonna meet up with the Mob boss?" Deck inquired.

"My brother's settin' up a time," Reese informed him, then looked at Brantley. "I don't think it'll be tomorrow."

Based on the bits and pieces of the conversation he'd overheard on the drive from the hotel, Brantley figured as much. It was a spur-of-the-moment request, so he understood, even if it irked the shit out of him. He wanted to get this over with so they could move on. Finding Tobias Land was a task that he'd expected to have completed already, but the man was proving to be elusive. That or he was dead, and they were going to find a body at some point, but he hoped that wasn't the case. Considering the goons had ransacked Toby's house, he got the feeling the man had slipped away before anyone—authorities or bad guys—could grab him. So the hunt would continue.

"I made a few calls," Slade said, wiping his mouth with a napkin. "Tried to get a feel for anyone else searchin'."

Brantley glanced down the table at him. "And?"

"There's at least one guy with a bead on him, but he's workin' the Austin angle."

"Maybe he'll find him," Brantley mused, although he didn't think that would be the case. For whatever reason, after seeing Toby's house, he got the feeling the man had hightailed it out of Dodge. He also didn't think they'd find him in Dallas, but since the Mob angle was the only viable lead they had right now, it was worth pursuing.

"I've got a question," Elana piped up, leaning forward to look down the table at him.

"What's that?"

"Do we … uh … get the bounty if we find him?"

Curious why she would ask, Brantley put down his fork and met her gaze. "According to Z, yeah. Why?"

Her freckled cheeks turned a rosy red. "I was thinkin' maybe we could use it to do somethin' fun. I mean, it's not a normal job for us, and the money would be a bonus, right?"

Interesting idea. "Yeah," he confirmed. "It would."

"So maybe we could use it to have a team-building exercise or something."

"You don't think we get enough team building just sittin' in the same building all the time?" Baz teased.

Brantley looked at Reese, noticed the man's permanent scowl had disappeared, and he seemed interested in the idea. Or maybe not the idea so much as the fact that the team was rallying together as they usually did.

He wouldn't deny things hadn't been the same when Reese was gone. For the six months Reese had been recovering in Dallas, they'd been focused primarily on work and little else. At least that Brantley saw. Based on their interactions tonight, the friendly banter and witty comments, he got the feeling they were spending quite a bit of time getting to know one another.

Funny how he'd never imagined his life without his SEAL teammates, but this… Although the abrupt end to his career hadn't been ideal, nor was it something he'd want to relive, this was a damn good consolation prize as far as he was concerned.

SLADE SAT QUIETLY AT THE TABLE, LISTENING to everyone else talk. He was just off-center, with three people on his right and two on his left, so he was bombarded with more than one conversation, none of which he was contributing much to.

Truth was, he didn't have much to say. The ride up from Coyote Ridge had been eerily silent for the most part. Slade had refrained from giving Evan a hard time about Becs because he hadn't been too keen on the idea of walking, and he didn't doubt for one second that Evan would've tossed his ass out of the moving vehicle just to shut him up.

It hadn't helped that Slade's cell phone had been blowing up with texts from his ex-wife for the better part of the afternoon. He hadn't responded to any of them. Hell, he hadn't read half of them, either. Whenever he thought about Jennifer, he was flooded with both anger and pain, neither of which he wanted to deal with right now.

Another half hour passed while Slade sipped tea and wished they would finish up so he could move on to something more interesting. More accurately, something that didn't involve him sitting shoulder to shoulder with Luca Switzer, who seemed intent on ensuring he was as uncomfortable as could be.

"Anyone up for a drink at the hotel bar?" Slade offered as they were walking out to their vehicles.

"I think we're gonna call it a night," Brantley said. "But y'all have fun."

"We're turnin' in, too," JJ announced with a grin. "Since I can't drink, not much fun to hang out at a bar."

"Well, y'all have a good night. But if you find you can't sleep, you know where I'll be," Slade told the group before detouring toward Evan's car, glancing over at the man. "What about you, big guy?"

If Evan meant to be subtle when he shot a glance in Becs's direction, he failed miserably. Slade managed to keep his mouth shut rather than razz Becs about whether she would be joining so Evan could make an informed decision.

"I'll join you," Holly said with a beaming grin.

"No, you won't," Luca answered for his sister, his dark blue eyes locked on Slade's face as though he'd been the one to ask her to join him.

Yeah, it was no longer a question as to whether the man was doing his best to ensure Slade and Holly weren't left alone in the same room together. He'd suspected it, but Luca's adamance now confirmed it. This wasn't the first time big brother had inserted himself into a conversation Slade was having with Holly. Overprotective seemed to be the guy's default setting.

Slade could've told Luca he had nothing to worry about, but what would be the fun in that? It was easier to let Luca think Slade might make a move on Holly than to inform him he had no interest. Not because Holly wasn't attractive. She was. Most definitely. But Slade had an iron-clad rule about screwing people he worked with. Shit like that got messy, and he had enough upheaval in his life already.

"Yes," Holly insisted. "I do want to join them. And that's exactly what I'm *gonna* do."

Slade smiled back at Luca, feeling as though he'd won this round, although, again, he hadn't been the one to ask Holly to join him.

"Then I'll get one, too," Luca said, still staring at Slade.

"I'll come," Becs announced as soon as Luca did.

"I wouldn't mind a drink," Evan chimed in, seeming to make a decision now that Becs had.

And just like that, it was a group thing when the truth was, Slade hadn't expected anyone to join him. He really wanted to go back to his room and call his ex-wife to find out what was going on. Her text messages had slowed, but he was still getting one every hour or so, none of them making a lick of sense. However, slinking away to sulk in his room wasn't his idea of fun. Nor was it something he wanted his team to know he did on occasion. They thought he was the fun-loving, drink-until-you-black-out kind of guy, the life of the party.

He wasn't and hadn't been for a long time, but he figured they didn't need to know that.

"We'll see you there," Slade told everyone as they started getting into their cars.

"You wanna ride with us?" Evan offered Becs.

Her blue eyes shot over to Luca instantly, a smile forming. "Would you mind if I rode with you?"

"I've got room," Luca said, seemingly oblivious to the fact that Becs had been coming on to him.

What the hell was going on here? If Slade didn't know better, he'd think he'd gotten caught up in some sorta weird love triangle.

Evan couldn't believe he'd gotten himself mixed up in this.

He was a fucking idiot.

When Slade had asked if anyone wanted to go to the bar, his first instinct was to turn down the offer, go to his room, call his daughter to say good night, then try to get some sleep.

Yet here he was, sitting at the bar because Becs had decided to go.

Oh, he hadn't missed the fact that her decision had hinged on Luca's willingness to go. In fact, it wasn't the first time he'd noticed that she tended to gravitate toward the man. Why wouldn't she, though? Luca Switzer wasn't only a good ol' country boy with his cowboy swagger and rugged good looks, he was also a fucking genius.

"If you're gonna sit over here and pout all night, why'd you even bother to come?"

Evan's head snapped up, his eyes landing on Deck, who was standing just off to the side, a bottle of Corona in hand. He started to say he wasn't pouting, but in his head, it sounded way too juvenile to allow to escape his lips, so he remained silent.

"Mind if I sit?"

"Free country," he grumbled, realizing too late that regardless of *what* he said, it sounded juvenile.

Decker Bromwell was the only member of the team Evan knew very little about. Most of the task force members tended to overshare, a trait he associated with small towns. Since Deck wasn't from Coyote Ridge like most of the others, he hadn't inherited the gene. For that reason, Evan hadn't interacted much with the man since he came on board a few weeks after Evan did.

"So, who're you pining over?" Deck jerked his chin in the direction of the others currently seated at tables scattered throughout the minuscule bar section.

"What?"

"I'm guessin' it's the cute little redhead," Deck noted.

Rather than answer, Evan tossed back what was left of his cheap vodka.

"Yep, it is," Deck concluded.

"Did you need something?" Evan wasn't about to talk about his personal life with this guy.

Deck exhaled heavily, leaning back in the chair. "It doesn't make sense to get mixed up with people you work with."

Evan narrowed his gaze. "Are you giving me dating advice? I didn't realize we were friends."

"Since everyone sees me as the enemy, I wasn't under that illusion either," Deck countered.

Evan detected a note of … well, he wasn't sure what it was he detected in Deck's tone. Could've been disdain or even hurt. The guy wasn't great with relaying emotions.

"No one sees you as the enemy," Evan told him, setting his empty glass on the table in front of him.

"A leper, then?" Deck sounded genuinely interested in an answer.

Curious as to what prompted this man to open up, Evan focused on him. "I think it's more like you don't give anyone a chance to know you."

"I show up every day. That doesn't count?"

Evan leaned back, studied him for a moment. "Do you even want to be part of this task force?"

"I didn't have much choice in the matter."

That was news to Evan. He'd honestly thought he heard someone mention that Deck had signed on for the job. "How'd you end up here?"

"Like I said, getting mixed up with people you work with doesn't make sense."

It almost sounded like deflection, but Evan sensed it was actually an explanation, so he went with it. "Bad blood between you and a co-worker?"

Deck snorted. "More like bad blood between me and the guy who wants that co-worker." Deck nodded his chin toward the group. "It's similar to Slade's situation with Holly."

Evan glanced over his shoulder at the others. "What about Slade and Holly?"

"It's obvious she's into him, but her brother's pretty damn adamant that not be the case."

Evan slowly turned in his chair, surveying Slade and Holly more closely. She was into him? How the hell had he missed that one?

"I don't think the feelin's mutual," Deck said, as though gossiping about the team was their new ritual. "But it doesn't matter. With Luca cock-blocking them at every turn, it's inevitable somethin's gonna happen."

"He's still hung up on his ex-wife," Evan noted, hating himself for revealing that fact when it was none of his fucking business.

"Yeah. That's a given. Guy's phone goes off all damn day. Only someone important in your life can keep you from turnin' the damn thing off or throwin' it into traffic."

Evan relaxed, watching Becs as she laughed at something Luca said.

"Same goes for her and him," Deck said. "She's into him, but he doesn't know she exists. Not in the way she wants him to."

He hated that his gut churned, pain radiating through his chest at the thought of Becs and Luca together. Yeah, he'd noticed her flirting, but he hadn't thought anything of it. Well, that wasn't entirely true. It was more like he was in denial, wishing like hell she would smile at him the way she smiled at Luca.

Deck chuckled softly. "Like I said…"

Yeah, yeah. Evan had heard him. It wasn't wise to mix things up with co-workers.

He got it.

Damn it.

CHAPTER SIXTEEN

Wednesday, May 4, 2022

"It's so good to see you," Cindy Tavoularis greeted when Reese's mother opened the door.

JJ offered a smile and accepted the woman's hug as she stepped into the house. This wasn't her first visit to Reese's mother's house, so she felt comfortable. She'd spent the holidays here back when she'd been running away from Baz and the overwhelming feelings she had for the man.

"Likewise," she told Cindy. "I didn't think I'd see you for a couple of weeks."

"Which tells me this visit isn't about the wedding," Cindy said sweetly, her gaze shifting to Baz and a beaming smile appearing. "And you must be Sebastian."

"Yes, ma'am." Baz held out his hand to shake hers. "But please, call me Baz."

Cindy peered down at his extended hand, then up to Baz's face. "I don't shake hands with family."

Before JJ could decipher what Cindy meant, she leaned in and hugged Baz, startling him enough to make his eyes go wide.

For whatever reason, that struck JJ as funny. Probably because she rarely saw Baz flustered. The man was the epitome of a smooth operator, but it looked as though other people's parents could trip him up. She filed that information away for later.

"Come on in the kitchen. I've got coffee, juice, and bagels if you'd like."

JJ glanced up at Baz as they followed behind Cindy. She mouthed, "I want coffee," which earned her a wicked grin.

"It's decaf," Cindy noted. "Since you're pregnant and all."

JJ stuck her tongue out at Baz and smirked. She would get coffee after all, although it didn't make a lick of sense to drink it if it didn't have caffeine. But it was the principle of the matter, she figured.

"I take it y'all are here to talk about Toby?" Cindy's brown eyes were wary as she glanced between them, motioning toward the table and pulling out one of the chairs for herself.

"We are." JJ took a seat across from her. "We think he might've gotten himself mixed up in something … uh…"

"Bad?" Cindy contributed, slowly easing into the chair, her gaze scanning JJ's face for clues. "Nefarious? Illegal?" Her face scrunched. "Taboo?"

JJ chuckled, realizing the woman was worked up with concern. Wanting to soothe her nerves somewhat, she answered with, "We don't know what it is at this point, but that's why we're here. Brantley and Reese are lookin' into some of the properties he owned up here, hopin' he might be hidin' out somewhere."

Cindy exhaled, then stood quickly, as though realizing she hadn't meant to sit down. "Would either of you like coffee?"

"I would, please and thank you," JJ answered, looking over at Baz.

"I'll take some, too."

JJ watched as Cindy poured three mugs of coffee and delivered them to the table. There was already a small container of sugar and a little glass pitcher of cream set up with a plate full of bagels and a variety of spreads to go on them. Her stomach rumbled.

"Go on, honey, get yourself some."

JJ didn't hesitate.

Because she'd spent a Christmas up here with Brantley and Reese, JJ'd gotten acquainted not only with Cindy but also Cindy's boyfriend, Hugh, and Reese's sister, Jensyn, who lived in California. At the time, she recalled being wildly anxious about being here, but it had only taken a few short hours in Cindy's company before she felt right at home. Enough that all those pesky nerves had been obliterated.

Grabbing a bagel, JJ went to work adding strawberry cream cheese to it, waiting for Cindy to join them at the table again.

"Where would you like to start?" Cindy asked when she took a seat.

Since JJ had just taken a bite, she couldn't respond, but she suspected Cindy had planned it that way because her eyes shifted to Baz. "I take it Reese has told you about my history with Toby."

The woman was very soft-spoken and ridiculously polite, but JJ noticed a fire banked in her eyes.

"High-level details only," Baz answered, shifting in his seat.

JJ wiped her mouth with a napkin, took a sip of black coffee. "Reese gets flustered when we bring it up."

Cindy's face brightened, her eyes shining as though that pleased her to some degree. JJ knew Reese had a good relationship with his mother and her boyfriend, so it wasn't that Cindy preferred her son to be uncomfortable. More than likely, she approved of the fact that Reese cared enough to let his discomfort with the situation shine through.

"I can only imagine."

"There's a story there," JJ accused with a grin. "And I wanna know what it is."

"JJ," Baz admonished.

"It's fine. Really." Cindy sipped from her own cup. "It's not as bad as you're probably imagining. Reese walked in on Toby and me kissing once."

"Do tell," JJ encouraged.

"God, it was years ago," she reflected with a smile. "Reese had just come home on leave, and Toby was on the tail end of one of his visits." Her gaze swept over JJ and Baz. "He would come to see Thomas and me on occasion, usually when whatever he was doing brought him to the Austin area."

"So he moved out of Coyote Ridge?" Baz asked.

"As soon as he could. Toby's always been the wanderin' sort. That's why it doesn't surprise me that he's in this mess."

"Y'all were close?" JJ asked, wanting to get Cindy back on topic because this was too juicy not to. Baz might not care to hear the story of Cindy's romance with Toby, but JJ did, despite what she'd promised Reese.

"You could say that." Her eyes took on a faraway look, as though she was lost in a memory.

"And Reese's dad was … close to him as well?"

JJ felt Baz bristle beside him. Thankfully, he didn't speak up.

Cindy's eyes locked on JJ's face and a smile pulled at her mouth. "He was, yes."

JJ cocked an eyebrow, hoping Cindy could translate the expression to mean she wanted more details without having to say it.

For the first time since Cindy had started talking about her previous relationship, the woman's cheeks turned a rosy red. "They … experimented. I guess that's the right word for it."

Wanting to ensure she understood correctly, JJ said, "With each other?"

"Only when I was with them, but yes, they were intimate."

"Reese doesn't know this."

Cindy chuckled. "I don't know if his heart can handle information like that."

"I'd agree with that assessment," Baz muttered over his coffee mug.

A laugh bubbled up from JJ's center. "No. No, it most certainly can't. But mine can."

Another blush infused Cindy's face. "Let's just say, if Reese had come home a couple of hours earlier than he did that day, he would've been horrified for an entirely different reason. Luckily, his timing only allowed him to find Toby and me kissing. Thomas had gone to the store to pick up a couple of things for lunch, left us there alone."

"Knowing what might happen?"

"My Thomas was a possessive man, but he knew I cared about Toby, and Toby cared about me. Plus, they had forged a bond that'd surpassed merely friendship."

"But it never got serious?"

Cindy's gaze drifted to the mug in front of her. "I think we each wanted something more, but no one knew how to voice it appropriately, so we settled for what we had. Plus, Toby wasn't the sort to settle down. He wanted to explore, to see the world, while I wanted to raise my kids and focus on being a teacher."

"I take it things ended after the accident?" JJ probed.

"It did. I was devastated, and I think Toby was, too. He came to visit soon after I called to tell him what happened. His visits lessened after that. I think it was too difficult for him to see Thomas like that, so he stayed away. Then I met Hugh."

JJ had to wonder what might've happened if there'd never been an accident. Would they have found a way to make things work eventually?

"Toby had a picture of you in his home," Baz noted. "A couple, actually."

"I heard." Cindy picked up her coffee mug and took a sip. "I've talked to him a few times over the years. I suspected he had regrets that things didn't work out between us." She looked up. "Don't get me wrong; I cared about Toby. There's a chance I even loved him, but it wasn't the same way I loved Thomas or even what I feel for Hugh. I think it had to do with his constant disappearances. It was hard to love someone who wasn't around."

"Is that your subtle way of tellin' us that you don't know what Toby's been up to?" JJ teased, picking up her bagel and taking a bite.

"I really wish I did. After I talked to Reese, I tried calling the last number I had for Toby. It's been disconnected."

JJ focused on eating while Baz filled Cindy in on what they'd learned so far, which was a whole lot of nothing. Cindy seemed genuinely surprised to hear that the travel agency was no longer in business, but not so much Toby's preference for full-nude cabarets.

"Part of Toby's appeal was his devil-may-care attitude. He wasn't ashamed of who he was, and that was refreshing. He was a lot like Thomas in that way, although Thomas didn't care for sex clubs. Just not his thing. He did embrace who he was and didn't make excuses for it, though." Another smile appeared. "Much like my boys did. I'm proud of them for that."

JJ felt tears well up in her eyes. Cindy's love for her kids always caught her in the heart.

And, unfortunately, these damn pregnancy hormones made it impossible for JJ to pretend she was heartless.

HAVING UNDERGONE A QUICK TOUR THROUGH THE Sniper 1 Security building to meet a few new people who'd been hired in recent weeks, as well as say hello to some of those they'd been working with over the past year, Brantley found himself relaxing a little. He'd woken up antsy because they didn't have a lead to follow, so when Reese suggested they come here, he had no excuse for why they couldn't.

Now that they were here, he was glad he'd come. Especially since it appeared Reese's older brother was enjoying Reese's discomfort with the recent revelation about their mother and her past love affairs.

"You realize she's gonna tell JJ everything." Z's wild grin said the man was happy about that.

Brantley followed Z as he led the way toward his office. "Oh, I know."

Reese grunted as he did anytime someone brought up the subject.

"Have a seat." Z motioned toward the two chairs in front of his desk before moving behind it to sit in the large leather-back executive chair.

"I take it you were already aware of your mother's relationship with Toby?"

Z's gaze swung to Reese, and he smiled again. "Oh, yeah. I knew."

"How'd you learn about it?" Brantley canted his head toward Reese. "Did you find out the same way Reese did?"

"You mean, did I walk in on them?" He barked a laugh. "God, no. I would've been scarred for life."

"I didn't walk in on them," Reese said through clenched teeth. "They were kissin'."

"But you saw Mom kissin' another guy." Z sat up and clasped his hands together on the top of the desk. "How did that make you feel?"

"Fuck off."

Brantley laughed, then patted Reese's arm. "All right, we'll stop fuckin' with you now."

"That'd be nice," he mumbled, reaching down to pet Tesha, who was lounging at his feet. Brantley noticed Reese did that frequently, as though using her as his emotional support animal.

Making good on his promise, Brantley changed the subject. "Did you talk to Max?"

Z relaxed in his chair. "I talked to Courtney. Told her to have Max call me."

"Did you tell her why?"

He nodded. "High-level, but yes."

"You think he'll agree to meet with us?"

"I figure he'll be too intrigued not to. If he doesn't already know about Hartwood, he's gonna want more details of a potential rival lookin' to make waves down south. She did say Max was busy today, but she's anglin' for tomorrow at the latest."

Brantley had only met Courtney Kogan once, and it had been here in the office. If he hadn't already been aware the woman was married to a mobster, he never would've guessed it. However, after a few minutes in her presence, he'd understood all too well what her appeal would've been to a man with power like Max Adorite. She certainly wasn't a wallflower.

"Max has been makin' some strategic changes to his organization," Z explained. "When he stepped into the role after his father … died, he'd been lookin' to take their businesses legit."

"How'd he die?" Brantley asked, curious.

Z cocked an eyebrow. "How do you think?"

Brantley glanced at Reese, wondering if that was a trick question. How the hell was he supposed to know?

"His family took him out," Reese muttered. "Although no one speaks of it."

Ah. So not a cohesive unit. Good to know.

He turned his attention to Z. "Did it work? The legit business avenue?"

"In some ways, yes."

Brantley found the whole thing fascinating. The fact that a straight-laced family like the Kogans could embrace their daughter's mobster husband proved that true love did exist.

"However," Z continued, "goin' legit only gets the Feds off his back some. It doesn't stop the other syndicates from wantin' to take him out at the knees. After Madison's attempted kidnapping, Max snapped."

Brantley didn't take his eyes off Z. He pretended he wasn't thinking about the night Reese had been shot. He'd watched the security video so many times, the scene was imprinted on his brain. But it was the *after* that still stuck with him. Namely, the fact that Reese had nearly died and Z hadn't bothered to call him to let him know.

Z was watching him when he added, "He's takin' drastic measures to gain control and to protect his family."

Could Z read his mind? Could he sense the animosity Brantley felt for not being told?

Beside him, Reese squirmed in his chair. "If we could talk about somethin' else…"

Z glanced between them, then his eyes flared as though he had just realized he was carrying on about a sore subject. "Sorry."

"It's fine," Brantley assured him.

"I'm still tryin' to figure out why y'all think Max might be able to help," Z said, relaxing in his chair.

"We don't know that he can." Brantley sighed. "But we're at a loss here. Tuggin' on this string's the only thing we've got right now."

Z sat up straight. "That reminds me. I did a little research on my own, found some property that I think belongs to Toby."

"You *think* it does?" Reese asked.

Z typed something on his keyboard, then turned the monitor so it faced them. "I've got one of the techs lookin' into it more because I honestly can't tell you how I got to it, but I think it's tied to him."

Brantley knew all too well how easy it was to go down a path that had nothing to do with your objective. It'd happened to him many times, but not following up on the lead was stupid because you never knew when you would strike gold.

"That's midway between here and Austin," Brantley noted, looking at the map on the screen.

"Yeah. About an hour and a half from here. Which is why I've got someone diggin' deeper. If it's—" Z's cell phone rang, cutting him off as he glanced down at the screen. "Sorry, I've gotta take this."

Z grabbed his phone and stepped out into the hall, closing the door behind him.

"We could always hop in the truck and head down there," Brantley told Reese. "Instead of waitin' for them to get more info."

Reese shook his head. "If it's all the same to you, I'd rather not go on a wild goose chase. I already feel like we're spinnin' our wheels here."

Brantley understood that. They'd been looking into Toby's whereabouts for the past five days, and they'd come up with nothing of substance besides uncovering the possibility of him working with the mob and the fact that he had a penchant for investing in rundown cabins. There was a good chance they'd gone too far off course already, and wasting too much time on it wouldn't help.

"We might have some time to kill," Brantley said, glancing over at Reese. "Any suggestions?"

"I thought we'd go to the simulation center."

The suggestion surprised Brantley, but he masked his expression carefully. "You sure you're up for it?"

Reese nodded. "That's to be seen, but I think it's a necessary evil."

Brantley continued to watch him. A second later, an idea came to him.

"I know that look," Reese stated, twisting in his chair. "What are you plannin' to do?"

He leaned over and kissed Reese quickly before getting to his feet. "I just need to find RT."

"For what?"

Brantley stopped with his hand on the doorknob. "Do you trust me?"

Reese didn't hesitate when he said, "With my life."

There was no denying his response made Brantley feel good. He said, "Then that's what I need you to do," as he opened the door and stepped into the hall.

"That tells me nothin', Navy boy," Reese called after him.

"It will. You'll see," he told Reese as he went in search of RT.

CHAPTER SEVENTEEN

REESE HAD NO IDEA IF THE PLAN was still to go to the simulation center or if Brantley had another idea, but he didn't care. Getting out of the Sniper 1 office, avoiding any conversations related to the Adorites … as long as he didn't feel like he was subjecting Brantley to that shit all over again, Reese would gladly go anywhere and do anything.

"Give me a sec, would ya?" Brantley asked when they stopped in front of RT's office. "Tesha, here. Let's say hello to RT."

Confused but a little curious, Reese nodded his head. "I'll wait by the elevators."

Brantley gave him a wicked grin, then slipped into RT's office with Tesha and closed the door.

Reese sauntered toward the front, passing through the bullpen that resembled a ghost town since most of their security personnel who used this space were out in the field, off on assignments. He continued until he was at the plush lobby with its expensive artwork and glossy-wood walls designed to greet their clients and put them at ease by making them believe that success equaled designer decor. Of course, Sniper 1 Security had the reputation to back their design, but he wondered how many other firms could say the same.

"We weren't expecting y'all to be here until Friday."

Reese turned away from the bronze wall sculpture he'd been eyeballing and smiled at Jayden Brooks, Sniper 1's receptionist.

Sitting behind that tall counter, you wouldn't know Jayden was five foot ten and preferred to wear four-inch heels, making her taller than most of the people in this office. But you couldn't miss the strawberry-blond pixie cut, her jade-green eyes, or her quick smile.

"We came up early. Workin' another case," he told her, resting his arms on the counter, trying to feign a casualness he didn't quite feel.

"Ah." She flashed a set of pearly whites. "I hope it's goin' well."

Reese genuinely liked Jayden. During his recovery time, he'd spent many hours here at the office, and during that, he'd had a chance to talk to several people who called this place home between nine and five. Jayden was one of those who liked to chat. And she had no qualms dishing dirt about anyone in the office.

Well, almost anyone. There was one person who was off-limits: Conner Kogan. Apparently, Jayden harbored a major crush on the guy—had for years—and talking about him, whether good or bad, wasn't allowed.

"One dead end after another, but you know how it goes."

Her eyes glittered. "Oh, I know." She canted her head toward the offices behind her. "I hear them complain about it all the time."

Reese wanted to tell her he wasn't complaining. He hadn't meant to sound negative, but the jumbled thoughts sent him in that direction, so he figured it was best to keep his mouth shut.

Footsteps sounded, and Reese glanced over to see Brantley strolling toward him. He caught himself staring at the formidable man for a little too long, something he'd been doing a lot lately. He couldn't seem to help himself. It was as though he was still making up for all the time they were apart, and looking at Brantley did something to him. He wouldn't go so far as to say it relaxed him—he was too wound up for that right now—but it eased some part of his soul that had been aching for the months they were apart.

"Hey, Jay," Brantley said with a chin nod toward Jayden.

"What's up, *Bran*?" she countered with a wide grin.

Reese's eyebrows popped. "Bran?"

"He hates it," Jayden teased. "The same way I hate when someone shortens my name." She shrugged, smirked. "Whaddya do?"

Brantley laughed as he touched Reese's arm and turned him toward the elevator. "Ready?"

"Be careful out there," Jayden called after them.

"Where's the fun in that?" Brantley countered as he stabbed the button for the elevator.

"Where's Tesha?"

"RT and Z are gonna keep an eye on her until JJ gets up here."

Reese nodded, more intrigued than before.

When the elevator arrived, Reese stepped in first, then turned to glance at Brantley when he pushed the button for the parking garage. "Everything good?"

His smirk was devious. "Peachy."

The elevator delivered them to the parking garage beneath the building. Reese strolled out, his curiosity getting the best of him. "Where're we headed?"

"The simulation building."

"Just checkin'," he said when Brantley looked at him sideways. "Never know what you've got up your sleeve."

Brantley stopped behind the truck and turned to Reese. "I had RT clear it out for us."

Reese frowned. "Why?"

One of Brantley's dark eyebrows rose slowly. "I think it's what you need right now."

Reese nodded, ignoring the churning that developed in his gut at the thought of being put to the test right now. He didn't want Brantley to know he'd been second-guessing himself since his reaction at the strip club the other day. His first instinct was to get defensive, but he knew that would only be his denial talking.

Brantley's voice lowered, and he took a step toward him. "It'll just be you and me for the next three hours."

Reese considered twisting Brantley's words into something dirty, but there hadn't been an ounce of seduction in the man's tone. Maybe a hint of promise, but if he wasn't mistaken, this was Brantley's way of offering to help him without broadcasting his concerns to the entire team.

"Unless you object," Brantley tacked on.

"No." Reese reached out and brushed his hand over Brantley's forearm. "I think it's a good idea. Thanks."

Seemingly content, Brantley smiled, then turned and walked to the driver's side, leaving Reese staring after him, wondering whether he would survive the next three hours without losing his shit altogether.

Twenty minutes later, they were pulling into the parking lot of the simulation center. The *empty* parking lot.

"We won't be wearin' any of the trackin' gear," Brantley explained as they strolled into the building. "Only the shot vests."

Reese wasn't sure that was the correct name for the vests that tracked whether or not the wearer had been shot by one of the laser guns, but it was an apt description. He wouldn't admit it out loud, but he was grateful not to wear the devices that monitored heart rate, temperature, and the like because he wasn't sure he was ready for Brantley to know his heart was already pounding like he'd run a marathon in record time. There was no doubt he was on the verge of a panic attack, and he wasn't even on the business end of a gun.

"If you're not up for it, we can leave."

Reese looked up to see Brantley was watching him closely, his expression concerned.

"I want to," he assured him. "I just…" Reese exhaled slowly. "I'm just not sure I can."

"Would it help if I took off my shirt?"

Reese's gaze slammed into Brantley's face. "That always helps."

The smile that formed on the man's mouth was slow and wicked and effectively eased some of the tension in his body. Of course, it caused a different type of tension, but Reese could handle that.

"Fine."

While Reese watched, Brantley reached for the hem of his T-shirt and slowly lifted it over his head, revealing that delectable upper body, thick slabs of perfectly sculpted muscle and sinew covered by smooth, sun-kissed skin.

"Better?"

Reese could only nod as he soaked up the sight of him, relying on his body's reaction to calm his nerves even more.

"Come on. Let's grab vests and weapons."

His brain processed the words, but thankfully Reese was too busy ogling him for panic to set in.

WHEN BRANTLEY HAD EXPLAINED HIS CONCERNS TO RT regarding Reese's need for reentry training, purposely not sharing that he'd witnessed Reese's panic in the field, the man had been more than willing to grant Brantley his one wish: clear out the training center. With a single phone call, Ryan Trexler closed the place completely, giving Brantley and Reese the space to themselves.

Three hours. That wasn't a long time in the grand scheme of things, but it would be long enough for them to work on a few scenarios that might ease Reese's mind a little. It wouldn't solve any major problems, but it would help to address the issue at hand, get it out in the open so they could talk more about it in the future.

Brantley knew bringing Reese here was a gamble, but he was hoping it would give them a chance to face a couple of scenarios together without the pesky interference of the real world and the dangers that lurked. Taking away the risk was key, he knew. There was a good chance this convoluted plan wouldn't work, but he was willing to do whatever it took to help Reese through this.

"We're gonna keep the lights on," Brantley explained. "And we won't be usin' the smaller rooms."

"So you're sayin' you don't want to work on my claustrophobia today."

There was a hint of humor in Reese's tone, but it didn't hide the trepidation Brantley could still hear underneath.

"We'll deal with that later." He grinned back at him over his shoulder. "When you're beneath me."

Reese laughed, just as Brantley'd hoped he would.

After passing one of the vests to Reese, Brantley put his own on. The small circular disc adhered to a light spandex fabric and covered only the chest region, reminding him way too much of the Arc Reactor on Iron Man's suit. The fact that he would even know who Iron Man was, much less an Arc Reactor, was a testament to Reese's insistence on watching Marvel movies. While their unit didn't power a fancy weapon suit, it did contain sensors that tracked the accuracy of a simulated bullet. And since they'd be coming up against virtual bad guys, it was necessary to determine whether or not they'd taken a hit.

He put on his own vest with ease, then turned to see Reese was fumbling with the clasp for his because his hands were trembling. His first instinct was to help him, but he didn't. The last thing he wanted was to draw attention to the fact Reese was already panicking, and they hadn't started yet. Instead, he made a show of looking through the selection of weapons. Every make and model of firearm had been modified and weighted to feel like a loaded gun, although they didn't have magazines or chambers, removing the possibility of potential accidents. Once that had been altered, they'd been set up with the laser system, giving the trainees plenty of options to ensure their success.

"I'm not sure a scenario with you as the bad guy is gonna help me," Reese said when he finally got the harness in place. "Especially bare-chested."

"It won't," he agreed. "Which is why we're gonna use the new toy."

"New toy?"

"It's a work in progress, but I got the go-ahead to turn it on. Dom and Austin have been workin' on it for a while now."

Dominic and Austin Trexler were two of Sniper 1's computer geniuses who'd ventured into tech design in recent years. Since Sniper 1 Security had been working with the government to test new weapons, they'd come up with the idea of an artificial intelligence system combined with a virtual reality program that would simulate whatever bad guy they programmed. They'd tried to explain how it worked, but Brantley had quickly cut them off. He wouldn't understand it, nor did he care to. The toys were their thing, not his. He just enjoyed shooting the bad guys.

"So how does this work?" Reese asked when they ventured back out into the warehouse designed as the training floor.

"We're goin' to the VR room," he said, leading the way.

Since the virtual reality room took up a significant portion of the training facility, Brantley knew the risk of a panic attack brought on by claustrophobia was small. From his interactions with Reese, the man only had issues when the spaces were small and dark. With this system, the scenarios would make it appear like they were in various locations—a mall, a restaurant, a park—and not inside a room.

"I'm gonna be your backup for this scenario," Brantley explained, swinging the door wide and urging Reese inside.

He tapped a button on the wall, which brought the room to life. He'd told Dom what he was angling for, and the man had promised to have it functioning before they arrived. He'd come through for them because the floor, ceiling, and walls took on a life of their own, reflecting a large shopping mall, complete with a few shoppers moving in and out of a variety of stores.

"Holy shit," Reese muttered.

"Looks real, huh?"

"Too real."

Yeah, in a way, it was kinda creepy. It was so lifelike that he felt he could reach out and touch the stand for the pretzel vendor beside them, although it was merely a three-dimensional simulation.

"If it helps, we've got about three minutes to peruse the place."

Reese peered over at him. "Seriously? We can go shoppin'?"

Brantley grinned. "In a sense, yeah. The program is synced to your vest," he explained. "So the room will shift based on your movements. To walk, just simulate taking steps in one direction or another. If you get too close to an actual wall, the virtual wall grid will appear as a warning, like on those Oculus goggles you made me try."

For the next few minutes, Brantley remained near Reese's side as he navigated through the upper level of a mall. Brantley had no idea what went into designing a system of this magnitude, but he understood RT's reason for wanting to keep this on the down low. They had yet to roll it out to the entire team, instead hand-selecting only a few to test it out. Brantley had been one of the few.

"There's gonna be a threat," he told Reese. "A man with a gun will appear in a moment. I'll be his target. He's not trigger-happy, but he is squirrely, so it's your job to talk him down."

Reese exhaled sharply. "Okay."

Brantley moved with Reese, keeping close, reminding him he was there as they passed various shops.

"There he is," Reese said, drawing Brantley's attention to a big bald guy wearing a jacket. Since everyone else was wearing summer attire—shorts, T-shirts, flip-flops—he was likely using it to conceal a weapon.

As had been the case at the strip club with the twitchy-fingered bouncer, the man shifted his jacket, revealing a gun, his hand settling on the butt of it. Beside him, Reese's breathing grew heavier.

"You," the holographic image said in a deep, gruff voice, pointing directly at Brantley. "You're coming with me."

It took effort not to laugh because it was a canned statement, like something out of a bad movie.

"I don't have all day," the image groused. "Let's go."

"Like hell," Brantley muttered, amused. In what world would he just put his hands up and surrender? He'd have to mention that to Dom and Austin. Maybe those two shouldn't be in charge of designing the scenes.

"The boss wants to talk to you," the image said, pulling his weapon free and raising it.

To keep with the program's design, in a move that wasn't something he would ever do, Brantley shifted to stand behind Reese as though using him for protection. That had the bad guy aiming his weapon directly at Reese.

"Reese? You okay?" Brantley asked when Reese was motionless, his breaths sawing in and out of his lungs as he faced off with a simulated loaded gun. "Remember, it's not real."

"My brain's not processin' that part," he rasped.

The bad guy took a step toward them, and Reese backed up one, his hand trembling as it hovered over his weapon still holstered to his hip.

Somewhere deep in his gray matter, Reese knew this wasn't real, but his fight-or-flight instinct had kicked in, flooding his system with adrenaline. The problem was, his parasympathetic nervous system wasn't counterbalancing the reaction.

He knew all of this, had studied it until his eyes would cross. Understanding what effects PTSD had on his body was crucial if he expected to return to the field, so he'd done his due diligence. But even in this simulated environment, his brain wasn't processing accurately, and panic was setting in.

"Talk him down," Brantley urged. "Get him to lower the weapon. This is a mall. There are civilians around."

Yes. Civilians. Bad guy. Gun.

It wasn't real, Reese reminded himself. *None of it's real.*

I can do this.

"Breathe, Reese. Slowly."

Brantley's voice sounded like it was echoing down a tunnel, but Reese tried to cling to the words and the deep, gruff cadence.

"We've got options here," Brantley continued.

"No, we don't," he countered. "We're too exposed. There's nowhere to go."

"He's exposed, too." Brantley's voice sounded near his ear, and Reese realized he'd move directly behind him. "He's antsy, not payin' attention. I guarantee I can put a bullet between his eyes before he gets a shot off."

Reese heard the conviction in Brantley's tone.

"We're not helpless. We're armed, Reese."

Moving his hand over the butt of the gun on his hip, Reese tried to focus on that. Brantley was right; he wasn't helpless this time. He was armed and capable of defending himself.

"Let's go," the bad guy said, waving his gun as though directing them. "Can't keep the boss waiting."

"Look how he's holdin' that gun," Brantley said firmly. "His finger's not on the trigger."

No, it wasn't, but he was twitchy, his eyes scanning their surroundings, straying from where it should be.

"What's around us?" Brantley asked. "Is anyone else in danger right now?"

Reese took a moment to look left, then right. There was one person crouching low behind what looked like a trash can. Another was ushering their child backward into a store and out of sight. There wasn't a family of four whimpering in the corner or a waitress frozen in place behind the guy. This wasn't the restaurant, and Reese wasn't on the floor.

As he told himself these things, his adrenal glands stopped flooding his system with adrenaline, giving him a moment of clarity.

"Put your gun away," Reese insisted. "We'll go with you, but not until you do."

The guy looked around as though expecting someone else to be there. When he met Reese's gaze again, there was a hint of concern. As though he just realized he hadn't thought this through.

The man's weapon slowly lowered.

"Turn it off," Reese pleaded to Brantley. "I need a minute."

Brantley didn't say a word, but a second later, the simulation ended, and Reese found himself standing in the center of a well-lit, empty room with concrete floors and cinderblock walls behind enormous green screens.

He heaved a breath, then bent at the waist, huffing as though he'd just run a hundred miles through quicksand.

A warm hand settled in the middle of his back, a reassuring weight.

"We're gonna get you through this," Brantley promised.

For the first time since that day when he'd been helpless on the floor, on the business end of the gun, Reese felt a glimmer of hope. It wasn't going to be easy, but with Brantley at his side, he couldn't help but believe him.

CHAPTER EIGHTEEN

"How'd it go with Cindy?"

Baz joined the others at the table, setting his plate down and meeting Brantley's gaze before glancing back to see if Reese was returning. When he saw the man at one of the food counters, he turned back to answer. "Good. I'm not sure we learned much about where Toby might be, but JJ unearthed *far* too many details about their relationship."

Brantley smiled. "Good stuff, huh?"

Baz shook his head. "Man, there are just some things you don't need to know about your friend's parents' love life."

That earned him a laugh from a couple of others who were listening in.

Taking his seat, Baz grabbed his napkin. "Let's just say, I think the fondness was mutual, although Cindy has moved on." He placed his napkin on his lap. "She's worried about him. I explained what we'd uncovered so far, and she said it sounded just like Toby. Apparently, he's a flight risk on a good day."

While Baz hadn't minded spending the day with Reese's mother or listening to JJ interrogate her about her past encounters and preferences for threesomes, there'd been a few times he had wanted to gouge out his eardrums to avoid hearing the details.

"Polyamorous relationships are fairly common," Evan chimed in from beside him.

"Are they now?" Brantley joked. "And you've got experience?"

"Well, no. But I'm from Miami, and I moved to Austin. The two cities are known for their diversity."

"He makes a good point," Slade added from his spot across from Baz.

"So now *you're* the expert?" Brantley scoffed.

"What if I am?" he countered with a shit-eating grin.

"Don't try to bullshit a bullshitter," Brantley retorted. "We both know you're a one-woman man."

"Doesn't mean my woman has to be a one-man—" Slade cut himself off with a laugh. "Nope. I can't even get the words out."

"I'm not sure this can be classified as polyamory."

Baz's head snapped over to see JJ pulling out her chair on his other side. He hadn't realized she'd returned.

"Then what would *you* call it?" Slade asked.

"More like a threesome, maybe. I guess it's all relative, but I do know that polyamory is more about having multiple committed partners. And often, the relationships are separate and far more complete than what Cindy shared with Toby. Plus, there's a hierarchy." She eased down into her chair. "There's a primary and a secondary relationship—or more than one—with other people. They know about each other, but one partner doesn't necessarily interact with the primary or secondary partners."

"She's a walkin' Wikipedia, that one," Slade mumbled around a mouthful of food.

"I didn't realize you knew so much about it." There was humor in Brantley's tone. "You been doin' research?"

"It interests me," she told him.

"Interests you?" Slade asked. "As in, you're *interested* in havin' one?"

"No, dumb ass," she said with a grin. "I've got my man. I definitely don't need another."

Baz felt that all-too-familiar warmth fill his chest just from her acknowledgment. It was still hard for him to believe that he'd come this far with JJ, that they were in a committed, monogamous relationship, considering she'd been opposed to them from the jump. To complicate matters, they'd veered wildly off track, breaking things off before they really got started. Baz had ended up screwing a random woman—or believing he had, anyway—and he'd thought he had lost JJ forever.

So to hear her claim him so easily after all they'd been through … well, that made him feel about ten feet tall and bulletproof.

"Besides, Cindy wasn't havin' a separate relationship with Toby. The only time they were together was with Thomas present."

A groan sounded, drawing all eyes to the end of the table where Reese was pulling out his chair.

"Time to change the subject," Brantley announced.

"No, it's fine," Reese grumbled, dropping into the chair. "But if I hear one person mention my mother, sex, or Toby's name in the same sentence…"

Baz grinned as he forked food into his mouth. He understood Reese's pain to a certain degree. He'd grown up in a house with parents who preferred intimate relationships with other people over one another. Although they'd continued a very close friendship, neither of them had tried to hide their affections for other people. Now that he thought about it, they hadn't tried to hide their affections for one another either.

"Cindy cared about Toby," JJ said, her tone reflecting her desire to tread lightly on the subject. "But they did not communicate with one another directly when he wasn't around. Only through Thomas. According to Cindy, she loved her husband, and Toby was his friend. She never would've done anything to jeopardize that relationship."

While the others continued to discuss the merits of open and polyamorous relationships, Baz's thoughts drifted to his parents. He remembered a conversation he'd had with his father. He'd been fresh out of the academy, if he recalled correctly. His father had asked if he'd met anyone special or more than one person because, according to Wes, there was no shame in finding love more than once. Wesley Buchanan truly believed that humans hadn't been meant to settle down with one person. He claimed that a person's propensity for love outweighed their desire to be monogamous.

Baz could admit, his father had made a compelling argument, and he could've almost agreed with him at one point. Then he'd met JJ, and all that nonsense about needing variety to keep the flame burning seemed downright asinine. Baz couldn't imagine a life with anyone other than Jessica James.

"Cindy did mention there was a time Toby talked about settlin' down up here," JJ was saying. "Said he'd even looked at various properties. When I asked her where they were, she didn't know, but she did say he had a preference for solitude, so he'd been looking for houses in rural areas."

"That explains why we're chasin' our asses lookin' at these cabins he's purchased over the years," Brantley told her.

JJ nodded. "I figured I'd do a deeper search of properties up this way, see if he happens to have any that we haven't uncovered yet."

"Sounds like a long shot," Brantley said.

"It is. But since we've got nothin' to go on so far…" She shrugged.

Baz knew JJ had been disappointed that they hadn't learned Toby's whereabouts after spending hours with Cindy. Evidently, she'd hoped that one conversation would solve the case and they would move on to the next. Baz hadn't been quite so optimistic, nor was he now. There was something about this entire thing that didn't sit well with him. Everyone was going on the assumption that Tobias Land was innocent in all of this and had gotten pulled into a bad situation. Baz wasn't so sure that was the case.

Maybe it was the hardened cop in him, but he found the idea of someone accidentally getting mixed up in Mob activity a little too loose of a theory for his brain to process.

An hour later, Baz was sitting on the hotel bed, staring at the wall while JJ finished getting ready for bed. His mind was still tossing around their conversation about polyamorous relationships. More accurately, he was thinking about his parents. He couldn't help but wonder if they'd ever considered being in an open relationship rather than being apart. Then it had dawned on him that there was a good possibility they had, and that was what they'd been doing all this time.

"What's on your mind, Detective?" JJ asked, coming out of the bathroom after flipping off the light.

He peered up, taking in the sight of her wearing one of his T-shirts, her legs bare. All thoughts of his parents and relationships with other people faded instantly.

"What're you wearin' underneath there?" he asked, his voice huskier than he'd expected.

She smiled, a sexy grin that made his cock twitch. It wouldn't be too much longer before the damn thing would be throbbing eagerly for her attention.

"Under here?" she teased, lifting the T-shirt an inch or two, revealing more bare thigh.

He groaned, flipping the blankets back, a silent invitation for her to join him in the bed.

JJ crawled over to him, but rather than lie beside him, she kept going, forcing him to lie back as she straddled his hips. He rested his palms on her silky-smooth thighs as he stared up at her. She was the most beautiful woman he'd ever met in his life, from her long, dark hair and those intriguing green eyes to the pouty mouth that always made him think of wicked, dirty sex.

Gauging her mood, he slid his hands higher on her thighs, his fingertips reaching her hips. He cocked an eyebrow when he was met with more bare skin, which told him she was not wearing panties, and he suddenly wished he had shucked his boxers before he'd gotten into bed.

"Mmm," she moaned softly. "Don't stop doin' that."

He continued to caress her thighs, his thumbs gliding along the insides while his fingers curled over her leg, brushing the rounded globes of her ass. The higher he went, the more sounds she made, telling him she was feeling frisky tonight. He loved that about her. The fact that she didn't hold back, didn't try to hide her desire for him. She was an exquisite creature, secure in her sexuality, and she made no attempt to hide it.

"Take off the shirt, JJ."

Her eyes met his, and he saw the glimmer of promise in the light green orbs. She began slowly lifting the shirt, revealing her belly, which was starting to round and swell with their baby inside her, then higher until her full breasts came into view. If he wasn't mistaken, they were a little bigger, a little heavier than before she'd gotten pregnant.

When she pulled the shirt over her head and tossed it aside, Baz's hands began to wander higher, his eyes skimming over every delectable inch she'd revealed.

"God, you're beautiful," he whispered in awe. His eyes lifted to hers. "You take my breath away, JJ."

She smiled sweetly, staring down at him with so much love he could practically feel it. "You make me feel beautiful."

"What do you want me to do to you tonight?" he asked, noticing her chest was rising and falling more rapidly as her arousal intensified, her soft, cool fingers grazing his lower abdomen, teasing beneath the waistband of his boxers.

"Is it like dinner?" she teased. "Do I have a selection to choose from?"

Baz laughed. "Just think of me as your all-you-can-eat buffet."

Her lips parted on a sigh when he brushed his knuckles over her nipples.

"That," she whispered. "You can keep doin' that."

Since her pleasure was his one and only goal in life, he followed her lead, letting her tell him what she enjoyed as he teased her body with his fingers.

JJ HAD NEVER FELT MORE BEAUTIFUL THAN she did when Baz looked at her. It helped that he never tried to hide what he was thinking from her. The man was an open book, his eyes always expressing his true feelings for something.

Leaning into his touch, she encouraged him to fondle her breasts, making her pussy clench with need. She loved the way he touched her. There was a hesitance she sensed that told her he was careful because he didn't want to hurt her. Then there were the times he took her with undeniable passion, as though he couldn't hold himself back.

Tonight, she wanted this. The slow build, the burning anticipation that fizzed in her veins because his touch made her ache in the best way possible.

"Cup your tits," he said, his tone thick with authority and desire.

JJ did, watching him the entire time. He slowly rose, his hands palming her ass to keep her in place on his lap. She was mesmerized by the way his tongue grazed each of her nipples, lightly licking at first. He continued to lave her breasts with that wicked mouth, sucking, licking, nipping her until she was grinding her hips down, trying to increase the friction on her clit.

"More," she whispered, her head falling back as he drew one taut nipple between his lips and sucked hard.

She reached for the back of his head, holding him to her, never wanting him to stop. She whimpered when she felt his fingers slide between her legs, parting her slick folds.

"God, Baz," she cried when he circled his thumb over her clit.

He hummed softly, a sexy, throaty sound that sent shock waves through her body. His lips glided higher, pressing soft kisses on her chest.

"I didn't have dessert yet," he mumbled against her skin.

JJ was panting and breathless, but she managed, "Did you have somethin' specific in mind?"

"Oh, yeah." He sucked the skin on her neck. "I want your sweet pussy in my mouth."

That specific part of her body clenched in response, her clit pulsing with hopeful glee. She loved this man's dirty mouth, the way he seemed to know just what to say to make her body catch fire.

"Is that what you need?" he mumbled, his lips caressing her jaw. "Do you need me to lick that tight little cunt until you come all over my face?"

JJ moaned loudly, her body coiling tightly just from his words.

"Tell me, JJ."

"Yes. God, yes."

His lips began a reverse trek, moving back down her chest, pausing to tease her aching breasts before he reclined on the bed once more. Cupping her ass, he pulled her toward him. Tipping forward, JJ was forced to put her hands on the headboard to keep herself steady as he repositioned her so she was straddling his face. When he dragged his tongue along her cleft, she cried out as pleasure tore through her body. The man's tongue was a masterpiece, a work of art, and he'd long ago mastered the skill of bringing her to orgasm with it.

JJ whimpered and moaned as he worshipped her clit, teasing her relentlessly with light licks followed by urgent flicks. When he suckled the little bud, drawing it between his lips, JJ felt the tension building. He didn't let up, even when she began grinding down against his tongue, fucking herself on his face.

"Baz!" The orgasm ripped through her, sending shards of electricity arcing through her limbs as she cried out in sheer ecstasy.

Her breaths were sawing in and out of her lungs as satisfaction stole over her body. She was boneless and limp, allowing Baz to gently ease her off him and onto her back. He didn't waste time, moving over her after stripping off his boxers.

As he was settling between her thighs, JJ's eyes opened, and she took in his beautiful face, those glittering teal-blue eyes as he watched her with so much adoration it made her heart swell in her chest.

"I love you," she said.

He returned her smile, his eyes locked on hers as he pressed the head of his cock against her entrance. No words were spoken as he pushed inside, a delicious stretch making her blood rush in her veins. His hand curved over her hip, then down her thigh before lifting her leg as he slid deeper, filling her in a way no one ever had before. Not only with his body but with the love she saw glittering in his beautiful eyes.

Baz rocked his hips slowly at first, and JJ knew he would've maintained that pace if she let him. She had plenty of times, but there were moments—like this one—when she wanted to feel his hunger for her, to see him come apart at the seams as he brought them both to climax.

"Fuck me," she whispered roughly, knowing it would trigger his primal instinct.

It did, too. His hips bucked forward as he drove in deep and hard.

JJ clutched his arms, digging her fingernails into his skin as he rode her hard and fast, adrenaline flooding her veins, giving her the high she'd only ever found from this man. She hung on for as long as she could until she felt another orgasm cresting. When it broke free, she arched her back and cried out his name as she came so hard she wondered if she'd be able to walk come morning.

"Oh, fuck, JJ," Baz growled. "Fuck … you feel so good. I want you to come again. One more, baby. Come all over—"

JJ dug her nails into his skin as he triggered another orgasm from his words alone. When her body clamped down on his, Baz threw his head back and came with a dark, thundering rumble that had her already anticipating doing this all over again.

CHAPTER NINETEEN

Thursday, May 5, 2022

"HAVE YOU BEEN HERE BEFORE?" BRANTLEY ASKED Reese as they ventured up to the enormous house that felt more like a fortress than a residential dwelling.

It'd taken them a good ten minutes to get from the front gate, which was an impressive twelve feet tall and topped with wrought iron spears, following a concrete driveway that wound through thick trees, past a wide stream that bisected a portion of the property until finally, they'd come out the other side where the house was visible. Brantley couldn't help but wonder how many enemies the man had made over the years to require such security.

"If you mean to Max's house, then no," Reese answered, his tone lacking any sort of emotion at all.

"He has more than one?"

"No idea, but I know they recently upgraded to this one." Reese dropped his head as though ashamed to know that. "I heard Courtney talkin' about it at the office one day. Evidently, when a Mob boss is interested in startin' a turf war, security is key."

Yep, it appeared to be.

Brantley stopped on the first step leading up to the house. He turned to face Reese. "We're here on a job. Nothin' more, nothin' less."

"I just don't want it to be weird for you."

"It's not." And for whatever reason, that was true. He had no fears that Reese would go running into the arms of his ex anymore. Those had been diminished when Reese returned, but he knew Reese wouldn't believe him even if he repeated that a million times over. The man's guilt still hovered just beneath the surface. Brantley wished he could relieve him of that, but only time could diminish it, and even then, it would chip away bit by bit.

Brantley nodded toward the house. "Come on. Let's get this over with so we can get back to our hunt for Toby."

Reese nodded, his eyes shifting but never meeting Brantley's.

With a sigh, Brantley started up to the next step, stopping when Reese grabbed his arm and urged him to wait.

He glanced back as Reese stepped up to join him. "I'm not gonna hide this from them."

Pretending he didn't know what *this* was, Brantley cocked an eyebrow.

Reese clarified by leaning in and pressing a kiss to his lips, which made Brantley smile.

"Everything's gonna be fine," Brantley told him, gripping Reese's forearm and squeezing lightly. "I promise. He's got information we need. Once we get that, we'll leave and never look back."

Reese responded with another nod, this one a bit less jerky than before.

They made their way up the stairs to the wide front porch. Any other time, Brantley might've been impressed by the sprawling modern structure that reminded him of a castle in Wales, complete with a fountain courtyard and garden terraces. The only thing it lacked was gargoyles to ward off evil spirits, but he figured there were armed men to handle that part for Max.

Just as they reached the front door, it opened slowly, and a big black man stepped out. He was enormous, probably clocking in at six and a half feet tall with shoulders the size of an NFL linebacker on steroids.

Brantley was about to introduce himself when the man glanced at Reese, and what could've passed as a smile tilted the corners of his mouth.

"Tavoularis," the man said with a voice so deep Brantley expected the earth to rumble beneath his feet.

"Rock," Reese greeted in return. "This is my partner, Brantley Walker. Brantley, meet Max's head enforcer, Rock."

The man Reese referred to as Rock looked him over from head to toe, his eyes pausing briefly on Brantley's sidearm before lifting to his face.

"That your real name?" Brantley asked, wondering if they would ever make it past the entryway.

Rock smiled, flashing pearly white teeth. "Might as well be. Only my mama calls me Taye anymore."

When Rock turned away, venturing into the house, Brantley took that as a good sign. He didn't figure Rock was the sort to turn his back on a threat, which meant he deemed them safe to enter the house. The guy probably didn't know Brantley knew a dozen ways to end his life using only his bare hands. Not that he would. Probably.

Once inside the cavernous space, Brantley took in the decor. The inside was even more impressive than the outside, although they'd left the castle feel behind. The interior was modern, with minimal decor and clean lines. The stained dark gray concrete beneath their feet had been polished to a glossy shine, the smooth walls painted a light flat gray, offset by a few art pieces one would expect to see in the Louvre.

Brantley made note of exits—you could never be too careful—as they followed Rock past a curved staircase that led to a second-floor landing, then through a sprawling living space set up with ivory leather couches that faced a wide electric fireplace set in a dark gray wall that soared up to the ceiling a good twenty-feet above.

He had to admit, he was impressed. Max Adorite might belong to the dregs of the earth, but the man had good taste.

Expecting to be led to a stuffy office right off the set of *The Godfather*, Brantley was pleasantly surprised when they entered the kitchen, where Max Adorite was sitting in a breakfast nook, his wife, Courtney, beside him.

Max's gaze shifted to them, and Brantley saw the moment he recognized Reese. The man's face softened instantly, his golden-brown eyes warming as he got to his feet and moved toward them.

"Reese," Max said easily, holding out a hand. "It's damn good to see you."

Reese nodded, clearly not as thrilled to see Max if his lack of reciprocation was any indication.

Max took Reese's rejection in stride, shifting his attention to Brantley, his extended hand moving toward him.

"And you must be Brantley Walker."

Not wanting to be discourteous since they were in need of information, Brantley shook Max's proffered hand. "I've heard a lot about you."

"All lies," Max said with a smirk.

Brantley relaxed. He'd come here under the pretense that he would despise Max Adorite at first glance but found himself both impressed and amused, a combination he wasn't familiar with.

This was going to be interesting.

FROM THE MOMENT BRANTLEY AGREED TO SEEK Max's help in finding out what was what with the mafia business down in Austin, Reese had been dreading the thought of facing off with him again.

Sure, it had something to do with the fact that Max was Madison's brother, and by being here, his two worlds—past and present—had collided once again, which was something he'd hoped would never happen because he wanted to spare Brantley from having to relive what they'd already been through.

"Please, have a seat," Max said, waving toward the vacant chairs at their breakfast table.

Reluctantly, Reese moved around to the chair adjacent to Courtney's—opposite Max—and eased into it while Brantley took the one next to him.

"Can we get you somethin' to drink?" Courtney offered, smiling over at them.

"I'm good, thanks," he said quickly, wanting to ensure them this wasn't a social visit.

Max took a seat next to his wife, shifting so that he was close to her, as though being too far away was a discomfort he couldn't tolerate.

Maximillian Adorite looked the same as he always had, and if Reese didn't know better, he'd say the guy hadn't aged a day since the first time Reese had been introduced to him years ago. At thirty-five, he still had the youthful features of a man a good decade younger. He was clean-shaven, with a jaw hard as granite and a celestial nose that gave him an air of confidence and cockiness. His thick dark hair reflected the light, gleaming a brilliant blue-black beneath the overhead lights. But his honey-gold eyes shrouded by thick, arched eyebrows told the truth about his age, reflecting knowledge of a life that wasn't entirely on the up-and-up, a life filled with pain and deceit, not to mention fear regardless of how well he masked it.

"What can I do for you?" Max asked, glancing between them.

"We're workin' a case," Brantley explained. "One that involves a man we believe might've gotten himself mixed up in some business dealings in Austin."

"I assume these business dealings are similar to mine?" Max's eyebrows rose slowly, his gaze shifting to Reese. "Otherwise, why would you be here?"

Reese didn't answer, leaving it to Brantley to speak.

"To a degree, yes. This might be a stretch due to the geography, but we were wonderin' if you know a man named Johnathan Hartwood."

There was a spark of recognition that flickered in Max's eyes.

"I'm not acquainted with him, no," Max clarified. "But I've heard of him."

"Is he a major player?"

Max snorted.

"You can drop the pretense," Brantley said before Max could offer a denial. "We work with your wife, not to mention her family. We know full well what you're involved in, and it's none of our business. The only thing I'm interested in is finding Tobias Land, and right now, this is the only real lead we have."

Max seemed to consider this for a moment before glancing over at Courtney. When she nodded, Reese figured that was her way of saying they could be trusted.

With a sigh, Max reached for his coffee mug. "It's my understanding Hartwood works for Sabrina Moroso."

Well, fuck.

"Sabrina Moroso?" Brantley's tone was hard. "The woman who hired those men to kidnap your sister? The two men who shot Reese?"

Max waved a hand. "They were hired thugs." An eye roll followed, as though the two assholes who'd shot him were nothing more than cockroaches to be exterminated. Max's eyes hardened as he met Brantley's stare. "And I assure you, they've been dealt with."

"At least *some* justice prevailed."

Reese frowned, glancing over at Brantley, surprised by the approval in his tone, not to mention the bitterness he harbored for Max.

"How's your case related to Hartwood?" Max inquired.

"He owns the Red Room Revue, a strip club down in Austin."

"It's nothin' more than a front," Max muttered.

"For?" Reese asked, curious as to what all the man was into.

Max took a sip of his coffee. "I'm sure you'll figure it out sooner or later."

Reese had expected him to be evasive. When they said there was no honor among thieves, they hadn't met Maximillian Adorite. He was synonymous with discretion. Perhaps that was the reason the Feds had never been able to pin anything on him.

Brantley spoke up. "We believe that's where Toby Land met him. We don't know the nature of their business dealings, but Toby owned a travel agency, and we suspect it's tied to that somehow."

"And Toby Land?" Max glanced between them again. "How'd he get on your radar?"

"He's a friend of my family," Reese answered. To avoid having to elaborate on the subject, he said, "He skipped bail, and we've been asked to find him."

"Bounty hunting," Max mused. "Sounds interesting."

"It's not," Brantley stated firmly. "However, it's our job to hunt him down, and our efforts thus far lead us to believe he's either gone into hiding or he's dead. Either way, we need to find him."

Max's gaze lingered on Brantley for a few heartbeats before shifting to Rock, who was standing sentry in the doorway. He gave a clipped nod toward the man.

"I'll make a few calls," Rock stated, then disappeared.

Brantley's gaze remained on the empty doorway for a moment before he turned back to Max. Reese was watching him, which was how he knew whatever came out of his mouth wouldn't have anything to do with Toby.

"He's your go-to guy, huh?"

Max's dark eyebrows lowered. "You could say that."

Brantley's tone was thick with hatred when he said, "He the one who came to Madison's rescue the night Reese was shot?"

Max didn't respond, which was an answer in itself.

"So he's the one who left Reese for dead?"

Reese put a hand on Brantley's arm. He could feel the tension, the way his muscles were coiled as though he might leap across the table and strangle Max with his bare hands.

"He had one job," Max stated, his tone hinting at defiance.

"Save the princess and let her white knight bleed out on the floor?"

"Brantley, it's not like that," Courtney said, speaking up for the first time and looking sincerely remorseful about what had happened.

Brantley's gaze shot to her, the blue-gray irises dark with fury. "It's exactly like that." His gaze snapped to Max. "And you didn't give two fucks, did you?"

Max's countenance smoothed out, and Reese knew this was going to turn into a knock-down, drag-out if he didn't do something. Unfortunately, the words that might ease the tension didn't come because his guilt strangled him.

"I nearly lost him because he defended your sister, and your guy left him for dead," Brantley seethed.

"Which is why you're here," Max said with an understated calm. "I owe Reese for what he did. This is my way of payin' that debt."

Brantley barked a laugh. "Adorite, you're gonna owe him for the rest of your fuckin' life. Don't think you're gettin' off this easy."

The two men stared at one another for an uncomfortably long time while Reese remained motionless, wishing not for the first time that he could go back a year and change history. If he had that superpower, he would start by deleting that first text Madison sent him.

After all, it was what had set the dominoes in motion.

CHAPTER TWENTY

Brantley had intended to come here, to keep things professional. His goal was to get the information that might lead them to Toby and get out. Unfortunately, his hatred for this man had bled through his good intentions and left a red haze of fury obscuring his vision.

It was one thing that Reese had gone to meet Madison that night. Another for those who'd left Reese for dead to keep living as though nothing had happened. For months, Brantley had imagined this exact scenario, confronting Max about his actions. He wanted nothing more than to reach across the table, grab Adorite up by his neck, and rip his head clean off his body.

He might have if it wasn't for Reese's hand curling around his forearm, soothing some of the anger that coursed through his veins.

"Tell us what you know about Johnathan Hartwood," Reese insisted. "And don't leave anything out."

Max's gaze bounced back and forth between them for a moment before settling on Reese and that eerie calm smoothing out his features.

"Hartwood's a small fish in a big pond, but he's lookin' to make a name for himself."

"You've met him?"

"No," Max said simply. "And I haven't done business with him, either. Until recently, he wasn't in my way."

"But now he is?"

As he had numerous times already, Max glanced at his wife as though seeking her approval. Brantley wondered why that was. He seriously doubted Max was asking for permission because he got the feeling the man didn't bow down to anyone, not even the woman he loved. Brantley did, however, believe that Max trusted Courtney enough to accept her approval as fact, which was why, when she nodded her head again, Max turned his attention back to them.

"Moving anything from Mexico requires the use of the interstate. And since I-35 runs through Austin, it's a major thoroughfare. Since Sabrina Moroso is makin' an attempt to impede on my business dealings, she's makin' a play for territory to the south of us."

Meaning Sabrina was trying to interfere with Max's shipments, although the man had been far too vague for anyone to pin that on him. He was good; Brantley would give him that.

"And Hartwood's her go-to guy?"

"No." Max took another sip of his coffee. "But he works for a man she wants to do business with."

"Who?"

"An Irishman by the name of Patrick O'Brien."

"You're tellin' me Hartwood works for the Irish Mafia, and Sabrina Moroso's tryin' to get in bed with him?"

"I'm tellin' you if there's anyone who'd know where your friend is, it's O'Brien."

Brantley wasn't buying it.

Oh, sure, he could believe the Irish Mafia had a foothold in Texas. Hell, half the country was moving to Texas as of late for a variety of reasons, many of which were tech companies looking for tax breaks. However, he also knew the cartels had populated the region, which meant there wasn't a lot of room for more mobsters to fit in.

"Why's Sabrina workin' with the Irish?"

"She's not." Max set his coffee mug down. "At least not yet."

"So it's a romantic relationship?"

"She believes it to be," Max said, as though he had a secret not even Sabrina knew.

"What *aren't* you sayin'?" Brantley insisted.

Max sighed. "I didn't agree to lay out my business for you. You asked for information; I've given you what I have."

Maybe, but Brantley knew there was a hell of a lot Max *wasn't* saying.

Before Brantley could pop off another question, he heard footsteps. More accurately, high heels clicking on concrete.

"Max? Are you in here?"

At his side, Reese's entire body went rigid, which told Brantley the visitor was none other than—

"Madison," Courtney said, pushing to her feet instantly, her expression wary.

"Sit, baby," Max crooned to his wife, easing her back down in her chair.

Brantley watched the interaction, curious as to why he was coddling her.

"You know what the doctor said."

Even more curious, Brantley wanted to ask for details, but his attention shifted to the woman standing in the doorway. He'd seen pictures of Madison Adorite plus witnessed interactions between her and Reese on that grainy security video, but none of those had done the woman any justice. She was beautiful in the traditional sense, even momentarily shocked, her brown eyes locked on Reese, midnight-black hair falling like a silk curtain down her back. She looked like the lawyer he knew her to be, dressed impeccably in a red silk blouse, black skirt, and red heels. It was her mouth that gave her away, the way it opened slightly as though a silent surprise had escaped.

"Reese," she said in a breathless whisper.

"We should go," Reese told Brantley as he pushed his chair back and stood.

Brantley was still staring at Madison, so he caught the expression on her face. While her voice had sounded intimate, her eyes glittered with something that resembled remorse and relief, not a burning desire.

"I've been tryin' to call you," she said, taking a hesitant step forward. "I wanted to see—"

"We should go," Reese repeated, putting his hand on Brantley's shoulder.

The move drew Madison's attention, her gaze lingering for long seconds before lifting to his face.

Yeah, that was definitely recognition, all right.

Brantley slowly stood, watching her intently.

"Walker," Courtney warned.

He glanced back and frowned for the simple fact Courtney could even believe he would do something to harm a woman. If she'd been wielding an AK aimed at his head or had a bomb strapped to her chest, that would be a different story.

Courtney cocked an eyebrow as though promising to do him harm if he so much as tousled a hair on the woman's head. It was almost enough to make him smile. Instead, he turned his attention back to Madison as he moved out from behind the table, making his way toward her. He could feel Reese just a few steps behind him, the man's tension radiating from him.

"Brantley Walker," he said gruffly, holding out a hand as he approached. "I'm Reese's partner."

She eyed him cautiously, then reached out and took his hand. "Madison Adorite."

"He's my fiancé," Reese corrected, stepping up beside Brantley.

Brantley wasn't sure whose head snapped over faster, his or Madison's, as they both stared at Reese in surprise.

IF THIS DAY COULD GET ANY WORSE, Reese didn't know how.

"Fiancé?" Madison said in a rough whisper. A soft chuckle followed soon after. "That makes so much sense."

He wasn't sure how he'd expected her to react to such a revelation, but it wasn't with a resigned understanding. Her gaze warmed, and she seemed to relax.

No one spoke for the longest time, and Reese wished the floor would open up and drag him down. Better yet, he wanted the power of invisibility so he could slink out of the house without anyone being the wiser.

Madison's eyes slowly grazed his face in an effort to read his mind. Thankfully, she couldn't do that.

"We were just leavin'," Reese told her, nudging Brantley as he glanced back at Max. "Thanks for your time."

Max didn't respond because he was too busy watching the train wreck taking place in his kitchen. Reese couldn't blame him.

When Reese turned back, he found Madison still staring at him as though she couldn't believe he was walking upright and talking.

"I'm glad to see you're all right," she said softly, her gaze liquid, a sheen of tears coating her nearly black irises.

"I am," he assured her. "Now, if you'll excuse us. It's time we got back to work."

Madison slowly stepped out of the way.

"Tell me somethin'," Brantley said, still doing an impression of a statue beside Reese.

Madison looked up at him. "Anything."

"Did you feel bad for leavin' Reese for dead at that restaurant?"

She swallowed hard, her eyes widening. "I've never felt worse."

Reese looked at Brantley, wondering what was going through his head. He continued to stare at her, every muscle in his body coiled tightly.

"You should," he finally said.

Madison's mouth opened, but no words came out.

Brantley finally broke the staring contest, glancing behind him at Max. "Thanks again for your time. I'm sure it won't be the last time we seek you out."

"I'm sure it won't be either," Max said with a sigh. "After all, it appears I'm still in Reese's debt."

"For a lifetime," Brantley stated, then stepped around Madison and headed for the door.

Reese followed, praying his heart would start beating again once they were outside.

"WHY WAS HE HERE?"

Max made a mental note to kick Rock's ass for not warning him that his sister was there. He hadn't been expecting her. If he had, he would've ensured Madison's path never crossed with Reese Tavoularis. It was bad enough she'd been harping on him for the past eight months for his part in whisking her out of that restaurant the night Sabrina's thugs attempted to kidnap her.

If he had to do it all over again, he wouldn't change a thing. If Reese had died that night, he would've been a casualty of war, and Max had long ago learned those were a necessary evil in his world.

"He's workin' a case," Courtney answered for him. "Come sit down. Have some breakfast."

"I'm not hungry," she muttered, pivoting on her heel as though she might follow Reese.

"Madison. Sit," Max demanded.

His sister's head snapped around, her eyes sparking with fury. She did not like to be told what to do. None of his siblings did, but Max didn't much care about that either.

Thankfully, Rock returned, drawing Madison's attention away from the man making a hasty retreat from the house.

Not that this situation was any more comfortable since now Max was forced to watch as Rock and Madison squared off, their eyes speaking far more than their mouths as they stared at one another. He didn't know what, exactly, was going on between them, but he had a feeling he wouldn't like it either way.

"Get her some coffee," Courtney instructed him, her soft, cool fingers brushing his forearm.

His wife was good at providing a distraction, he would give her that. If it weren't for the fact she was supposed to be on bed rest, he would've rolled his eyes and left the task to her. Okay, that was a lie, but still.

With a heavy sigh, Max got to his feet and headed for the coffeepot. He grabbed a mug from the cabinet above it, then returned to the table, setting the carafe and mug down. If Madison wanted coffee, she could pour it herself.

"What did you find out?" Max asked Rock.

Rock's eyes shifted away from Madison briefly, his expression masked as he morphed back into the professional he was rather than the lovesick fool who thought he could hide his feelings for Max's sister.

"Was Tobias Land workin' for Hartwood?" Courtney asked, her tone reflecting her curiosity.

"Yes, but not willingly," Rock answered her quickly, urging Madison to move into the kitchen as he took a step forward.

Max watched the interactions, noticed the way Madison's eyes narrowed infinitesimally. Clearly, she didn't like taking orders from Rock, and she wanted to ensure he knew that.

The smile that tugged at his mouth said he was amused by her reaction.

Max shook his head, wondering when the fuck these two were going to get with the program. They'd been doing this dance for years, pretending they didn't have feelings for one another. Even when Madison had been dating Reese, Max had known she was secretly in love with Rock. Hell, he suspected that was why she'd taken a different path. But when Reese had proposed, she'd been shocked back to reality, deciding it was time to give up the ruse rather than risk hurting Reese any more than she had.

Or so Courtney had told him.

"From what little I could get, Tobias Land was pressured into doing business with Hartwood."

"It was the travel agency," Max mused. "They were usin' it as a front for somethin'."

"That's my guess," Rock agreed. "I'm just not sure how."

Laundering money was Max's guess, but it could've had something to do with travel to Mexico. He'd heard Patrick O'Brien was inadvertently working with the cartels, attempting to move more weapons through the state. Then again, it could also be drugs since they went through the same pipeline. The problem was, Patrick O'Brien appeared to be a ghost. Every time Max thought they had a bead on the guy, that they might learn who he was or where he came from, the guy disappeared into the ether. Almost as though he didn't exist, just a figment of everyone's overactive imagination.

"You find out where he is?" Max inquired, refilling his own coffee mug as Madison pulled out a chair at the table.

"No."

Max nodded in understanding. He didn't figure he'd been much help to Brantley and Reese; however, he had gleaned some valuable information for himself.

Information that was going to help him fortify his stronghold and ultimately eliminate Sabrina Moroso once and for all.

CHAPTER TWENTY-ONE

Rather than return to the S1S office, Brantley drove straight to the hotel.

"Maybe we should talk about it," Reese said from the passenger seat.

"Nothin' to talk about." There really wasn't. Brantley wasn't upset about the encounter with Madison Adorite. Not even a little. And fine, his stern tone of voice probably didn't relay his true emotions all that well, but at the moment, he was feeling a tad fragile after what he'd just witnessed. Fragile enough to know he needed to be alone for a few minutes—just a few—with the man he loved.

"I'm sorry," Reese muttered as they were pulling into the hotel lot.

Brantley didn't say a word. He parked the truck and got out. Reese wasn't far behind him, following him through the lobby. Brantley opted for stairs because he didn't have the patience for the elevator.

By the time he opened the door to their room, his heart was pounding, and it had nothing to do with the exercise they'd gotten going up four flights.

No sooner did the door close behind Reese than Brantley pounced on him, shoving him up against the door and slamming his mouth over his.

This. This was what he needed. To taste and touch and *feel* this man, to have him all to himself. To reassure the painful ache in his chest that Reese was alive, that he didn't die all those months ago, that Brantley'd been given a second chance at a happily ever after. A real life, a real, heart-wrenching love.

He swallowed Reese's muted *hmmph* from the sudden jolt, but that was where his surprise ended. Reese grabbed his hips, jerked him forward, then slid his palms up his back, holding on to him as their tongues thrashed around the moans that escaped.

"I *need* you," Brantley growled softly against Reese's lips, his voice a rough grind thanks to the fragile grasp he had on his control. "Right. Now."

With two hands firmly on Reese's head, holding him close so their mouths didn't venture far, Brantley managed to walk them toward the bed.

"You're not mad?" Reese asked when Brantley released him in order to tug his shirt over his head and toss it to the floor.

"Mad?" Brantley shook his head and smiled. "Horny as fuck?" He nodded and smirked. "Desperate to be inside you?" He nodded again.

Reese's gaze raked over his face. Brantley could feel his uncertainty, his need for clarification.

"Get naked, Reese," he insisted. "I'm gonna fuck you. Right now. Right here. And I'm not gonna stop." *Maybe not ever.*

Reese's brown eyes flared with the same hunger Brantley felt churning like the wild sea in his veins.

He briefly wondered if it would always be like this between them. A devastating hunger sparked by a gleam in the eye or the sound of Reese's voice. Brantley wasn't sure what the triggers were, but there were times he couldn't contain what he felt for this man. And it always … *always* … took tremendous effort to restrain himself because what he felt for Reese overwhelmed him on a base level, incited that deeply ingrained primal instinct. Never had a man made him feel like this. Not before Reese, and he knew with certainty no other man ever would.

Neither of them spoke as they stripped off their clothes. As soon as they were naked, Brantley didn't hesitate, grabbing Reese and pulling him down with him. He bore the brunt of Reese's weight as he dragged him in for another kiss, letting his hands roam all the velvet smooth skin he could reach. His hands were rough, but Reese didn't seem to mind, so Brantley didn't aim for gentle.

When he felt as though he would spontaneously combust, he pulled back and stared up at Reese.

"I don't trust myself not to hurt you," he said truthfully. "So you're gonna ride my cock and make yourself come."

A rough groan rattled in Reese's chest as he pushed himself up, straddling Brantley's hips. He reached back for the lube they'd left on the nightstand and made quick work of lubing Brantley's cock. When Reese's hands curled around his dick, stroking slowly, Brantley felt his spine tingle. It wouldn't take much, he knew.

"Ride me, Reese," he ordered. "Put my cock inside you."

As Reese sat astride him, Brantley didn't move, recalling the first time they'd done this. It had been at Reese's request that time, but it was a moment Brantley would never forget. Watching Reese as he sank down on his cock was a pleasure in itself. The way his mouth opened on a moan, his eyes closing as the skin on his face tightened from the sheer ecstasy of it.

Placing his hands on Reese's thighs, Brantley kept his touch gentle. Doing so used a significant amount of his quickly vanishing self-control.

"Oh, fuck, yes," Brantley hissed through clenched teeth when his cock sank into the tight, hot depths of Reese's body. For a brief moment, he regretted giving Reese all the power because he wanted to roll them over and ram deep inside the man, desperate for a modicum of relief from this overwhelming need.

But he remained still, watching, breathing, listening to the roar of blood in his ears as his pulse skyrocketed.

When their eyes met, Brantley saw so much in Reese's golden-brown gaze. Love, lust, and the same need that warred inside him. It caused that now familiar tightness in his chest, the one that he associated with a love so great it defied nature. He wasn't sure humans were supposed to love this much, to *need* this much, to feel so wildly out of control because of one person.

"Fuck me," Brantley rasped, sliding his palms over Reese's washboard stomach, up to the hard planes of his chest.

He swept his fingertips over smooth skin while Reese began to lift and lower on his cock, taking him deeper each time he sank down.

When Reese reached for his hands, Brantley let him link their fingers. Brantley locked his elbows when Reese leaned into him, using his extended arms to brace himself as he fucked himself on Brantley's cock. The friction and heat of Reese's body sent chills shooting through his body as pleasure consumed the hunger in his veins, filling him with a feeling so intense he briefly wondered if he'd survive the aftermath.

Reese remained fully in control of the pace and the depth.

"Stroke my cock," Reese groaned, releasing one of Brantley's hands. "Stroke me, Brantley. Fuck … oh, fuck … touch me."

Brantley wrapped a hand around the iron-hard length, jacking Reese's cock to the rhythm of Reese's body moving atop him. Heat swamped him, and the hair on his arms stood on end as the pleasure crested. His cock jerked inside Reese, that telltale tingle in his spine a warning that he wouldn't last much longer. He didn't try to fight it, welcoming the release that was inevitable.

He applied more pressure to Reese's cock, tugging and stroking while Reese panted and moaned above him.

"Come for me, baby," he groaned, teeth clenched as he fought to hold on just a moment longer. "I wanna watch you come."

He didn't bother telling him it would be the detonator because he sensed Reese already knew that.

"Oh, fuck…" Reese's movements were jerky and jarring as he tried to move faster. "More … I need…"

Brantley knew just what he needed. He released Reese's cock and gripped his hips, urging Reese to lift himself up.

When Reese leaned forward, bracing his hands on the bed beside Brantley's head, Brantley held tight to his hips and drove his own up, impaling Reese. Again and again, he fucked Reese from beneath him, taking what was rightfully his. This man. His body, his heart, his very soul … Brantley had claimed that a long time ago, and he would never let him go. Not in this lifetime.

His hips pistoned as he drove them both to the sharp-edged cliff that would take them into ecstasy. He fought to hold on, needing it to last another second, two. He never wanted this feeling to end, never wanted to lose what they shared because it was the most he'd felt in his entire existence.

Reese reached between them and gripped his cock, jerking himself harder, his eyes closing, head tilting back while Brantley continued to bottom out inside him, driving his hips up, delving as deep as he could.

Seeing Reese like that, hovering above him, in the throes of passion, set Brantley off. He drove into him once, twice…

The instant Reese let himself go with a choked cry, Brantley impaled him one final time, driving in as deep as he could go and coming so hard he was pretty sure he blacked out for a moment.

AFTER ONE OF THE MOST INTENSE EXPERIENCES of his life, Reese figured a shower was in order. He extricated himself from Brantley's hold, went to the bathroom, and grabbed a washcloth. He wet it with warm water then took it to Brantley before returning to the bathroom. He didn't linger in the shower, but he cleaned up, grateful—and quite frankly, surprised—his legs were strong enough to keep him upright.

Afterward, Reese returned to the bedroom to retrieve his clothes, expecting to find Brantley dressed and ready to head out again. He couldn't have been more wrong. The man was in the bed, this time propped up on the pillow, the blankets shoved to the floor, still gloriously naked.

Reese couldn't resist joining him when Brantley patted the mattress beside him in invitation.

As he had many times before, he moved in close, resting his head on Brantley's chest, draping his arm over his stomach, a leg over his thigh. It was a peaceful position, one he'd never imagined himself being in. Not before he'd met Brantley, that was. From this spot, he could soak up Brantley's warmth, inhale his rich, musky scent, and comfort himself with the steady thump of his heart.

Brantley's arm came around his back, his fingers teasing lightly over his shoulder, down his arm. "Should we talk now?"

Reese smiled. "I think you said everything you needed to say."

"You sure?"

"Hmm. I might need to have the same conversation a couple of times to ensure I caught every word."

Brantley grunted a laugh. "Is that right?"

Reese patted Brantley's stomach. "Later, though. Much later."

Brantley chuckled, a soft sound that resounded against Reese's ear.

Neither of them spoke for the longest time, the steady hum of the air conditioning unit the only sound in the room.

"I didn't know she was gonna be there," Reese finally said, knowing they did have to address what had happened back at Max's house.

"How could you know?" Brantley sounded flippant. "And I told you, it's all in the past."

Reese wasn't so sure about that. Sure, it seemed as though Brantley had forgiven him for meeting Madison for dinner, but he hadn't forgiven anyone for the fact that they'd left Reese to take a bullet and nearly die. He'd sensed the man's fury when he'd called Max to the carpet.

"I wasn't tryin' to be her white knight," Reese said, tilting his head back in an attempt to look up at Brantley.

Brantley's arm tightened around him, keeping him from moving too far. "You were doin' what you needed to do."

"I wasn't gonna let them take her."

Brantley's swallow was loud in Reese's ear.

"If I'd been armed, it wouldn't've been an issue."

"But you weren't," Brantley countered, an edge creeping into his tone.

"I wasn't," he concurred, relaxing once again as he swept his fingers across Brantley's rigid abdomen. "Truth is, the second she was out the door, the only person I could think about was you. No, that's not true."

Reese heard Brantley's sharp inhale, but the man remained quiet.

"You were the only person I was thinkin' about the entire time. I wanted to tell her. I *needed* to tell her. For me. Because I wanted it to be out there. But I couldn't."

He took a deep breath, cleared his throat, and wrangled his emotions back down.

"And when I got shot…" He swallowed the emotion clogging his throat. "When I got shot, the only thing I thought about was seein' you again. You were the only thing that mattered."

Brantley's arm tightened behind him, pulling him in closer as his chin pressed to the top of Reese's head. "It still pisses me off that I damn near lost you that night," he whispered. "That I couldn't've helped even if I'd wanted to because I didn't know where you were."

Reese felt the tsunami of emotion churn in his chest. It was the same thing that happened whenever he thought about how badly he'd fucked up that night. The thought of losing the most important thing, the most *precious* thing in his life … it stole his breath and made his heart ache.

"You can't blame Max for that."

Brantley grunted, his grip loosening somewhat.

More silence descended, and Reese remained quiet until he felt some of the tension leave Brantley's body.

"When I think back on that night, I see myself starin' down the barrel of that gun." Reese had to inhale slowly and deeply to keep his composure. "I remember thinkin' that I was gonna die, and I wasn't gonna get the chance to apologize for bein' a jackass."

When Brantley didn't move, Reese lifted his head, propping himself up on his elbow and staring down at Brantley. He dragged a finger along Brantley's jaw, met his steel-blue gaze.

"I was so scared. Before that moment," he amended. "I was terrified because not once in my life had I felt the way I do when I'm with you. Truth is, I never thought it was possible to truly fall in love, to have what my mom and dad had. Then I saw you for the first time, and somethin' clicked inside me. A light came on, and a new possibility presented itself."

He took a deep breath, got lost in the emotion churning in Brantley's eyes.

"It scared the shit outta me, Brantley. It didn't make sense. I mean, Z's gay. Not me, right?"

When Brantley's gaze cut away, Reese turned the man's chin, forcing him to look at him.

"Gay, straight … whatever label you wanna put on it, I didn't understand how I could've gone my entire life and never known. I questioned everything I did, everything I felt, tried to understand how I'd repressed such an important part of myself." Reese's gaze bounced over Brantley's face. "It wasn't until I hashed it out with my therapist that I realized I hadn't repressed anything. I just hadn't met you yet."

He saw the surprise in Brantley's eyes.

He kept his voice soft and even as he continued. "It wasn't that I was straight; I just hadn't met the one person I was meant to be with to know any different. But that night at Moonshiners, when I first saw you for the first time … I felt a connection to you before I knew who you were. I knew you were gonna change my life." He smiled, ensuring Brantley saw the love in his eyes. "You did. In ways you can never imagine."

Brantley's hand slid over the back of his head, his fingers gliding through Reese's hair. "You didn't come back," he rasped, his voice tight, tormented. "I thought you were never comin' back."

Leaning in, Reese pressed a kiss to Brantley's lips. "I was always comin' back. I had to get right in the head first. You deserved more than I'd given you, and I wanted to be in the right frame of mind to give you everything you deserve. You've given me your whole heart from the very beginnin', and you deserved the same from me."

Brantley's eyes danced over his face, and Reese hoped he saw the sincerity behind his words. Nothing in this world had ever felt as right as being with this man. He'd endured hell and walked out the other side, but it wasn't until he met Brantley that Reese realized there'd been a reason for that, a reason he hadn't died in that hellhole he'd been locked in for months, the endless days and nights of torture. He'd endured and prayed for one reason.

His name was Brantley Walker.

CHAPTER TWENTY-TWO

"WHATCHA WORKIN' ON?" BAZ ASKED JJ AS he approached the desk she was seated at. He glanced down to see Tesha snoozing at her feet, and he smiled. His woman loved that dog, and he knew the feeling was mutual. Sure, Tesha still preferred Reese and Brantley, but her time with JJ was special.

JJ's fingers stopped flying over the keyboard as she looked up at him and smiled. "I was thinkin' about that burner phone we were tryin' to track. You know, for Toby Land. It's impossible to trace it, but I thought maybe he had another."

"More than one phone?"

She offered a slight shrug. "It seems like he's into somethin' shady," she said, as though her thoughts needed defending. "Not that he is. I don't know for sure, but…"

"I'm with you, JJ. I think there's more to this than meets the eye."

Her eyes softened. "Glad I'm not the only one."

Baz nodded his chin toward her computer. "What'd you find?"

JJ took a deep breath. "I figure if he's not on the up-and-up, why wouldn't he have more than one? Let's him dispose of one if necessary and still have a backup."

Baz didn't like where this was going, but he understood what she was saying. He frowned, stepping around behind her so he could massage her shoulders while she turned her attention back to the computer monitor.

"And?" he prompted. "Does he?"

"I was tracin' the serial number to see where he bought it."

"Find anything?"

"More than I thought I would. The phone we know about was bought at a convenience store not far from Toby's house. And yes, my hunch was right. The good news is, he bought more than one that day. Three, actually."

"I don't suppose you pinpointed his position, and we're about to swoop in and pick him up?" Baz would be happy to put this case behind them so they could get back to their lives, back to Coyote Ridge.

"Not that lucky, Detective." JJ glanced up at him over her shoulder. "However, I do know he's been usin' one of 'em."

"That's good news?"

"Since it pinged cell towers along the route up here, I'd say it is. It means we haven't made the trek for nothin'."

"So he's here? In Dallas?"

"Unless he dumped it along the way, that's my best guess. Maybe not *in* Dallas but close." She slumped against the seat. "Bad news is, he hasn't turned it on in the past twenty-four hours, so I don't know where he went once he reached Red Oak. That's about half an hour south of here. Twenty minutes with no traffic."

"You tell Brantley yet?"

JJ sighed, shaking her head. "No. There's not a whole lot to go on yet. I'm runnin' a program that'll notify me the moment it pings off another cell tower, but for that to happen, he has to turn it on."

"That's more than we had before," he told her, wanting to ease her disappointment. "You hungry? Want me to grab you some lunch?"

JJ tipped her head back and looked up at him. He couldn't resist smiling down at her. This woman, she undid him in so many ways. Her brains, her beauty. He was in awe of her, and his feelings for her intensified each day, growing stronger the longer they were together. He sometimes couldn't believe he was building a life with this woman, that he'd gotten so fucking lucky, yet here they were.

"I wouldn't say no to lunch, although…" JJ tilted her head back down to glance at her watch. "Could you give me another hour?"

Baz kissed the top of her head. "Sure can."

"GO LEFT," EVAN INSTRUCTED SLADE AS THEY made their way through the maze of cargo containers that filled the inside of the S1S training facility.

They were being put through the paces by Z Tavoularis, Reese's older brother, today. Usually, RT oversaw their simulated missions, and Evan could admit he preferred RT's laid-back methods to Z's overexuberance. Sometimes it was hard to believe that Z and Reese were even related. They were like night and day. Where Z was quick with the jokes, Reese always seemed more reserved. And Z's overdramatization of everything certainly wasn't a trait little brother had inherited from their parents.

With night-vision goggles casting everything with an eerie green glow, Evan continued to make his way through the maze, doing his best to focus on the task at hand and not let his mind wander to Becs. For some ungodly reason, she'd been plaguing his thoughts more than she should. He figured it had to do with the fact he'd caught her flirting relentlessly with Luca last night at the bar. He had no right to be jealous in the first place, but there was a spark of envy every time he saw them together.

It wasn't like he intended to make a move on the woman. Hell, she was far too young, too inexperienced for the likes of him. Who wanted a washed-up, thirty-eight-year-old detective who'd spent the past seven years mourning the death of his wife and plotting his revenge on the bastard who'd killed her? Becs deserved someone young and energetic, someone who could make her laugh all the time. Evan wasn't that guy, but damn it all to hell, there'd been a few times lately that he wondered if he possibly could be.

A strong vibration in the center of his chest had Evan jolting out of his reverie and standing tall. "Son of a bitch."

"You're killin' me here, Smalls," came the gruff voice in his comm.

"Shut up, Slade," he grumbled, yanking off the glasses seconds before the main lights were flipped back on.

Another voice sounded in his ear, this one Z's. "You killed the hostage and yourself, Vaughn. Nice job."

With a heavy sigh, Evan started back toward the control room. He knew he would spend the next hour getting ribbed by both Slade and Z about being lost in his head and taking a bullet from the bad guy. It wasn't the first time it had happened. Hell, it wasn't the first time it had happened today.

"What do you say we grab some lunch and call it an early day?" Slade asked when he appeared around the corner. "I'll buy the first round of drinks."

Evan glared over at his partner even as he considered the invitation. A drink would go a long way to easing some of the mental strain. And perhaps more than one would help him to put the thoughts of Becs out of his mind completely.

"Fine."

Slade smirked. "I knew you had a fun side. It's just takin' me a while to dig it out."

Evan could've argued, told Slade there was nothing fun about him, but why bother? They'd spent enough time working together that Slade would've picked up on it by now.

An hour later, Evan was sitting at a table with a margarita the size of Texas in front of him. He'd somehow let Slade talk him into this Mexican food place rather than the sandwich shop Evan had been hoping for.

"What's on your mind, city boy?" Slade said as he shoved a chip in his mouth.

Evan glanced at his partner, considered shrugging off the concern he heard in Slade's tone like he always did. He had a rule about getting close to people, and if Slade kept at it, Evan knew they were going to cross that line between business and friendship.

He took a sip of his margarita and wondered if that was all that bad. He hadn't had a real friend in years. Not since he left Miami and relocated to Texas, trying to get as far away from his old life and the pain and misery that had become his constant bedfellow.

"She was murdered," he heard himself say before he could stop the words.

Slade's lazy expression sobered, his smile fading as he sat up straight and gave Evan his full attention. "Your wife."

Evan nodded, stared down at the vibrant green liquid in his glass. "But not before he raped and tortured her."

"Fuck, man," Slade hissed. "I'm sorry."

"It's been seven years," he admitted. "Sophie was just a baby." He looked up, met Slade's gaze. "We believe he targeted her. Knew her routine, waited until she was alone. She was just his type. Petite, blond. Like all the other women he's raped and killed."

"They haven't caught him."

It wasn't a question, but Evan shook his head anyway. "He vanished into thin air."

"And you haven't stopped lookin' for him."

He wasn't surprised that Slade had picked up on that. The man came across as not having a care in the world, but Slade Elliott wasn't an idiot, he merely portrayed one to keep everyone at arm's length.

"I'll never stop lookin' for him," he admitted, his voice raw with emotion. "I will search for him until either I'm dead or I've put a bullet between his eyes."

Slade leaned in, his eyes serious. "If you ever want help, just say the word."

Evan swallowed, realizing for the first time in a long time that he was no longer on his own. He didn't have to forge this path by himself. He was building friendships, despite his efforts not to.

And maybe, just maybe, that was part of the reason the spark that had died inside him was flickering back on, returning him to the land of the living.

JJ'S HOUR TURNED INTO TWO, BUT BAZ finally talked her away from her desk. She needed to eat, and she knew if he didn't intervene, she'd be snacking on cheese puffs from the vending machine, and afterward, she'd still be starving. Since she'd made no progress on her hunt for the elusive Toby Land, she welcomed the idea of getting out of the office for a little while.

With RT promising to keep an eye on Tesha for a little while, Baz took her to lunch at one of her favorite Mexican food places close to the Sniper 1 Security offices. It was a popular place today because across the way, she could see Evan and Slade chatting over a basket of chips and margaritas. She was a little envious of their drinks, but being that she had months and months to go before she could have one, she shoved it to the back of her mind and focused on Baz.

They discussed what they knew so far about Toby, which was a whole lot of nothing, and he listened while she speculated about the nature of Toby's relationship with Reese's mother. He seemed content to listen to her try to work things out in her head, to unravel the mystery in the only way she knew how.

"What I can't figure out is how he ended up in Hartwood's crosshairs," she mused, forking off a piece of her enchilada. "I mean, I know how their paths crossed, but beyond that, I'm lost."

"The strip club," Baz inserted. "That's where they met."

"I agree. In my head, Toby visited because he enjoys the scenery and probably became a regular after meeting Serendipity. They get to talking, she flirts for the money at first, then things heat up between them."

"You think it was real?" Baz asked, sipping his iced tea. "Their relationship."

"Depends." She smiled. "Define real."

"You don't think she was playing him, stringing him along for the money?"

JJ shrugged. "It's not like he had much. The guy bounced from one job to another."

"He had to have some money, though. He's never worked for anyone but himself."

JJ hadn't considered that, but yeah, based on what they knew of Toby, he'd spent his entire life coming up with grand ideas for new business ventures. His first attempt had been with a coffee shop when he was fresh out of college. From what she'd uncovered, Toby had purchased a small shop in Round Rock that was in dire straits. He made an attempt to revitalize it, but it failed within the first six months. He sold it off and moved on to the next thing, which was a mobile dog grooming service. That hadn't worked, either, but she wasn't sure if it was because he wasn't building a client base or because he didn't have the motivation for it. After that, he bought a laundromat. A freaking laundromat of all things. *Who does that?*

Then it hit her. "Wait." JJ frowned. "What's the one thing all his professional ventures have in common?"

Baz was watching her closely, but he didn't respond, so she continued. "He started with the coffee shop, then the mobile groomer. There was a laundromat, the self-service kind, but he didn't hang on to that for more than a year."

Baz's eyebrows lowered. "Don't forget the nursery."

Yep. He'd tried his hand at that, but JJ figured he didn't have a green thumb, so it hadn't lasted long.

She recalled a few other of his wild schemes. "The delivery service he tried lasted the longest. Two years, I think."

"Landscaping company," Baz filled in. "And the resume service."

That one had tripped her out because seriously? "Convenience store, then the food truck." She met Baz's gaze. "They were all cash-heavy businesses."

Baz sat up straight. "You're right. They were."

"One where he interacted with people directly."

His nod encouraged her to keep going.

"So why the travel agency? I mean, what does he do? Schedule people on cruises? Plan their vacations?"

"That'd be my guess."

"Who uses a travel agency?" she asked, trying to wrap her head around what would make it appealing to a man who'd spent his life taking on small businesses that would net him next to nothing.

"People who don't want to do the work themselves?" Baz mused.

"Yeah." JJ took a drink of Baz's tea since her glass hadn't been refilled yet. "It's probably easier to have someone who knows what they're doing plan the trip, right? Take care of the airfare, the hotel, sightseeing tours, and whatnot." She cocked her head. "What about cruises? They probably handle a lot of those, huh?"

"Probably."

"And they pay by credit card." She laughed. "Or check, you know, back in the day."

Baz's eyes relaxed, and she liked that he found her amusing.

"So why go from these cash-heavy businesses to one that doesn't deal in cash at all?"

"You're goin' down a whole different path than Brantley and Reese," Baz said.

Yes, she was, and JJ figured that was what had been bothering her all along. She couldn't wrap her head around how a travel agency would help someone get weapons from Mexico. It wasn't like he was providing an actual bus tour service. He didn't have a fleet of vehicles that gave him a free pass to move in and out of the country. Toby was setting up vacations for people. He was making airline and hotel reservations, maybe having flowers delivered or whatever when planning someone's anniversary trip. She honestly didn't know. JJ had never been on vacation, much less had one planned out for her.

"What's on your mind, JJ?"

She pushed her chair back. "I need to get back to the office."

Baz sat up straight and began looking around for their waitress. "Somethin' wrong?"

"I think I know what Toby Land was doing."

"You gonna enlighten me?" he asked with a smile.

JJ shook her head, her mind running a million miles a minute. "I need to look at somethin' first. If I'm right…"

Turning, JJ waved the waitress over when she appeared too busy flirting with a couple of guys in suits. She didn't have time for this chick to earn a bigger tip. She needed her computer. Stat.

CHAPTER TWENTY-THREE

"THAT WAS JJ," BRANTLEY INFORMED REESE WHEN the man came out of the bathroom, no longer naked. "She wants us to meet her at Sniper 1."

Reese picked up his wallet, tucked it into his back pocket. "She find somethin'?"

"She didn't say. Somethin' about wantin' to do some research."

"We should look into Patrick O'Brien."

Brantley agreed. He'd been thinking about the Irishman Max had mentioned. He wasn't sure the guy played any part in this case, but he figured it was worth checking out since they didn't have much else to go on.

"Send his name to Holly," Brantley told Reese as they were heading for the door. "See what she can dig up."

Reese nodded, pulling his phone out and tapping on the screen as they made their way down to the main floor and outside.

Fifteen minutes later, they were parking in Sniper 1 Security's underground garage. Neither of them had said much on the drive from the hotel, but Brantley figured words weren't necessary. They'd said plenty back in the room. Reese's revelation about what had happened that night—more specifically, his feelings and why he'd done it—had left Brantley with a sense of peace he hadn't realized was missing. When he'd told Reese the past was the past, he truly believed it. That's how he lived his life, and it worked for him. Or so he'd thought, anyway. He hadn't realized how much he'd needed to hear the things Reese had revealed.

They took the elevator up to the Sniper 1 offices. As soon as they stepped out, Jayden informed them that the team was waiting in a conference room.

"You call them in?" Reese asked as they headed in that direction.

"Nope."

The team had settled into one of the bigger conference rooms, everyone gathered around the large table, laptops in front of them.

"Oh, good, you're here," JJ said when he reached the open doorway. "I think we might have somethin'."

As soon as they stepped into the room, Tesha got up and ambled over to Reese, nudging his hand with her head to get some attention.

"Please tell me it's the whereabouts of Toby Land." Brantley wanted to get this done so they could get back to Coyote Ridge.

"Unfortunately, no, but I've got Charlie and Jay doin' some research on that front," she explained.

"Did Adorite have anything useful?" Evan inquired from his spot at the table.

Brantley perched on the highboy near the door since there were no other chairs to be had. "A little."

He went on to explain what Max had told them about the Irish Mob and the possible ties to Sabrina Moroso. As soon as he mentioned Patrick O'Brien's name, Baz's head snapped up.

"What did you say?"

"Patrick O'Brien," he repeated. "You know him?"

"I know *of* him, sure." Baz frowned, leaning back in his chair. "The APD vice unit was working with the FBI a few years back. I remember hearing his name come up."

"Do they have anything on him?"

Baz shook his head. "I don't think so. I just remember them bein' impressed because he's elusive. Whenever they thought they were onto him, they'd come up empty. And I mean, like, Sahara Desert dry. They don't even know what the guy looks like."

Brantley wasn't sure how that was possible. How'd they get onto the guy in the first place?

"I think I might know why," JJ announced, looking up from her computer screen.

Brantley crossed his arms over his chest and regarded her. "Whatcha got?"

"I was talkin' to Baz at lunch," she explained, "and I started thinkin' about all the businesses Toby's owned. Then I realized they all have one thing in common."

He cocked an eyebrow, encouraging her to continue.

"Every endeavor he took on was a cash business. Laundromat, coffee shop, convenience store."

"So? I'm not seein' the red flags."

"The cash businesses don't raise red flags. It's the fact that everything in his past was a relatively small cash business. More specifically, he moved on to a travel agency."

"An anomaly," Reese noted.

"Exactly. Why go from a business that interacts directly with customers with an exchange of money for every transaction to a business that deals with setting up travel arrangements and entertainment packages for cruises? It's the lack of connection that was the red flag."

Brantley considered that. It didn't make much sense, but he'd thought so as soon as they learned about the travel agency. He'd chalked it up to Land's cooky behavior as a whole. The guy didn't have a good track record with sanity, so why wouldn't he launch himself into a new venture without anything to back him up? Regardless of how or why, Brantley couldn't see how it tied into anything.

But maybe that was the problem. They were trying to tie it into Toby Land's quirky little life. What if it had nothing to do with that at all? What if—

Reese's cell phone ringing broke through Brantley's thoughts. He glanced over at the man, saw him frown as he stared down at the phone. He tapped the screen, then put the phone to his ear.

"Hey, Hugh. What's—"

Brantley couldn't hear what was being said on the other end of the line, but he could easily read the expression on Reese's face, and the sheer horror that widened his eyes and blanched his skin told him everything.

"When?" Reese barked, moving toward the door.

Brantley got to his feet and stepped out of Reese's way. Before Reese passed, he met Brantley's gaze and mouthed, "Someone took her."

Ice filled his veins, but he kept himself level as Reese slipped out of the room.

Brantley turned to the team. "Evan, Slade, Deck, and Baz, you're with us. The rest of you, keep diggin'."

"What's goin' on?" JJ called out from behind him, but Brantley didn't stick around to explain.

REESE GLEANED AS MUCH INFORMATION OUT OF a frantic Hugh as he could moving through the building in search of his brother.

"Stay calm," he told the anxious man on the phone.

"I'm trying," he said, his tone belying that statement. "She was here one minute, gone the next."

It was stupid to ask, but Reese knew he could leave no stone unturned, so he asked, "Are you sure she's not in the bathroom?"

"I had one of the waitresses check," Hugh insisted.

"Did she see someone she knew? Did she talk to anyone?"

"No. We were having lunch, talking about work. There was no one, Reese. One—Wait." Hugh was silent for a moment. "Something distracted her while we were talking. She looked past me, and I swear her face went white. When I asked her what was wrong, she assured me it was nothing."

"Did you see who it was?"

"No one. I mean, I saw a guy, but only the back of him. He looked like he was talking to someone else, though."

"Hugh, I want you to stay there," Reese stated firmly. "I need to talk to her bodyguards."

"Her *what*?" Hugh exclaimed.

Well, hell. It looked as though his mother hadn't filled Hugh in on anything that was going on.

"I don't have time to explain right now. Let me make a coupla calls, and I'll call you right back."

"Reese, what's going on? Tell me what's happening."

He wished he could take the time to do that, but Reese needed to fill Z in on what had happened. He knew for a fact that Cindy Tavoularis would not just walk out of a restaurant and leave Hugh in the lurch.

"I'll call you back," he repeated, then disconnected the call as he rapped his knuckles on Z's closed office door.

"Come in."

The door swung inward, and Reese moved inside, doing his best to remain calm so he could relay what had happened to his brother. As soon as he did, Z shot up from his chair, sending it rolling backward into the wall of windows.

Reese heard footsteps behind him, so he glanced back. Brantley was heading toward him with RT at his side. Behind them, Evan, Slade, Deck, and Baz were pulling up the rear.

"What's goin' on?" RT asked, glancing between Reese and Z.

"I think Toby might've gotten in touch with my mother," Reese relayed, trying not to jump to the worst possible conclusion.

"He took her," Z blurted.

RT frowned. "What?"

"My mother disappeared from the restaurant," Reese informed him, then looked at Z. "You need to call the guys you had watchin' her."

Z's expression fell, and a surge of anger shot through him.

"You didn't." Reese threw his hands up in exasperation. "Fuck, Z. What's the point of keepin' an eye on her if you're just gonna call 'em off when she might need 'em the most?"

"She asked me to, all right? Just for a few hours," Z said, eyes wide, face pale. He clearly understood the ramifications of that. "She didn't want Hugh to freak out until she could tell him what's goin' on."

"Well, I think he gets the gist of it now," RT mumbled softly.

"What's the team have?" Z insisted. "Where's Toby?"

"We don't know."

"Actually," a female voice sounded behind them, "we might."

JJ.

Reese turned as the others parted in the hall, allowing her to move through.

"I just got a ping on a burner phone I was tracking." Her eyes bounced between him and Z. "I think I know where he is right this minute."

"Where?" Z insisted.

JJ met Reese's gaze, ignoring his brother. "But that's the good news."

Reese did not like the sound of that.

"And the bad?" Brantley prompted, coming to stand behind Reese.

JJ swallowed as a sympathetic gleam glittered in her eyes. "I don't think Toby Land's as innocent as everyone wants to believe he is."

Reese stared at her, willing her to hurry the fuck up before he lost his shit.

"Reese," she said softly. "I think Toby Land is…" She swallowed again. "I think *he's* Patrick O'Brien."

WELL, THIS CERTAINLY WASN'T HOW CINDY TAVOULARIS thought her day would go. When Hugh had sprung an impromptu late lunch on her, she'd been giddy to spend some time with him. Never in a million years would she have thought Tobias Land would come along and ruin that for her.

Considering the trouble she'd heard he was in, she should've known. Trouble was this man's middle name. Wherever he was, it seemed he found it, or it found him.

"Where are we going?" Cindy stared at the man's profile, recognizing instantly what she'd found so appealing about him. Toby had always struck her fancy with his physical appeal. The dark blue eyes, the thick dark hair, and the interesting symmetry to his face. He was nice to look at, both back then and now. And she could recognize that, even though she was a little peeved at him.

So yes, from a physical perspective, he was certainly good-looking, but to be fair, she'd always been more attracted to his personality. He was boisterous and witty, but he could be smooth and charming in an instant. Even his scatterbrained reputation had been alluring in some way.

However, this hard-as-nails tough-guy thing he was pulling on her now wasn't sitting well.

"Just to talk," he said smoothly.

"Toby, hiding isn't going to help the situation," she said, wishing she could convince him to turn himself in. "The police are still looking for you."

"The police are the least of my worries right now."

"What does that mean?" She didn't understand what was going on with him. She did know, however, that she didn't recognize this man anymore. He was not the Toby from her past, the man she'd allowed herself to develop feelings for because her husband had encouraged it.

Her heart constricted as she thought about Thomas. She still missed him. Then again, she figured she would always miss him. He was the love of her life, and while she was moving on, trying to find happiness to fill her remaining days on this earth, she knew no one would ever replace him in her heart.

"It's okay, sweet girl," Toby crooned, reaching over to pat the top of her hand. "You have nothing to worry about."

The instant his fingers touched hers, she pulled away. How could he dare touch her when he'd just forced her out of that restaurant at gunpoint? Did he really think she would willingly leave Hugh behind and ride off into the sunset with him?

"What do we need to talk about?" she asked, trying to remain calm. She figured that was the only way to get herself out of this mess. Or, worst case, to give her sons time to find her. Which they would, she knew. As soon as Hugh realized she was gone, he would call Z or Reese and let them know. Since they'd assigned bodyguards as protection, they'd obviously suspected this might happen.

Damn it.

She mentally kicked herself for thinking there was no threat, for insisting Z call off the bodyguards because she didn't want to worry Hugh. Just for a couple of hours, she had told him. Just long enough for them to share a nice meal at a restaurant so she could hear how his day was. She adored the man, and she always felt safe with him. It was one of the reasons she loved him. Poor Hugh. He was probably worried sick right now.

Cindy rode in silence for a little while, and with each passing mile, the tension ramped up another notch until she began to shake.

"Toby?" she prompted when she feared she was going to break down in tears. "Tell me what's going on."

"I will," he said firmly. "I promise."

She watched him in profile as he drove. "Reese and Z can help you. If you turn yourself in, they can ensure you're safe until your court date."

His gaze cut to hers, and she saw something on his face, something she'd never seen before. It made him appear harder, more intense. Gone was the good-natured silly man who'd made it his mission in life to tease her back when they'd been friends.

"I can't turn myself in, Cindy."

"Why not? I read what happened. I'm sure the police—"

The muscles in his neck tightened, his jaw bunching. "None of it's real, Cindy."

"I don't understand."

He peered over, and his expression cooled somewhat as though he knew he was frightening her. "You will. I promise. I'll explain everything as best I can." With his attention back on the road, he added, "Although you won't understand. Hell, I don't understand it anymore."

Cindy frowned as she processed what he'd just said.

What was going on here?

CHAPTER TWENTY-FOUR

"We're not gonna sit around and talk about this," Reese declared.

Brantley moved to stand beside him. "I agree with Reese. We need to find them. If Toby is who you think he is, we don't know what his next move is gonna be."

From the moment JJ told them she believed Tobias Land and Patrick O'Brien were one and the same, Brantley hadn't questioned it. Too many things about this hadn't felt right from the beginning. All the pieces of the puzzle hadn't fit in their neat, tidy spots. If Toby was the reclusive mobster, it definitely helped to fill in some of the blanks. Of course, it presented a shit ton more questions, none of which they had answers for.

Worst of all, he wasn't sure what any of this meant for Cindy Tavoularis. What the hell did Toby/Patrick want with her? Why kidnap her? What would it gain him?

"JJ, run a trace on Cindy's cell phone," Brantley barked as the mission became clear. "And send me the coordinates for the land you mentioned before."

"Which one?" she prompted. "Z found one, too."

"The one closest," he decided, figuring it made more sense to check that out first.

"It's half an hour from here," she informed him even as she took a seat and placed her laptop in her lap.

"Then we should get goin'." Brantley glanced at RT. "You happen to have a chopper handy?"

RT's gaze slid to his husband briefly before returning to Brantley. "I can get one. Give me a few," he said before he turned and walked out of the office. It was clear by his body language that he wanted to console Z, but he was smart enough to realize time was of the essence.

"A chopper won't hold all of us, so we'll start that way," Baz said.

"Good idea." Brantley watched Reese, waiting to see if he wanted to insert anything. He was more than willing to let him and his brother lead this investigation, but he knew exactly what shock and fear could do to a man. They were worried about their mother, rightfully so.

"I don't wanna wait for a chopper," Reese inserted, meeting Brantley's gaze. "Let's just go."

Brantley nodded. "Okay then."

Leaving JJ behind to work, Brantley followed Reese toward the elevators. Evan, Baz, and Slade were sticking close, none of them speaking as they made their way to the parking garage. Deck stayed behind to talk to Z about God only knew what, and while he wished Deck would get with the program, Brantley didn't have time to worry about his insubordination. He liked Deck, he did, but the guy seemed to have one foot out the door at all times.

"South on I-35," Baz instructed as they walked to their vehicles. "That's all we know right this second."

"It's a start." Brantley considered offering to let Reese drive but realized it wasn't a good idea. The man looked lost in his head, his thoughts likely scattered as he tried to piece it together as Brantley had been doing.

"Hold up!" someone shouted from behind them.

Brantley turned to see Z and RT strolling toward them, both carrying two motorcycle helmets each, with Deck walking behind them, carrying one of his own.

"I can't get a chopper right now," RT informed them as he passed one of the helmets to Brantley. "But this'll be faster."

Brantley glanced at Reese, noticed the man was taking the helmet Z thrust in his direction. He didn't hesitate, so Brantley didn't either.

"We'll take Tesha with us," Baz offered, veering toward them rather than the SUV.

Reese passed over her leash, and for a second, Brantley wasn't sure the man even realized he'd had the dog with him.

"Connect your phone to the helmet's Bluetooth," Z instructed as Baz led Tesha away. "That way, you can make a call if necessary. It'll also automatically read any text messages you receive."

Well, wasn't that just fancy?

"When we get there, we'll switch to comms. You have yours?"

"Always."

Without hesitation, Brantley pulled out his phone. It took only a moment with minimal instruction from Z to get the two linked.

"You ever ridden one of these things before?" RT asked as they headed for a row of Ducatis and Yamahas parked along one of the interior walls.

"I have," he confirmed, not bothering to add that there weren't many vehicles in existence that he hadn't driven at some point in his lifetime.

"Good." RT reached into his pocket and pulled out a key. "This one's Conner's. You break it, you buy it."

Chuckling, Brantley took the key then buckled the helmet securely before straddling the sleek, matte black Yamaha YZF-R1 while Reese moved to another. He had no idea who that one belonged to, but likely it was one of the Trexlers or Kogans since this was their thing.

He felt the power of the bike the moment he started it. He welcomed the rush of riding and secretly wondered if this would be the deciding factor in whether or not he got one for himself.

With a glance in Reese's direction, he waited for him to settle on his bike. Their eyes met briefly. Brantley nodded, letting him know he was here and he was ready.

A minute later, the five of them were weaving through downtown traffic, leaving Evan, Slade, and Baz somewhere in the distance.

IT HAD REQUIRED SOME UNNECESSARY ASS KISSING, but Evan talked Baz into letting him drive. He'd known there wasn't a chance in hell they'd be able to keep up with the crotch rockets, but he was making every effort not to let them get too far ahead.

"JJ just texted," Baz informed him from his spot in the passenger seat. "She's got the coordinates of the last place the burner phone pinged from."

Slade's head appeared between the two front seats like a golden retriever seeking attention. "She get a location for Cindy's phone?"

Evan kept his attention on the road. Dallas traffic wasn't the easiest to navigate on a good day.

"Yeah." Baz sighed. "It's at the restaurant. He probably made her leave it behind."

"Why does she think this Toby guy is … whatever she said the name was?" Slade questioned.

Evan listened with half an ear as Baz laid out the facts as they knew them. He was having a hard time making the connection, but he'd worked with JJ long enough not to question her judgment. The woman didn't jump to conclusions, so he figured there was something that connected the dots. Something they weren't seeing right now.

"How the fuck would Reese's mom not know she was hookin' up with a mobster?" Slade mused. "I thought he was from Coyote Ridge."

"Do you know everyone from there?" Evan asked, glancing in the rearview to make eye contact with Slade.

"Most of 'em, yeah."

"But not everyone."

"Probably not, no. I also don't know anyone who's pretended to be from there, either."

Evan didn't know about all that, wasn't sure why it even mattered. He doubted anyone had looked too close since it had been part of the details provided to explain how Reese's mother knew the man with the bounty on his head.

"What do we know about Patrick O'Brien?" Evan asked Baz.

"Not enough." Baz's fingers were moving over the keyboard. "And when I say that, I mean there's not much to find. Like I said earlier, not even a picture."

"So we don't know for sure they're one and the same?"

"No, but if JJ thinks they are, I'm tempted to believe her," Baz explained.

Again, Evan agreed. JJ had a way about her. She could piece things together that the rest of them overlooked.

"What I don't understand is why kidnap Cindy?" Baz muttered, his attention glued to the computer. "How's this gonna help him?"

Another good question. It would have to go in the pile with the rest since they had no real answers. And they wouldn't until they found the guy and asked him.

JJ PARKED HER BUTT IN THE CONFERENCE room after the others left. With Holly's help, they were trying to nail down a specific location for where Toby might be taking Cindy. She hated that they didn't have an exact spot.

"Charlie might have somethin'," Holly noted from her spot across the table.

JJ looked up. "What?"

"She's been doin' research on the area. She found some cabins on the outskirts of a state park near Joe Pool Lake?"

JJ wasn't sure why Holly phrased it as a question because she knew nothing of the area. "Why does she think that's it?"

"She's been lookin' into the phone history for that burner. Evidently, it pinged from there at some point since he got it."

Figuring it was a better place to start than a twenty-mile radius, she pulled up her text messaging app and shot a note to everyone, giving them the locations Holly read off.

"Do you really think Reese's mom's friend is a mobster?"

JJ looked up from her computer, met Holly's curious gaze. "It makes sense. The guy's never held a real job, and besides a checking account and a social security number, there's not a whole helluva lot to this guy."

Holly's gaze dropped to her computer screen. "But there's even less for Patrick O'Brien."

That was true. And that was the part JJ didn't quite understand. If she'd had more time to research him, she could probably pinpoint exactly where the two intersected because if she was right and Toby was Patrick, she'd be able to find where the alias was created.

"They said Toby was from Coyote Ridge," Holly added.

"Yeah," she agreed. "Look into that some more, would you?"

"Like what? Try to find a yearbook picture or something?"

"Or something," she muttered, needing to stay focused on narrowing down exactly where this man was taking Cindy. He had to have a place, and she was confident he did. If he was an Irish mobster in Texas…

She snorted because the idea sounded ludicrous. Why in the world would an Irish mobster embed himself in Texas and take on this squirrely identity? And how in the world had he become mixed up with the Tavoularises? She recalled what Cindy had said, how Toby had been best friends with Thomas. She never said when that friendship had been established, but JJ assumed when they were kids.

They were missing something; she knew it. The question was, what? And did it even matter at this point? Finding Cindy Tavoularis was now the objective. She no longer gave a shit what happened to Tobias Land or whoever the hell he was.

THE FARTHER TOBY DROVE THEM INTO WHAT the sign said was a state park, the more concerned Cindy became.

He'd been silent for the majority of the trip, but she had noticed the tight grip he had on the steering wheel. He was hiding his nervousness but not well.

Was he going to hurt her? Kill her? And if so, why? What would that gain him? She still didn't understand how she fit into all this. Or if this was a knee-jerk reaction by a man who'd reached the end of his rope. She was leaning toward the latter because it made sense to what she knew of Toby.

But did she really know him at all? Would the man she'd been intimate with years ago kidnap her? Cindy wanted to believe he wouldn't. No, that he *couldn't.*

The only positive in the whole mess was that they weren't too far from Dallas. Half an hour, maybe. Which meant Z and Reese would not have to look far to find them. And they would. She knew that with absolute certainty. She had the utmost faith in them, and she knew they would not hesitate to turn over every rock until they figured out where she was.

Cindy peered out the window at the tall trees looming overhead, lining the one-lane dirt road.

"What is this place?" she asked, keeping her anxiety out of her tone as best she could.

"Home away from home," Toby replied, pulling the car behind a large cabin.

The good news was, it wasn't run-down. In fact, it looked as though it had been recently remodeled. Off to the side was a small shed. Based on the color of the wood, it was a new addition to the property.

Cindy was tempted to make a run for the wooded area behind the house but figured she wouldn't make it far. She had no idea what the terrain was like behind it or what, if any, wildlife might be out there. Since Toby had put his gun away, and he hadn't restrained her in any way, she figured she had a better chance of sticking with him and hopefully being able to talk him down.

When he got out of the car, so did she. Cindy made an effort to appear compliant, not wanting him to pull out that gun again. She found she didn't much care for being held at gunpoint, thank you very much.

"I like this," she said, trying to make polite conversation. She figured it would help if he didn't see her as his captive and more like a willing participant, which she wasn't, regardless of the act she was putting on.

"Thanks. I had to do a lot of work on it, but I enjoy it."

"Is this where you live?" she asked as she marched up the steps to the wraparound porch. He remained close behind her, so she made no sudden moves, simply taking it all in.

"One of them."

When she reached the front door, she didn't bother trying to turn the knob. Based on the biometric dead-bolt lock, she knew this wasn't just a home away from home or a temporary retreat. The security alone told her Toby wasn't who she'd thought he was.

"Welcome to my humble abode," he said after he unlocked the door and urged her inside.

Cindy watched as he closed the door and locked it, this time with a matching interior contraption that also required a fingerprint to unlock. Great. Well, if she hadn't felt like a prisoner before, she certainly did now.

"Toby?" This time she couldn't hide the tremble in her words. "Can we please talk? Let me figure out how to help you."

When he turned to look at her, Cindy didn't recognize the man. Gone was the slight hunch of his back, which she'd always found endearing. His jaw appeared harder, too. He looked tired, defeated, as though he'd run out of road and gas simultaneously. This was not the man she'd given her body to, and yes, if she was being honest, a little piece of her heart to go along with it.

"You can't help me, Cin. God, I wish you could," he said, his voice a hint deeper than usual and lacking that cool drawl she'd always found appealing. "But not this time."

For some reason, she believed him.

Which explained the fear that slithered down her spine and made tears spring to her eyes.

Who was this man? And what did he want with her?

CHAPTER TWENTY-FIVE

FLYING DOWN THE ROAD ON THE BACK of a machine was a rush Reese hadn't experienced in a long time.

Not since the day he'd met Brantley.

Or the days that'd followed.

Beneath the visor of his helmet, he smiled. Okay, so maybe Brantley provided him this same rush on a daily basis, but there was still something exhilarating about this. A sense of freedom, perhaps.

He made a mental note to suggest they invest in motorcycles of their own. Might make traveling for work a little more exciting. At least every now and then. Then he thought about Tesha and decided that might not be the best idea. He liked having her with them, and this method of transportation didn't allow for it.

An image of a sidecar had his grin widening.

Yeah. Probably not that either, although she would be cute as hell with some goggles and a doggy helmet.

Reese managed to keep pace with RT and Z, who were leading the way, while Brantley was staggered directly in front of him, and Deck pulled up the rear. Once they left the city, the traffic thinned enough to allow them to violate the speed limit and probably a few dozen other motor vehicle laws, but he didn't care. His mother had been taken, and he was bound and determined to get to her before Tobias Land or Patrick O'Brien or whatever his fucking name was did anything to hurt her.

Would he hurt her? Had she always been a mark for him? If so, why? How?

There were too many questions, and they remained on constant repeat in his head for the entire drive. He'd thought going into this that he knew who Toby was. He was the happy-go-lucky guy who used to swing by the house for beer and pizza with the folks. He would hang out with Reese's dad in the garage, tinkering with whatever project his father was messing with. Never anything that required too much time or effort because Thomas Tavoularis didn't do that. He didn't invest his time in something that wasn't his family. That was the way he was built.

Reese felt a pang in his chest, the same one that consumed him when he thought about his dad. He missed him so fucking much, even all these years later. The world had lost a great man when his dad's life was cut short, taking him from an animated character and placing him in a bed, oblivious to the world around him, for the seemingly never-ending days until he finally passed on.

He recalled the many times he'd visited his dad in the nursing facility, sitting with him, talking to him. He hadn't spent as much time with him as Z had, but he'd dropped by whenever he could. He'd always imagined what his father would be saying if he could've opened his eyes to speak. He would've told him and his brother and sister to watch over their mother. Admittedly, Reese hadn't done a good job of that, but he liked to think he was there when she really needed him.

Up ahead, he saw Z motion with his arm, pointing off to the right, seconds before his blinker turned on and he took the exit from the highway. RT was right there with him, the rest following close behind.

The two-lane road they took was less traveled than the highway, so they got more speed, pushing the limits of the motorcycles and likely tempting fate. He was sure there was going to be a small-town cop hiding behind a copse of trees, just waiting to take them down.

Thankfully, if there was, he chose not to give chase, so Reese considered them lucky. He did not have time to explain who they were and what their objective was. Without a badge, they had little leeway when it came to local cops. Something they'd learned soon after the task force had disbanded and they'd gone into the private sector.

Another four miles later, RT and Z began to slow, so Reese mirrored them until they were in a small bait shop parking lot. There were three trucks, one of them an antique, one that looked to be on its last leg, and another that was brand new. Gunmetal gray, shiny wheels, and more than a little out of place. On the side of the building, a bicycle leaned against the wall, chained to what appeared to be an ancient pay phone that had been gutted.

"JJ sent a map of the area," Z explained, glancing at his phone. "There's a handful of cabins, but the one closest to the water is Toby's."

Reese pulled out his phone to look at what JJ had sent. It was a satellite map of the area, but most of it was obscured by dense brush and trees.

"We have no idea what we're walkin' into," Z noted, his gaze swinging between all of them. "But we do this calmly and rationally. No hero shit, understood?"

A few choice words for his brother hovered on the tip of his tongue, but Reese refrained from telling him he'd do whatever the hell he wanted. Z was right. They had to be cool about this. Yes, Toby had taken Cindy, but that didn't mean she was in any immediate danger. They didn't know what they were dealing with yet, or what Toby's mental state was, so they had to go in with the intention of talking him down.

RT took the lead when he said, "Brantley and Reese, y'all go in from the front. Z and I'll go in through the back. Deck, you secure the perimeter and wait for the others."

Reese wished they had a floor plan for the cabin, but JJ hadn't worked that kind of magic yet. If she'd had enough time, there was no doubt in his mind she would have.

"And remember, we're here to *talk* to him," Brantley reiterated. "That's all."

Reese looked at his brother. He wanted to say he wouldn't do anything rash, but his mother's life was at stake here. If Toby had hurt her…

"Reese?"

Jerking his attention to Brantley, he schooled his expression. "I'm good."

He could see the concern in Brantley's eyes, but thankfully the man kept his opinions to himself.

If Brantley could've come without Reese or Z, he would have. He figured RT was thinking the same thing right now, too. It was a gamble to bring them since they were too close to the situation. Based on what little information they had, their mother had been kidnapped in a crowded restaurant by a man who was on the run from both the police and some goons who wanted something from him.

They were lacking on the information front, and that bothered Brantley. He didn't know what they were up against because there were still too many gaps in the story, so much that didn't make sense. So far, everything they'd come up with was based on assumptions and theories, not cold, hard facts. For all they knew, Cindy could've wanted to be whisked away by her former lover.

Well, maybe not the last part. Brantley didn't believe that one for a second. Cindy Tavoularis was a woman of integrity and class. She wouldn't dump her current boyfriend to run away with an old flame. And if by some strange chance she had, she would've had the decency to tell Z and Reese, at the very least.

It only took a few minutes for them to reach the cabin. They left the motorcycles, along with their helmets, at the edge of the property. After inserting their comms, they moved in on foot, taking it slow as they assessed the area, ensuring no one was hiding in the trees or monitoring the perimeter. Considering how elusive Toby'd been throughout this whole ordeal, Brantley wouldn't put it past the guy. And if he *were* Patrick O'Brien, the infamous Irish mobster no one seemed to know anything about, as JJ had said, it would make even more sense.

"Found a small shed," Z's voice rang in his ear. "Give me a sec to clear it."

"Roger that," Brantley responded, slowing his pace and watching as Reese did the same.

They continued forward but waited to see if Z would need backup. A moment later, an "all clear" came through, signaling for them to proceed.

Brantley picked up the pace, scanning his surroundings, his hand on the butt of his gun. He wanted to avoid moving in hot on the off chance this wasn't Toby's place. The last thing he wanted was to scare some unsuspecting family with guns.

He came to a stop when he saw a parked car at the rear of the structure. Glancing to his left, he signaled to Reese that he would check it out. When Reese nodded, Brantley moved forward. He glanced in the windows, back seat first, then front. Empty. No cups, no empty food containers. And no woman's purse to signify that, yes, they were here. He felt the hood of the car to see if the engine was hot, something to tell them how long they'd been here.

He caught Reese looking at him expectantly, so he shook his head, letting him know it was cool to the touch. They'd been here a while.

"Car's clear," he relayed to the others before moving toward the cabin.

Using hand signals, he directed RT and Z to stay with the plan, taking the rear while he and Reese moved around to the front. Brantley kept to the shadows and away from the windows to avoid being seen from inside. He moved slowly up the steps to the wide front porch, praying there weren't any loose boards that would give away their presence.

As soon as he saw the state-of-the-art lock on the front door, he knew gaining entry wasn't going to be as easy as they'd thought. There would be no kicking this one down. They could try for the window, but if the past told him anything, it never gave them the proper vantage point.

Glancing at Reese, he nodded toward the biometric lock and raised his eyebrows, seeking his input on how he wanted to handle this. Brantley was all for knocking shit down and making his own entrance if he had to, but not when Reese's mother's life hung in the balance.

"Back door's secured with state-of-the-art technology," RT's voice came through his earpiece.

"Same for the front," he replied softly.

As they were standing there trying to figure out a way in, the locks began to disengage on the front door.

Brantley stepped back, taking cover to the side of the door and aiming his gun at head level, preparing for the threat that appeared.

"I'm unarmed."

The door opened slowly, and a man appeared. He was dressed in all black and holding… Was that a bag of frozen vegetables pressed against his head?

"Who the fuck are you?" Reese demanded, his gun aimed directly at the man's face.

"Whoa, Nelly," the guy said, holding up his hands in a sign of surrender and wincing as he did. "Name's Atticus James." He released the door as he stepped back into the cabin. "My ID's in my pocket if you want it."

Brantley cut his gaze to Reese and nodded before stepping forward to reach into the guy's pocket.

"Don't be too handsy, big fella," the guy joked. "I might like it."

Ignoring him, Brantley pulled the wallet out of his jeans pocket and skimmed the ID. The name matched the one the guy gave, and there was a Garland address, meaning he was from the Dallas area. His date of birth put him in his mid-twenties based on Brantley's quick math. Funny since he'd adopted the language of someone three times his age.

Brantley skimmed the other items in the wallet: two credit cards, twenty-two dollars, and a business card for a bail bondsman. He flashed the card in Reese's direction so he could see what they were dealing with.

When Atticus held out his hand, Brantley tossed the wallet back to him.

"Where's my mother?" Reese demanded.

Atticus stumbled toward the sofa and flopped down on it. Brantley followed Reese inside, then began sweeping it for others.

"You mind puttin' the gun down? I said I'm unarmed."

"As soon as you tell me where my mother is."

Brantley watched as Reese wielded that weapon like a man determined. There wasn't a hint of panic in his body as he stood there, finger on the trigger.

"Do you work for Toby?" Brantley asked when it was clear they weren't getting anywhere. He already suspected he knew the answer but figured he'd give the guy a chance to be honest.

Atticus's tone was cool, amused when he said, "Toby? No." He looked up, green eyes glittering with amusement. "To*ny*? Yes."

He sounded far too cheerful to currently be a human target. Almost as though he was used to having guns pointed at his head.

Atticus sighed. "I work for Tony Stark." He looked between them as though expecting a comment.

Brantley didn't know who that was.

"And no, not Iron Man," Atticus tacked on with a smile.

Brantley could feel Reese's tension rising.

"Geez. Tough crowd." Another sigh from the dark-haired stranger before he clarified. "Tony Stark. A bail bondsman. I'm here to take Toby in." He blew out a breath and lowered the frozen bag from his head.

"You're a bounty hunter," Reese stated.

"Day job," he said smoothly. "By night, I'm Batman."

Brantley rolled his eyes. And sure, he might've smiled but only on the inside.

"Where's my mother?" Reese repeated, his words spoken slowly, each syllable wrapped in a threat of bodily harm if the guy didn't get to explaining.

"I take it she's the home run hitter?" Atticus's gaze bounced between Reese and Brantley. "She nailed me good when I came in. Woman would give Hank Aaron a run for his money."

Brantley lowered his gun but kept it at the ready, moving toward the bedroom. He did a quick look through the space, then the bathroom, clearing them before returning to the living room. As he joined Reese, footsteps sounded on the front porch, and a second later, RT and Z were coming in through the front door.

"You brought friends," Atticus said, dropping his head back. "How nice."

"It's clear," Brantley relayed, then nodded toward the man on the couch. "This is Atticus James. Bounty hunter."

Atticus tipped his chin up, meeting their hard stares. "Nice to meetcha. Wouldn't happen to have some aspirin on you, huh?"

Brantley tapped Reese's shoulder, a silent request for him to lower the gun. There was no danger. At least not for the moment.

Atticus repeated what had happened when Z demanded to know, but he didn't look the least bit concerned that four armed men were standing over him. In fact, Brantley would go so far as to say the guy looked entertained by the turn of events.

"She hit you with a baseball bat?" Z inquired.

"She did."

Which told Brantley that Cindy wasn't being held against her will. "Where'd they go?"

Atticus pushed to his feet, holding on to the arm of the couch for balance. "Hightailed it while I was unconscious would be my guess," he said with a grimace.

Z began launching his own questions, most of them the same as what Brantley and Reese had already asked.

"That your car parked out back?" Brantley asked when the interrogation ended.

Atticus frowned, black eyebrows lowering over his eyes. "Car?" His hands went to his pockets. He rummaged in them for a second, then threw his hands up as though accepting defeat. "Son of a bitch. He stole my truck."

"Gunmetal gray? Shiny rims?" Reese said.

Atticus's eyes widened. "Yes."

Reese jerked his chin toward the door. "Saw it back at the bait shop. They haven't gotten far."

Brantley wasn't sure if he was supposed to find this amusing or worrisome, but he couldn't contain his smile. This had been an odd case from the jump. Looked as though it wasn't over yet.

REESE WOULDN'T LIE. HE FOUND THE FACT that his mother had taken a baseball bat to this man's skull kinda funny. Then he had to wonder whether or not he was losing his mind because *his mother had taken a baseball bat to this man's skull.*

For fuck's sake, what was going on here?

He'd honestly expected to find his mom curled in a ball, scared for her life. Instead, it appeared she was on the run with a wanted man, and she'd been the one to secure their freedom by taking *this guy* out. Was it her idea to steal the truck, too? Were they now a modern-day version of Bonnie and Clyde?

Honest to God, he hated where his thoughts were drifting. This was not how he'd expected this day to go.

"When did they leave?" RT asked, pulling Reese from his wandering thoughts.

"Depends," Atticus chirped. "What time is it?"

Reese glanced at his watch when Z said, "Three forty-five."

"Then I guess it's been about half an hour." He flinched and rubbed the spot on the back of his head.

"You should probably get that checked out," Brantley said, clearly done with this as he marched out the front door.

Reese found him standing on the front porch, his phone in his hand as he spoke into it. He was explaining to JJ what was going on.

"So the question is," she said, "did they head south to Austin or north to Dallas?"

That *was* the question, Reese figured.

He met Brantley's inquisitive gaze and gave a subtle shrug. He honestly had no fucking idea. He was still confused about his mother clubbing this guy upside the head. What was she thinking?

"We were hopin' you'd tell us," Brantley told JJ.

"Might help if you'd get me the license plate of the truck they stole. I might be able to track it."

Well, why the hell hadn't they thought of that?

He rattled off the series of numbers and letters he'd memorized earlier, earning a confused look from Brantley.

"I saw it at the bait shop. Seemed outta place. Habit to memorize the license plate."

"Good job, Tavoularis," JJ said from the phone.

"Yeah." Brantley's smile was slow and sexy. "Good job, Tavoularis."

The sound of tires crunching gravel had Reese pulling his gun out of its holster at his back. He moved to the edge of the porch and peered around the side of the cabin.

"It's Baz," he announced, re-holstering his weapon.

For the next few minutes, while JJ searched for Atticus's truck, Reese filled the others in on what happened. Once they were all in the know, they took some time to search the cabin. It was neat as a pin, and there was nothing that would tell them where Toby had gone or whether Cindy was his accomplice or his hostage.

"We should head back to the office," RT stated. "Regroup. Once JJ pinpoints where they're at, we'll proceed from there."

"Any chance I could catch a ride with y'all?" Atticus asked when they were closing up the cabin, securing it behind them.

Reese didn't bother to answer as he headed for the motorcycles they'd left back near the dirt road. If Baz wanted to let the guy hitch a ride, that was his business. Right now, Reese wanted to find his mother, and standing around with his thumb up his ass wasn't moving things along.

"You good?"

He turned to see Brantley strolling toward him. "As can be expected, yeah."

"You did good in there."

Reese studied Brantley's eyes, looking for a hint of what he was referring to.

"You didn't kill the guy," Brantley tacked on with a smile. "If my mom was missin'…" Brantley shrugged as though to say he wasn't sure he would've done the same thing.

Reese grabbed the helmet from its perch on the seat of the bike.

"Let's head back to Sniper 1," Brantley said. "We'll grab the truck and figure out where to go from there."

Reese nodded.

"Oh, and I asked JJ to call Hugh. Give him a heads-up."

"He's gonna freak."

"I told her to keep it high-level," Brantley added. "I figure Cindy can fill him in on her antics."

Great. Now Hugh was going to know that Cindy was complicit in a crime. Regardless of her reasons, she had hit a man over the head with a bat. Plus, she was in a stolen vehicle with a man who was on the run from the law. And God only knows who else.

If this was the universe's way of ensuring his life didn't get too routine, it was doing a damn good job.

CHAPTER TWENTY-SIX

"TELL ME YOU FOUND THEM," BRANTLEY SAID when he encountered JJ in the bullpen at the Sniper 1 Security office.

They'd returned from the cabin a few minutes ago, and he was ready to be on the move again. He knew Reese felt the same because the man was practically vibrating with nervous energy. He was worried about his mother, which was understandable, but Brantley worried his anxiety was going to escalate if they didn't get a bead on Cindy's location soon.

JJ turned in her chair and peered up at him, her expression solemn. "I wish I could."

"Do you know if they went north or south once they hit the interstate?" That would at least give them some idea.

She shook her head.

"Son of a bitch." He looked around. "Where's Luca?"

"With Dom and Austin," JJ said. "He's helpin' them do some updates to the simulation program they designed. The one y'all tested out the other day."

"And the others?"

"Darius and Becs are at the trainin' center, helpin' them from that side. Holly and Elana are still in the conference room. I have them diggin' up information on Patrick O'Brien. Figured we needed all the ammo we can get."

"Does Charlie or Jay have anything?"

JJ shook her head. "I talked to them a little while ago. They're at HQ. I've sent them some stuff to look into. Why?"

Brantley shook his head. He had no reason, but he wanted to ensure that his team was dedicated to finding Cindy. All of them. He didn't like the idea of any of them sitting around, doing nothing while Reese's mother was missing. He didn't give a shit if she was helping Toby at this point, she hadn't volunteered for the duty, which meant their job was to get her back as quickly as possible.

"What's your gut tellin' you we should do, boss?"

Brantley pivoted to see Evan perched on one of the desks nearby. He hadn't even noticed the man.

"My gut's fuckin' silent," he admitted regretfully.

Which was the problem, wasn't it? Usually, Brantley was dialed into the case and could figure out where to go next. This one felt a little too personal, what with his future mother-in-law involved. He didn't want to make a mistake and risk something happening to her, so he was playing it safe. And that was getting them nowhere fast.

"What would Cindy do?" JJ prompted.

Brantley glanced over at her. "What do you mean?"

"If she hit that guy over the head with a bat, it doesn't sound like she's bein' held hostage," she said, her tone careful and measured, her eyes reflecting a hint of concern when she peered past him.

He could feel Reese approaching, knew the man was interested in what JJ had found out.

"When I say that," she clarified, "I mean, she likely wants to help him in some way. He would've kidnapped her, sure, but that doesn't mean Cindy's gonna play the victim." Her gaze moved to Reese. "She's a strong, smart woman. If she's helpin' him or protectin' him, it's only because she thinks he needs it."

"Or he's forcin' her," Reese noted.

"True." Her eyebrows rose slowly. "But can he really force her to hit a guy with a bat?"

She had a good point, but Brantley already believed Cindy was helping Toby. At least helping him to evade arrest.

"Would she talk him into going back?" Evan asked. "Confronting whatever it is he's gotten himself mixed up in?"

Brantley didn't know the answer to that, so he looked at Reese to see if he wanted to weigh in. He didn't.

"Maybe she's got a safe place he can hide," Baz mused. "She have any property? A vacation house or something? Friends who might let her stay with them?"

"No," Reese answered without hesitation.

"We do know that Toby has other property," JJ chimed in. "They could've gone to one of those."

Yeah. They could have. But Brantley didn't have the manpower to traipse across Texas to see if Toby was holed up in some abandoned shack on a piece of property he owned.

"Or there's a good chance they circled back to the cabin," Slade offered.

Brantley looked over at him. "What?"

Slade's eyes shifted between each person before returning to Brantley when he said, "It happened to me a few times, actually. When I was lookin' for someone." His shoulders shrugged, and he smiled. "You'd think I'd learn to just hang out at the first place I thought they'd be."

Brantley hadn't considered that they would double back. Made sense, though. Why not? Since he hadn't even considered that option and likely wouldn't have, it made a hell of a lot of sense.

"We can go back," Brantley told Reese. "Wait 'em out if they're not there. See if they turn up."

He could see the indecision in Reese's eyes, knew he was as unsure as Brantley was.

It felt like an eternity passed while he waited for Reese to make a decision. He finally nodded.

"Okay then," Brantley said, taking a deep breath. "Reese and I will go back to the cabin. Evan and Slade, you two round up the others and head back to Coyote Ridge. Y'all can work things from there. We've got RT and Z if we need backup."

"Sure thing, boss," Slade said, standing up.

Brantley looked at Baz, then to JJ. "You two stay put. Work the case from here."

She nodded. "You want us to keep Tesha?"

Brantley looked to Reese again for a decision.

"She'll go with us."

At least they had a plan of action. It might net them nothing, but it was a hell of a lot better than sitting idle.

"What's on your mind, Tavoularis?"

Reese glanced over at Brantley, who was behind the wheel. They'd swung by the hotel, grabbed their things, and checked out since they didn't know where they'd be when night fell.

"I'm tryin' to understand what my mother was thinkin' when she nailed Atticus with a bat."

Brantley chuckled. "She was thinkin' that she's a badass."

Reese couldn't help it, he smiled. He'd never thought of his calm, reserved, schoolteacher mom as a badass, but yeah, he could see it. She was tough as nails when she needed to be, there was no doubt about that. She'd raised three hellions without batting an eye, and all three of them had turned out fine because of it.

"Oh, shit," he bit out.

"What?"

"No one told my sister what's goin' on," he said, grabbing for his phone.

"JJ did," Brantley replied. "I asked her to before we left the first time."

Reese sighed heavily and leaned into the seat.

"I didn't want her to hear it from Hugh and panic before she had all the details."

Another reason he was grateful for Brantley. The guy thought of others first, more often than most people even realized.

"Thank you."

He should've known Brantley would be keeping an eye on all the angles while Reese was caught up in the chaos in his own head. It was nearly impossible to see past his fear for his mother's safety. The only reason he was functioning now was the simple fact that his mother had beaned some guy with a bat. It meant she wasn't chained to a bed somewhere, being tortured and beaten.

"You think they'll go back there?" he asked Brantley.

"It's what I would do. It's already been searched and cleared, so there's no reason anyone would come back and find them. They'd be safe there."

That offered him some relief. Not only because it meant there was a good chance they would find his mother but also because it meant Cindy was safe. There was at least one bounty hunter after Toby, plus the authorities would be on alert since there was a warrant out for his arrest. Since JJ'd managed to find the cabin, as had Atticus, it was only a matter of time before Hartwood and his goons did too. The only positive was that Hartwood was down in Austin taking care of his own businesses. More than likely, he'd bide his time and wait for Toby to return.

If they were lucky.

Half an hour later, after Brantley parked the truck in an alcove at the edge of the property, Reese was leading Tesha toward the cabin on foot, Brantley off to his right.

He would've preferred they be under the cover of night for the approach, but the sun hadn't yet set on the horizon, although it was close. Thankfully, the trees provided some cover, keeping them concealed for the most part.

"The truck's not here," Brantley noted, his voice whisper soft.

No, it wasn't, but Reese hadn't expected it to be. Toby would've been smart enough to dump it somewhere in the event it had Lojack. Maybe. At the moment, Reese was concerned about Toby's mental state in general. The fucker had kidnapped his mother, for fuck's sake.

The good news was, the car that'd been here earlier still sat in the same place. So they hadn't doubled back and bolted. At least not yet.

As they'd done earlier, they approached the cabin quietly, slipping past the windows without looking in. It wasn't until they were about to round the corner to the porch that Reese heard voices coming from inside.

He tapped Brantley's shoulder to get his attention. When he turned, Reese saw his nod, meaning he'd heard them, too.

So Slade was right. They had returned.

At least something was going their way today.

CHAPTER TWENTY-SEVEN

Brantley's gaze shot to Reese's when he heard Cindy's voice coming from inside the cabin. He couldn't make out what she was saying, but her tone was calm. At the moment, anyway.

When Reese moved around him toward the porch, Brantley fell into step with him. For the second time today, he found himself staring at a state-of-the-art lock, wondering what the best method would be to get through the door. Considering it was a cabin, meaning it was built with solid logs, making a hole in the wall wasn't an option.

Reese solved the problem a second later when he knocked on the door. The voices inside went silent.

"Open the door, Mom," Reese shouted. "It's me and Brantley. We're here to talk."

Brantley listened for the sound of movement, but he heard nothing. There was a good chance that Toby was bolting out a window, and they'd be off on a wild goose chase again. He hoped not because he was fucking tired. Chasing down Tobias Land hadn't been the easy case he'd anticipated. Nor did it lack that sense of urgency he'd been looking forward to. Not since the asshole had kidnapped Cindy.

"Mom!" Reese called out again. "Open the door. Let's talk."

When the lock clicked, Brantley took a step back, moving to the side of the door for cover, while Reese and Tesha did the same on the other side.

"Please don't shoot him," Cindy said firmly when a slit in the door appeared.

"Open it, Mom," Reese insisted.

Brantley figured it would've gone a long way if Reese had assured her he wouldn't shoot, but Brantley didn't bring it up. If Reese wanted to shoot the guy who had kidnapped his mother, Brantley damn sure wasn't going to stand in the way. Hell, if the roles had been reversed, Brantley would've probably gone in hot.

Cindy's eyes were pleading as she met Brantley's gaze. He could feel her concern for what was about to happen, and he couldn't say he blamed her. There was no way Reese was going to go about this with any sense of decorum when he feared for his mother's life.

"Where is he?" Brantley asked.

"Sitting on the sofa," she said, slowly pulling the door wide. "And he's not armed. Not anymore," she tacked on under her breath.

Brantley nodded, urging Reese to enter first because it was clear he wanted to. He followed, neither of them lowering their weapons.

"Is Z with you?" she asked.

"No, Mom. I told you, it's just us."

Once inside, Cindy locked the door and peeked out one of the windows.

Tesha remained right at Reese's side, her full attention on him as she waited for a command. She'd come a long way in her training, which was most obvious in situations such as this one.

Brantley took the opportunity to clear the place again because that's how he was trained. He glanced in the bedroom, the bathroom, and the single closet before returning to find the three of them still in the living room. Reese was glaring at his mother and Toby like a parent would after their kids had been caught sneaking out at night.

Since no one was speaking, Brantley took over, turning to Cindy, who was sitting on the sofa to Toby's right, about a foot of tension between them. "Are you all right?"

She nodded, and he sensed she was relieved they were there but also scared that something might happen.

"Where's your weapon?" Brantley asked Toby.

He jerked his chin in the relative vicinity of the kitchen but never looked up as he continued to stare at the stone fireplace that covered one wall of the cabin.

No one appeared to be in a hurry to move or talk, so Brantley headed toward the kitchen to find the gun. He lifted the Ruger that was lying in plain sight on the small butcher-block island. He unloaded it, tucking the magazine in his pocket and releasing the chambered round before setting it back down.

"Mom," Reese drawled. "Would you mind tellin' me what the fuck is goin' on?"

"It's complicated," she said, her tone defeated as she peered over at Toby. "You need to talk to them. They can help you."

Brantley joined Reese on the far side of the room, wanting to be able to look Toby in the eye when he explained.

"Yeah, Toby," Reese growled. "Or should we call you Patrick O'Brien?"

Clearly, he hadn't expected them to have tied the two together if his wide eyes and raised eyebrows were any indication.

"Talk," Reese barked. "Now."

"It's all right," Cindy crooned, glancing over at Toby. "You can tell them everything. They'll help."

"That or we'll shoot you," Reese grumbled. "Your choice."

Brantley held back his smirk. He was impressed by the way Reese was handling things. He hadn't lost his temper—at least not yet—nor was he trying to manhandle Toby into the truck so he could deliver him to the cops. Again, not yet.

However, the muscle in his jaw was ticking, so Brantley figured it was only a matter of time before the guy snapped.

And when that happened, because it would sooner or later, Brantley didn't want Cindy to be caught in the middle.

THE ABSOLUTE LAST FUCKING THING REESE EXPECTED was to find his mother consoling her kidnapper, urging him to seek their help.

How she wasn't terrified, he had no idea, but Cindy looked as in control in this situation as she had on the first day of school when any of them panicked and begged her not to make them go. Reese had always admired his mother, loved her beyond measure, but he'd never realized she had a spine of steel and nerves of iron.

Then again, she was a teacher, and if a teacher wasn't capable of handling whatever life tossed their way, he wasn't sure who was.

"It's a long story," Toby said, his gaze lifting for the first time, shifting from Reese to Brantley then to Cindy as they all stared, waiting not so patiently for him to enlighten them.

"We've got time," Brantley noted, always the levelheaded one. "Start by tellin' us why you didn't make your court date."

Reese continued to watch his mother and Toby, trying to determine what the relationship was. Had they been wrong? Had Toby not taken her at gunpoint from the restaurant? According to the witnesses the police spoke to, he had, but she sure wasn't acting like a woman who'd been forced to help him against her will.

Then again, she also wasn't acting like a woman who was all that thrilled to be here, so maybe she was just a good actress, too.

"If he's not gonna talk, we're done here. We just need to get him into police custody," Reese decided when it was clear Toby was clamming up.

"No!" Toby snapped, his eyes pleading as they met Reese's. "If you take me in, they'll kill me."

"Who?" Reese asked. "Who's gonna kill you, Toby?"

"Sabrina Moroso's guys."

Reese shared a look with Brantley. Of all the people he could've mentioned, Moroso wasn't on the list. Sure, he recalled what Max had told them, but he still didn't know how Toby tied into the Mafia nonsense.

"You're not runnin' from Hartwood?" Reese asked.

Toby waved a hand. "He's a small fish who wants to be taken under Sabrina's wing. I'm more worried about her."

"Why's she wanna kill you?" Brantley sounded completely chill and not at all bothered by the turn of events that had led them here.

"Because I'm not who she thinks I am."

"Patrick O'Brien?"

Toby nodded.

"Why the fuck does she think you're O'Brien?" Reese asked, his tone gruff. He was still irritated with it all, and his patience was frayed beyond repair. He wanted to know what the hell was going on so they could get his mother out of this mess.

"Because he is," Cindy said, meeting his gaze. "But he's not."

"Oh, Jesus fuck," Reese huffed. "Could someone start makin' some damn sense?"

"Don't you take that tone with me," Cindy shot back at him.

Reese pinched his lips together to avoid smiling. There was certainly nothing funny about this situation, but his reaction was ingrained in him since he was a kid. He was just glad Z wasn't here to see this. His brother would've been laughing his ass off, something he always did when Reese got in trouble.

"What's your real name?" Brantley asked, stepping in to lead as he was prone to do.

"Tobias David Land," Toby answered quickly, settling back against the couch cushions, his expression that of a man who was tired of running.

"Then who's Patrick O'Brien?"

Toby's eyebrow quirked slightly. "A myth, a figment of my imagination. Take your pick. I made him up to protect myself."

Ah, hell. It was getting weirder by the second.

Brantley frowned. "Protect yourself? From who? Moroso?"

He shook his head. "From Hartwood. And then, yes, ultimately Sabrina. Although, I got in over my head on that one." He sighed. "I didn't mean for it to go this far, but the more I fabricated, the more interesting the imaginary O'Brien became. At least to them."

Reese would have to agree, considering even the Adorites believed that O'Brien was real, that he was an Irish mobster working with Sabrina Moroso to take over Adorite territory.

"I pretended to be O'Brien's front man when I realized it offered me some protection. The last thing Hartwood wanted to do was piss off the Irish Mob, so he believed me. Sabrina, not so much."

"The rumor is Sabrina's sleepin' with O'Brien," Reese told him, recalling what Max had said.

"That's all it is," Toby admitted. "A rumor. Fabricated by me when Hartwood started asking questions. Bought me a little time."

"Let me guess," Brantley mused, "he suspected you were lyin', but then he figured out the truth the night you stole his car and wrecked it."

Toby leaned forward, dropping his head in his hands. "It was so fuckin' stupid. I know it." His tone was tormented. "And yes, he figured it out that night. Vowed to eliminate me when he thought I was arrested. I told his goons I wouldn't talk." His eyes lifted. "And I didn't. I swear it. I didn't tell the cops anything."

Reese narrowed his eyes. "Did you have somethin' to tell?"

Toby shrugged. "I might know some things."

"Somethin' pertinent enough to take him down?" Brantley inquired.

"Probably."

Reese shook his head. How in the fuck could one man get himself in so much damn trouble? All from a lie?

Then again, based on what JJ had uncovered about Toby's past business dealings, he was starting to believe the man's entire life was a lie. He wasn't a salesman or an entrepreneur like Cindy and Thomas had always led Reese to believe. No, Toby Land was a con man.

And based on the hot water he'd landed himself in, he was a pretty fucking shitty one at that.

Cindy could understand why Brantley and Reese were staring at Toby like he'd sprouted a third eyeball or maybe a second set of ears. She'd felt the same disbelief when he'd revealed the truth to her. She still didn't understand why a man would be compelled to create a fictional life for himself in order to impress others.

Then again, there wasn't much about Toby Land that she believed was real. She couldn't help but wonder how he'd managed to snow Thomas all those years. Had her husband known? Had Thomas realized Toby's entire existence was built on a fictional house of cards? They'd been close growing up. Wouldn't he have seen it? Cindy had heard the stories of their childhood, which was the only reason she knew there was some good deep inside Toby, even if it was wrapped in lies and deceit.

"What's your plan?" Reese prompted Toby as all eyes remained locked on the man who was practically cowering into the sofa cushion.

His gaze lifted and his brow furrowed. "What do you mean?"

"You can't run forever. Hell, I'm sure the bounty hunter y'all knocked out earlier will be back sooner or later."

Cindy's eyes widened as she stared at her son. "Bounty hunter?"

Reese nodded. "Atticus James. Came to take Toby in and collect his money."

Oh, dear.

Toby had told her that man was coming to kill them, which was the only reason she'd hit him the way she had. It had been a natural survival instinct that had caused her to grab the nearest object—in this case a bat—and whack him over the head with it.

"Is he all right?" she asked.

"Probably has a headache," Brantley chimed in, his tone somewhat amused. "And he wants his truck back."

"It's at a gas station on the interstate," Toby mumbled.

Cindy sighed, recalling how Toby had insisted they dump the truck and steal another car. She'd managed to convince him that stealing wasn't necessary when they could call an Uber. Of course, she hadn't used her own account because that would've led everyone right to them, and she'd been hoping to protect Toby for a bit longer. At least until they could figure out how to safely get him out of this mess. So Toby had created a fictional one on the fly like it was a regular, everyday task he was used to. They'd had the driver drop them at the next cabin over, and they'd walked the short distance over to be safe.

"Hugh's worried about you," Reese noted.

A hot ball of remorse formed in her belly. "I know."

"And Jensyn," he tacked on.

Cindy met her son's gaze and narrowed her eyes. "You can tell them both that I'm fine." He could guilt her like the best of them, and the last thing she needed right now was any more piling on her head. When she woke up this morning, she certainly hadn't expected to be kidnapped by a former lover.

Admittedly, when Reese had called to talk about Toby, she'd been intrigued. The man represented a good time in her life, a time that was filled with love and new experiences. Just thinking about him brought back memories of Thomas, and truth be told, Cindy still missed her husband fiercely. She'd learned to cope without him, but it hadn't been easy. And while she genuinely cared for Hugh, knew he would make her happy for her remaining time on this earth, no one would ever replace Thomas in her heart. And because Toby was part of the time she'd had with Thomas, she didn't mind the interruption to her regularly scheduled life.

Granted, the guns and the kidnapping, and the threat of violence weren't something she was all that keen about, but they did add just a hint of spice to her mundane routine.

Not that she would admit that to Reese, or anyone else for that matter.

"So what's the plan?" Brantley asked, glancing between them. "You won't be safe for long. Certainly not here."

Cindy watched her future son-in-law, saw the concern in his eyes. It wasn't for Toby's safety, she figured. No, his concern was for Reese, and ultimately her by proxy. From the day she'd been introduced to the man who had stolen her son's heart, she'd known he was the very best of them. There was no doubt in her mind that he loved Reese with everything he was. Which meant he was along for whatever roller coaster ride Reese found himself on.

Including this one.

"The first thing we're gonna do is get you back home where you belong," Reese said, his tone rife with determination as he peered directly at her.

"I can't argue with that," Toby chimed in. "She shouldn't be here."

"Then why the fuck did you kidnap her?" Reese snapped.

"I have no excuse, other than I was desperate." He peered up at Reese. "I needed something good in my life. Even if only for a minute."

Cindy felt her heart swell with love for this man. Not the forever sort of love but an emotional one all the same.

"Something good?" Reese snorted. "And you're not above taking by force if you have to, huh?"

"I wasn't thinking," Toby muttered.

"No," Reese agreed. "You weren't."

Reaching over, she gripped Toby's hand and squeezed. "We'll figure this out."

Toby glanced her way. "You do have to go home."

"I know, but that doesn't mean I can't help them figure out a way to get you out of this."

"Maybe it's meant to be this way," he said, his lids lowering, more defeat wrinkling his expression. "It might be easier just to let Sabrina take me out."

"That's not gonna happen," Reese declared. "We won't *let* that happen."

She was surprised by his conviction, although she wasn't sure why she was. Reese was a stand-up guy, a man any mother would be proud of. Then again, all her kids were. She liked to believe she'd played a part in making him that way.

"So what do we do now?" she asked, taking a deep breath, committed to doing whatever was necessary to get this day over with so she could return to her house and the man who loved her. Mundane though it might be, she still loved every minute of the life she'd built.

And truth be told, she got enough drama at school. This was a bit more than she'd bargained for.

CHAPTER TWENTY-EIGHT

As he drove, Brantley continued to eyeball the man in the back seat. He didn't trust Toby Land as far as he could throw the guy. The only reason he wasn't cuffed to the headrest was because Reese was riding back there with him. Tesha was in her element, keeping the seat between them warm, while Cindy was in the passenger seat.

No one said a word during the entire drive. There really wasn't much to say, he figured. They'd set out to find Toby, and they had. Taking him to the police would be the final step to conclude this wild goose chase they'd been on for a week. Aside from the fact Cindy had been kidnapped, it felt a bit anticlimactic. And for that reason, Brantley couldn't help waiting for the other shoe to drop.

Thirty minutes later, Brantley stood outside the truck while Reese, Cindy, and Z were inside, relaying the events to Hugh. Tesha was sitting in the driver's seat behind him, staring up at the house, likely waiting for Reese to return so they could get on with the rest of their evening.

"Someone needs to keep an eye on them," Toby said from his spot in the back seat. "Sabrina will figure out she's the key to finding me."

Brantley turned around, glancing through the lowered window. "And why do you think that is?" He rested his arms on the door, glaring at Toby. "Could it be because you've led all your fuckin' enemies right to her door?"

He could see genuine regret on Toby's aged and wilted face. At one time, the man had been handsome. Based on the pictures Brantley had seen. But the years hadn't been good to him. Or maybe recent events were what had aged him more than usual. Whatever it was, Toby looked defeated, as though moving forward wasn't something he looked forward to.

"I didn't mean to."

Brantley snorted. "Do you mean to do *anything*, Toby? All I've heard outta your mouth are excuses. You won't get any sympathy from me if that's what you're lookin' for."

"I'm not."

"Bullshit. You've been lookin' for sympathy since the moment we came through the door."

Toby's eyes narrowed on Brantley's face, and for the first time since they'd found him in the cabin, emotion sparked in his eyes. "You can say it. I'd be better off dead."

Brantley rolled his eyes and turned around to watch the house. He had no time or patience for whiny assholes.

As he stared at Cindy's front door, willing Reese to emerge, Toby's comment ran on repeat inside his head.

"You know what, Toby?" he muttered, not caring if the man could hear him or not. "You might actually be on to somethin'."

REESE HAD KNOWN HUGH FOR A LONG time. Not once in all that time could he recall a moment when he thought he would have to hold the man back. As soon as Hugh learned that Toby was outside in the truck, that was exactly what he'd had to do.

"I'll kill him," Hugh rasped, the words coming out softly but with a knife-edge of fury.

Reese figured he was trying to keep Cindy from overhearing. The man would never want to do or say anything that might hurt her. He was a good guy, and for that, Reese was glad he'd come into his mother's life.

"He'll be handled," Z assured him. "Reese is gonna personally escort him back to Austin and turn him over to the police. He'll have a new bed to sleep in for a while."

Reese released Hugh and stepped back, glaring at his brother. "*I'm* drivin' him back? Why me? This is your case, not mine. We were doin' you a favor."

"There's a bounty to be collected," Z noted, mirth glittering in his eyes.

Reese found nothing funny about this situation. Based on what Toby told them at the cabin, there were some nasty people out to get him. Regardless of his idiocy or the cons he'd pulled on God only knew how many people, Reese didn't figure he needed to die at the hands of wannabe mobsters.

"I'm not interested in the bounty," Reese said with a sigh, his thoughts shifting in an entirely different direction.

"Maybe I should call Atticus James," Z mused. "See if he wants to escort him back."

Reese figured there was a good chance whoever took Toby back to Austin was in for a welcome home party from Hartwood and his trigger-happy goons. Since he had no intention of waking up dead, maybe it wasn't a bad idea for them to call Atticus in. The guy had found Toby, after all. It wasn't his fault he hadn't anticipated Cindy's wicked swing.

"Thank you," Hugh said, sounding calmer than he had a moment ago. "Thank you for finding her. For bringing her back safely."

Reese didn't need thanks. He'd done what any son would do, and he'd do it again in a heartbeat.

"Well, y'all have a long way to drive," Z told him. "Probably oughta hit the road."

Reese wanted to hit something, all right. His brother's smug face. However, he refrained because Z was right. They did need to get back to Coyote Ridge.

"You gonna be all right?" he asked his mother when she appeared in the doorway, a tissue clutched in her hand.

"Of course I will," she said with a forced smile. "I just need a good night's sleep."

He knew the feeling. A solid eight hours in bed with Brantley sounded like pure heaven right now.

Half an hour later, after he'd hugged his mother and said goodbye to Hugh, Reese was sitting in the passenger seat, Brantley behind the wheel. Tesha was keeping an eye on their guest from her perch in the back seat.

Reese continued to glance over at Brantley because he could tell he had something on his mind. He'd been quiet since they'd left his mother's house, and the silence was beginning to suffocate him.

"What's on your mind?" he asked, needing something to take the edge off his anxiety.

Brantley's gaze cut his way quickly. "You really wanna know?"

Curious, Reese smiled. "When you say it like that, yeah. I wanna know."

Brantley's attention shifted back to the road. "Toby needs to die."

A choked sound came from the back seat. "Wait, what?" Toby's voice was pitched high. "You're gonna kill me?"

Brantley chuckled. "I'm thinkin' about it."

Reese would've been worried if he didn't hear amusement in Brantley's tone.

"If you kill me, you won't get the money."

"What money?"

"The bounty."

"Hell, Land. We ain't in it for the money. Atticus wants it far more than we do," Brantley said smoothly, winking at Reese before peering in the rearview mirror again. "And it's in the cards anyway, right? You said it yourself, you're better off dead."

"But I didn't mean it."

"It *is* a foregone conclusion that you'll be dead within a day," Reese mused. "Once Hartwood learns you're in jail, he'll have someone take you out."

"Yep," Brantley agreed. "You'll get a shiv in the kidney and bleed out on the concrete floor."

"The guards'll pretend they don't hear you beggin' for help," Reese added, playing along. "They'll wait until you've stopped gaspin' for air before they rush in. By then, it'll be too late."

"I don't wanna die," Toby declared. "I really, really don't."

Brantley looked his way once more, and Reese could practically see the plan forming in the man's mind. "What devious scheme are you cookin' up?"

"I'll tell you later. Don't wanna ruin the surprise for Toby."

Reese glanced in the back seat, saw Toby's face was white as a sheet. "Don't worry, we'll make sure you don't feel a thing."

"IT'S A TEXT FROM REESE," JJ EXPLAINED to Baz as she stared at the phone, a smile forming. "They're almost home. They've got Toby with them."

Her phone chimed as another text came in.

"What else does he have to say for himself?" Baz inquired, patting the couch cushion in invitation.

With phone in hand, JJ headed over and joined him, easing down at his side, welcoming the warmth of his arm as he draped it around her, pulling her against him. She loved how he made her feel safe.

Admittedly, she was glad to be home, back in her own space. No, it wasn't the new house, but she'd come to find some solace in Baz's apartment. At least as long as he was here with her.

"He wants me to call Atticus," she explained. "Have him meet them at HQ first thing in the mornin'."

"The bounty hunter?"

"Yeah."

"For what?"

JJ shrugged. "Maybe they want him to take Toby in."

"He does, he'll collect the bounty."

JJ knew this case had never been about the money for Reese or Brantley. Then again, money wasn't what drove either of them.

Another text came in. "Now he says he wants you and Evan to be at HQ in the mornin', too."

"He say why?"

"Not yet." But JJ could think of a dozen reasons, her brain already conjuring up a thousand different things they could be planning. All of which were more interesting than the last.

Her phone chimed once more. This time the message had her glaring at her phone. "He says I'm not allowed to be there."

Baz's arm wrapped more securely around her. "I'll drop you by the new house on the way over. They're supposed to be finishin' up the master bathroom first thing. You can keep an eye on them."

Although she really wanted to know what Brantley and Reese were planning, JJ did like the idea of visiting the new house. She really wanted to check on the progress, see what they'd done in the past week. She was so ready for it to be finished, ready to move into it so they could start getting things ready for the baby. She was only fifteen weeks along, but it was all getting real for her now. She was starting to show more. Enough that she knew buying maternity clothes was next on her to-do list. She could no longer get away with using rubber bands to secure her jeans.

"Actually," she said, peering up at him over her shoulder. "I think I'm gonna have lunch with your mom tomorrow."

"Really?"

JJ nodded. "She texted me earlier, asked what my plans were for the weekend. I told her I'd make time. Seems as good as any, right?"

"She'll love that," Baz said, his hand rubbing her arm gently.

When her phone remained silent, she set it down and leaned into Baz, sighing her contentment. "You think maybe you could take me shoppin' after y'all are done?"

"Of course. Need somethin' specific?"

Smiling up at the ceiling, she covered his hand with hers. "Yep. Clothes. I'm startin' to grow out of what I've got."

Baz nuzzled her ear. "You could always go naked. I certainly wouldn't mind."

She smiled. "Maybe not, but I'm not out to scare the life outta the people we work with. Not to mention your parents."

A soft grunt sounded. "Good point. Plus, I'd have to kill them all if they saw you naked. Those sinful curves are for my eyes only."

God, she loved this man. He always knew just what to say.

CHAPTER TWENTY-NINE

Three days later...
Sunday, May 8, 2022

"You realize we're not alone," Reese said when Brantley walked into the bathroom, closing the door behind him.

"In here, we are," he assured him.

Reese stood beneath the showerhead, water sluicing down every gorgeous inch while Brantley openly ogled him. Two full days had passed since they'd returned from Dallas, and while he would've preferred to keep Toby locked in the barn until this was all over, it felt a bit inhumane. Which was the only reason he'd allowed the guy to stay in the house. They'd given him a pillow and a blanket and set him up on the couch in Brantley's upstairs office, hoping he would stay there. He should've known Toby couldn't sit still. For two nights, he'd listened to the guy moving around the house at all hours, pacing the floors.

While Brantley was capable of sleeping through damn near anything, he wasn't capable of resisting some of his baser urges. Namely, Reese.

"What if he bolts?" Reese asked, swiping the water out of his face.

Brantley began stripping out of his shorts and T-shirt, dropping them on the floor on the path to the shower. "Then we'll have somethin' to do next week."

Reese grinned, and that damn wicked smile set Brantley's body aflame. Things had been tense these past couple of days with Toby being there, but it was a good tension. At least compared to the anxiety that Reese had been battling for the days leading up to that. Brantley welcomed it because it allowed for a distraction, one they'd desperately needed.

But right now, he needed a different sort of distraction.

"For this moment," he told Reese, moving closer, "I don't care about anyone else but you."

He stepped into the shower, letting the warm water hit his back as he steered Reese toward the tiled wall. He pinned him there, crushing him beneath the weight of his body as he kissed him slow and deep, exploring his mouth with his tongue, relishing the soft, guttural moans that came from Reese's throat.

"How long do we have?" Reese asked when they broke apart.

"As long as it takes." Brantley had no intention of rushing. He'd wanted to get this man alone for days, and now that he had, he was going to spend every second he could getting them both off.

Dragging his lips along Reese's collarbone, he let his hands wander downward. He brushed his fingertips along the steely length of Reese's cock, teasing more of those rough groans out of him. The sounds filled the shower as Brantley went to his knees, licking and kissing every inch of Reese's chest and stomach, working his way to his prize.

When he took Reese's cock between his lips, he did so while staring up at him, loving how Reese's head tipped back, his eyes closing. Pleasure contorted his handsome face as he succumbed to the exploration of Brantley's tongue along his shaft.

"God, that feels good," Reese rasped, his hand sliding over Brantley's head, resting there, keeping him close.

Brantley let him guide him as he worked his cock deep in his throat, humming softly just to feel him throb between his lips. He took his time, never rushing because he was not ready for Reese to reach the finish line. Not yet.

When he pulled back, Reese's eyes snapped open, the light brown glittering with arousal. The man looked good like that.

"Wash me," Brantley commanded as he got to his feet. "Once I'm clean, I'm gonna take you to the bedroom, bend you over, and fuck you until you're beggin' to come."

A soft gasp escaped Reese, and the glaze in his eyes became more prominent. Brantley smiled. He knew Reese enjoyed when he told him all the wicked, dirty things he was going to do to him. He'd caught on to that a while back, hence the reason he'd started doing it more. Seeing Reese dazed with lust was one of his favorite things.

Brantley should've known Reese wouldn't keep things PG as he ran his soapy hands over every inch of Brantley's body. By the time he was done, and the water was rinsing all the soap away, Brantley was hanging on by a thread. He had enough presence of mind to turn off the water before grabbing Reese's wrist and dragging him out of the bathroom. He didn't bother with towels because it would require too much effort.

He led Reese to the bed, spinning him around so he was facing away. Brantley stepped up behind him, wrapping his arms around his chest, his palms gliding over smooth, slick skin.

"Do you want it slow and gentle?" he whispered near his ear. "Or fast and dirty?"

"Ah, fuck." Reese leaned back against him. "Do I have to choose?"

"Not at all." Brantley curled his fingers around Reese's cock, stroked from root to tip. "I can do this all day if you'd like. I can tease you until you cry."

Reese chuckled, then cut it off with a groan as he pumped his hips, trying to fuck Brantley's fist. "I'm sure you can."

"So what'll it be, Tavoularis? You want me to torment you, or you want to feel my cock in your ass right now? Buried deep…" He nipped Reese's shoulder. "Filling you … stretching you."

"Yes," Reese hissed.

Brantley laughed. "That still doesn't answer the question."

"It's all I've got right now," he said, panting as he continued to rock into Brantley's fist.

He slipped two fingers between Reese's ass cheeks, teasing his hole. "You're about to have more."

Reese's cock twitched in his hand.

"Are you close?" Brantley nipped his shoulder. "Are you gonna come in my hand?"

"You keep doin' that, yeah."

"Fine with me." He began to stroke Reese faster. "I'll let you come, but I'm still gonna bury my cock in your tight ass."

Reese was panting, leaning into him until Brantley had to bear some of his weight. He fucking loved watching this man come undone. He thought about it incessantly. Day, night. Every waking moment was spent with thoughts of Reese giving in to him somewhere at the forefront of his brain. He would never get enough of him.

Strong fingers curled around his wrist, halting his movements. "Not yet," Reese belted out. "Fuck me first."

"You wanna come with me deep inside you? Or you wanna come in my mouth after?"

"Both."

Brantley released him and smiled. "Your wish is my command."

REESE WASN'T SURE HOW THE MAN COULD play him like a finely tuned instrument. One second he'd been showering alone; a short time later, he was bent over the bed while Brantley teased him relentlessly, driving him absolutely mad with his touch and those explicit words coming out of his mouth. The more Brantley talked, the more Reese craved hearing his voice, willing him to do all the things he promised.

"Beg me, Reese," Brantley drawled.

It was hard to form words when the man was dragging the blunt head of his cock between his ass cheeks. He grunted, the only coherent sound he could make as he tried to press back, needing more, needing everything. They'd refrained for two fucking days because Reese had been hesitant with Toby in the house. Turned out, he didn't fucking give a shit where Toby was because this was what he'd needed, and nothing and no one was going to intrude on his time with Brantley.

"I didn't hear you," Brantley taunted, pressing the engorged head against his hole. "Beg. Me."

"Please," he groaned, leaning forward on his elbows, feet spread wide. He could feel the hair on Brantley's legs brushing the backs of his legs.

Clearly rewarding him for the effort, Brantley pushed in but retreated just as quickly.

Reese groaned his disappointment.

"Just beg me," Brantley repeated. "Beg me to fuck you, and I will, Reese. That's all you have to do."

His hands balled into fists as he clutched the comforter. "Fuck. Me," he managed through gritted teeth.

"That's not begging, that's demanding. There's a difference."

Reese grinned. He loved this man. Loved every damn thing about him, even this sensual torture he was so fond of.

"Please, Brantley," he said on a slow inhale. He relaxed on the exhale and said, "Let me feel you. Deep. In. Side. Me."

The next sound was Brantley's garbled grunt as he shoved his hips forward. Reese braced himself on the bed as Brantley filled him in one punishing thrust. It was heaven, as was every second that followed when Brantley rammed him from behind, driving in deep, retreating. Over and over, he impaled him until he was panting and pleading, his breaths racing in and out of his lungs as the pleasure consumed every inch of his body and mind.

Reese never reached for his cock, which was the only reason he didn't come. The delicious friction alone, the occasional grazing of his prostate, pushed him closer and closer to the edge, but he wanted to come in Brantley's mouth as the man had promised.

"Fuck, you're so tight like this." Brantley dug his fingertips into Reese's hips as he pulled him back each time he drove forward.

Time ceased to exist as he let the pleasure envelop his entire being, his heart pounding as he memorized every sound Brantley made as he drove them both higher and higher until…

"Tell me you love me," Brantley growled roughly.

"Make me," he countered, gasping as the pleasure overwhelmed him.

Brantley's thrusts became more urgent, and Reese felt his control slipping.

"Fucking tell me," Brantley ordered.

"I love you," he hissed, barely holding on. "So fucking much."

When he reached for his cock to relieve some of the pleasure, Brantley snarled, "No. You come without touchin' yourself."

Ah, hell. That was all it took. Reese's cock erupted, his orgasm obliterating him in an instant.

"Oh, fuck!" Brantley drove in as deep as he could, filling Reese nearly to the point of pain. A moment later, he felt his cock throb inside him as he came.

The moment Brantley pulled free, Reese rolled to his back, feet fumbling for purchase on the floor. He should've known Brantley would be there to steady him, gripping his thighs as he leaned down and sucked Reese to the root.

Holy shit. Wet heat bathed his dick as Brantley bobbed up and down, no doubt pushing Reese to the inevitable breaking point one more time as he'd promised. Although he'd just come, the sensation built again just watching this man suck him off. It didn't take much before the tension coiled inside him one more time.

"I love you," Reese told him as he gripped Brantley's head with both hands and pulled him down, thrusting his hips up at the same time. He loved that Brantley wanted to hear him say the words, and he loved even more than he could. "Always. Forever."

Brantley groaned, the vibrations causing tremors to ignite in Reese's spine. A minute later, he came, shouting Brantley's name and a few expletives to go along with it.

When Brantley collapsed on top of him, Reese ran his hands over his back, smiling up at the ceiling.

"You know you were loud, right?"

Reese chuckled. "Right now, I don't care."

"You will in ten minutes when you leave this bedroom."

Yeah. Probably.

Okay, definitely, but for the next ten minutes, he was going to enjoy the high.

CHAPTER THIRTY

Monday, May 9, 2022

"Are you sure this is gonna work?"

Brantley ignored Toby's question because it was the fifteenth time he'd asked in as many minutes. The guy was on edge about the plan, that was obvious. He figured he couldn't blame him since the foundation of Toby's life was about to be rocked, and whatever remaining time he would have was contingent on the success of their mission.

It would work. Brantley was confident in that. What was debatable was whether they could carry it out without raising suspicion or question from Toby's nosy neighbors because, according to the update he'd received from Slade a moment ago, the neighbors had already started trickling out to see what was going on, hovering nearby like flies.

Probably shouldn't have pulled up in black Suburbans. It was the equivalent of hovering black helicopters. No one knew who they were, but they suspected the government was behind them. They were right. Most of the time.

In this case, they'd rented five blacked-out Suburbans for the day, specifically for this. Three of which were currently in front of Toby's house while Brantley, Toby, and Baz were in this one, and Reese and Evan were in the one parked behind them. And no, they weren't working for the FBI, nor were there any FBI agents involved in the mission. Only a few guys who looked like they were FBI, thanks to the windbreakers they were wearing. Brantley'd given them explicit instruction not to impersonate an agent or to talk directly to any onlookers. It was all for show, to enhance the narrative.

"And what if it doesn't?" Toby pondered, seemingly talking to himself.

"Then you'll go to jail," Baz said from the passenger seat, his head shake signifying he was tired of hearing the man worry, too.

"Where's Atticus?" Brantley asked Reese over the two-way communicators they were using.

"He's on the way to the Red Room Revue now. Ten minutes out."

They'd sought out the bounty hunter's assistance in an effort to avoid his interference. Brantley knew the guy was hell-bent on taking Toby in, and rightfully so since his livelihood was dependent on the bounties he collected. It was actually Slade's idea to bring him in and compensate him accordingly to ensure he didn't get caught in the middle. Since Atticus was from Dallas, they were assured that Hartwood and his goons wouldn't be able to ID him from their previous interactions with the cabaret.

"Am I gonna end up dead, anyway?" Toby asked, his voice pitched higher with panic. "If I am, you might as well just let me take my chances with the cops."

"You're not gonna end up dead," Baz said through clenched teeth.

"You might," Brantley retorted. "Only 'cause I'm gonna kill you first."

"Can we go over the plan one more time?" Toby pleaded.

They'd already gone over it a dozen or more times since last night, but Brantley conceded anyway. Anything to get the guy to shut up.

"Darius, Deck, and Slade are at your house right now, making it look as though they're searchin' for something. As soon as Atticus and Jay get to the cabaret club, we're gonna pull up to the house, take you inside," Brantley explained. "Once we're in, I'll give the signal, then Slade's gonna make a scene to alert the others that he's found something. They'll retreat from the house with haste, urging everyone back. Jay will make a show of callin' in the bomb squad."

"And we'll be communicating with Atticus and Jay the entire time," Baz added, "so they can relay the concern to whoever's listening at the club, gettin' them to turn on the news."

Toby exhaled heavily. "And we're supposed to rely on JJ to do her part?"

"She'll do her part," Baz snapped. "She's never failed anyone yet."

"He's right," Brantley agreed, glancing at Toby in the rearview mirror. "She's tied into their Wi-Fi already. As soon as Atticus gives the go-ahead, she'll run the news clip we pre-recorded and tie in the live feed that Becs is streamin' now."

"So I just have to survive the explosion," Toby huffed.

Brantley grinned to himself. "We won't be inside when it goes off. Reese would kick my ass if I died tryin' to save your fuckin' life."

"So we'll be out by then?"

"We will."

"What about the cops? What if they show up?"

"They've been alerted to our drill," Brantley reiterated. They'd had RT put in a call to APD to notify them that Sniper 1 Security would be doing a live drill, and there was going to be some destruction. They hadn't been thrilled with the idea, which delayed their plan while RT worked out the details. There were currently two undercover APD detectives positioned at each end of the street to oversee things just in case.

"And Mr. Adorite?" Toby asked. "Can we trust him?"

Brantley couldn't confidently answer that, but he said, "Yes. He arrived early this mornin' with one of his enforcers to ensure it goes off without a hitch. He owes Reese. He won't fail us."

That had been the most challenging part of the plan, getting Max Adorite to go along with it. Thankfully, they'd had something to entice him with.

"You have the SD cards?" Brantley asked.

Toby nodded fervently. "All the watches are on me, yes."

"Good."

Brantley would let him go on believing he still had the original SD cards they'd only recently learned about. He still couldn't believe Toby had *conveniently* forgotten about them in all the chaos of the past few days. It wasn't until they were discussing the state of Toby's house and the fact someone had been searching for something that he *remembered.* Whatever. Brantley wasn't buying the kooky routine, but he would let Toby think he did.

It was the existence of the SD cards that Toby had hidden in his collection of stolen watches that had inspired this plan in the first place. Originally, they had intended to ship Toby off to Ohio or somewhere equally as rural to start a new life while they created a false trail in his wake. Then the guy had blurted out that he had leverage against Hartwood and Moroso.

Needless to say, their plan had changed.

Now it was time to kill Toby Land once and for all.

ATTICUS JAMES STROLLED INTO THE RED ROOM Revue like it was any other day and he was any other customer.

With Jay Hernandez, one of the analysts for the Sniper 1 Security team, at his side, pretending to be eager for an evening of debauchery and nude chicks, they headed toward one of the tables close to the bar, where their conversation would likely be overheard by one of Hartwood's enforcers, who were currently chatting it up like they were here for the entertainment as well.

They'd purposely waited for the goon squad—as JJ liked to refer to them—to arrive because they were the audience Atticus and Jay were gunning for.

Ten minutes passed while they ordered drinks and traded smiles with the ladies sauntering around the room. Atticus played his part as he'd promised, pretending to be interested while he was anything but. He preferred his naked entertainment to have a dick, not tits, but he was nothing if not accommodating. After all, he was getting a rather hefty payment out of this deal, far more than the bounty on Toby's head would've gotten him. Plus, he might've developed a slight crush on the Navy SEAL who was in charge of this task force. Not that he would admit that out loud. He valued his life, and he figured Brantley's fiancé wouldn't be all that keen on Atticus making a play for his man.

Atticus's phone, which was lying face up on the table, lit up.

"Show time," he muttered to Jay as he reached for the phone and made a show of staring at the screen. "Holy shit, man! You see this?"

Jay leaned in, acting as though he was looking at the screen.

"Holy fuck! That's an FBI sting, dude," Atticus shouted. "And it's live."

He twisted in his chair, glancing over at the bar, pretending to be looking for the television he already knew was mounted above the bartender's head. Without hesitation, Atticus launched to his feet and moved quickly, holding up his phone.

"There's an FBI sting goin' on right now." He pointed to the TV. "That thing work? Turn it on."

The goons were looking at him like he'd lost his damned mind, but he'd sparked the curiosity of the bartender, who reached for the remote.

"We're a go, JJ," Jay muttered beside him. "In three … two … show time."

The TV came on a second after the pre-recorded-to-look-live broadcast began to run.

All eyes moved to the television as Keegan Walker, one of Brantley's neighbors, began his spiel in his role as news anchor, alerting the viewers to the FBI raid of the wanted criminal Toby Land.

Atticus remembered watching them film, and he had to admit, Keegan was a natural behind the camera. It helped that the guy seemed to enjoy being the main focus of attention. It took a few takes to get it right, and they had more bloopers than actual footage, but they'd gotten what they needed.

"We don't have all the details about what the FBI is lookin' for," Keegan was saying into the camera, "but we do know they've been hunting for Tobias Land since they learned of his dealings with Patrick O'Brien, a suspected member of the Irish Mafia."

On the screen, Keegan put his finger to his ear as though he was listening to someone speaking directly into it.

He nodded, his eyes wide. "We've just learned that the FBI has Tobias Land in custody. He voluntarily surrendered last night, claiming he has information on…" Keegan's eyes widened even more. "He claims to be informing on Maximillian Adorite, the head of the Adorite family, also known to many of our viewers as the Southern Boy Mafia."

Atticus fought the urge to grin as he recalled Keegan's original taping of this part. He'd been highly amused by the Southern Boy Mafia part, although he couldn't explain why. Then again, he also couldn't stop laughing.

"We're gonna take you to the scene live right now. One of our field investigators has his camera trained on the action."

The image flipped to a live view of Toby's house, where Slade, Deck, and Darius were currently positioned out front. Glasses and hats obscured their faces so no one could identify them, and the camera was purposely not hovering on them for too long.

Atticus glanced around the space to ensure the goons were tuned in to the fake broadcast. They were watching raptly, and one of them had already headed for the back, where they'd seen Johnathan Hartwood disappear earlier. This only worked if they were watching the television in this building, so it was imperative he'd been in place.

"What're they doing?" Jay asked, pitching his voice loud as he leaned forward.

"Looks like they're waitin' for someone," Atticus added on cue, then lowered his voice so only the mic for his comms would pick up. "We're a go, team."

Now for the fun part.

CHAPTER THIRTY-ONE

"WE'RE A GO, TEAM."

"All set here," Reese told Brantley through the comms when Atticus's signal came through.

"Perfect," Brantley's voice sounded in his ear. "What about you, JJ? You good to go?"

"All set," she confirmed. "I'm watchin' the action through the button cam on Slade's shirt. Keegan's here with me, ready for his next segment. We're good on this end."

Reese took a deep breath and started the engine.

"Let's do this, and nobody fuck it up," Brantley said firmly.

Reese grinned. Leave it to Brantley to kick it off with that.

When the Suburban Brantley was driving pulled away from the curb, Reese followed right behind him. They didn't pick up speed until they were on his street. It was merely for dramatic effect since the point was to draw the attention of anyone watching to their vehicles.

They came to an abrupt stop directly in front of the house. Reese put the truck in Park and jumped out, meeting Brantley as they pulled Toby out of the Suburban and ushered him toward the house. They'd put a bulletproof vest on Toby and covered his head with one of the extra windbreakers, wanting to flash the FBI letters for the camera. Conveniently, it slipped, giving the camera a good view of Toby's face for verification purposes before Brantley jerked it back in place.

Baz and Evan were moving swiftly, one in front, the other in back, as they escorted Toby into the house.

Slade, Darius, and Deck closed rank behind them, guarding the front door from outside. Since their plan was more for show on the outside than the inside, they'd needed them in place for the camera.

As soon as they were inside, Reese closed the door.

Brantley went right for Toby's home office, where they'd set up the device that would detonate when they clicked the button. It had required some ingenuity and a little help from one of Brantley's former SEAL teammates, but Reese had been assured the blast was designed to destroy the structure from the inside, not cause too much external damage. It was a gamble, regardless, but Reese trusted Brantley knew what he was doing.

"All set," Brantley confirmed. "Adorite? You in position?"

"We're here," Max replied, sounding significantly put out.

"Make him promise he won't kill me," Toby pleaded.

"He's not gonna kill you," Reese said.

"I'm not gonna kill you," Max echoed. "Not unless you screw me over, Land."

"I won't. Swear it," he said as he pulled off the vest and tossed it at Baz.

Reese believed him. The man looked terrified, but he also appeared resigned to his future. Then again, working for Max Adorite would be a far better outcome than sitting in a prison cell waiting to be shivved by one of Moroso's informants.

Baz shifted into gear, dressing one of the remains Max Adorite had acquired from a morgue. Which one, they didn't know, but Max had assured them one of the bodies was the same height and body type as Toby. The other didn't matter since it was being staged as the FBI agent that had accompanied Toby into the house. Max had also told them the bodies were scheduled for cremation, so they had nothing to worry about. That was yet to be seen, but for this to work, Reese knew he had to trust the guy.

In all fairness, he still didn't trust Max—never would—but he didn't have much choice in this matter.

"All set, boss," Baz noted when he was finished draping the FBI windbreaker over the body.

"Time to go," Brantley told Reese. "You two head out the back. Keep low. I'll see you in a little while."

Reese nodded, meeting Brantley's gaze. "Be safe."

"Always."

"Let's go," Reese told Toby, gripping his arm and tugging him toward the back door. "You move when I move. Got it?"

"Thank you for this," Toby said, his tone sincere.

"Don't thank me yet. I gotta get you to Max first." Even saying it sounded like a death sentence for Toby, but again, Reese had to trust that Max would follow through with his promise to keep Toby alive for the foreseeable future.

Standing at the back door, Reese took a deep breath before opening it.

Show time.

AS SOON AS THE DOOR CLOSED BEHIND Reese, Brantley started the countdown on his watch. They were giving him two minutes to get Toby out of the neighborhood to safety. It was a relatively straight shot, so provided they didn't encounter any people, they should be good.

In the meantime, the rest of the team was creating a distraction outside.

"You're up, Slade," Brantley said into the comms. "Two minutes. Make it count."

"On it, boss."

Brantley stood by with Baz and Evan as they waited for Reese to get some distance and Slade to make a show of finding something outside.

"You're up," Brantley told Evan.

Evan took off out the front door, moving quickly as he hurried to help Slade look for something that wasn't there. The seconds ticked by painfully slow, but from the sound of it, they were doing a damn fine job of making it look like they'd found a bomb. Pointing fingers, urgent comments into their radios, whatever it took to look real.

"Our turn," Brantley called to Baz.

They flung the door open and hurried outside. He kept his face averted from the direction of the camera Becs was currently using to film the scene from one of the houses across the street. She'd volunteered to go with Charlie so they could keep an eye on things from nearby, as well as to hang back with APD, who would be checking the scene when all was said and done, part of the agreement RT had made with them.

"Go time," Brantley instructed.

On cue, Baz turned toward the house, shouting instructions for the others to leave. He was talking to an empty house, but the onlookers didn't know that. If they'd been paying attention, they would be expecting two more to emerge.

Now for the fun part.

Brantley shouted, waving his arms for the others to get back. Slade was currently on his phone, making a fake phone call to the bomb squad so the neighbors would hear and it would be picked up on camera.

"They're buyin' it," Atticus said in his comm. "Hartwood came out of his office to watch the show on the big screen."

Brantley smiled to himself. That was what they'd been hoping for.

"We're almost to the drop point," Reese said in his ear, a verbal confirmation that they were far away from the house.

A chorus of "Out of range" came through his comms from Darius, Deck, Slade, and Evan. When the final confirmation came through from Baz, Brantley started toward the door as though he was going in to help get Land out.

When he reached the designated mark, he pressed the detonator in his hand.

The house exploded, sending Brantley back a few feet. He hit the ground hard enough to knock the wind out of his lungs, but he'd been prepared for impact. He stared up at the house as it went up in flames. Although it would burn to a crisp by design, the explosion had been mostly for effect. Granted, it was real, which meant the risk was as well, but it was one Brantley had been willing to take. Killing Toby Land in the eyes of the viewing public was imperative.

"Oh, shit, there were people inside," Atticus said from his location at the cabaret club, playing his role as the stunned witness. "I think it was their prisoner."

Brantley rolled to his knees and forced himself to his feet.

This was the part Brantley wasn't looking forward to. The cleanup was always a bitch, but thankfully, Evan and Baz, former detectives with local PDs, had volunteered to remain back to talk to the fire department. They had one guy, a friend of Luca's, who said he'd do his best to keep it all on the DL, but that was yet to be seen.

Unfortunately, there would always be loose ends when building and executing a lie in public, but hey, if it meant Reese's family would be safe, Brantley was willing to go to any lengths to make it happen.

"Let's go," Brantley said, continuing the ruse by limping toward Slade, who rushed to his side and helped him to one of the Suburbans.

Deck and Darius got in the other vehicles, leaving the two Brantley and Reese had pulled up in out front. Evan and Baz would take those when it was all cleared out.

"We're exiting the scene now," Brantley said when Slade backed the Suburban down the road. "Reese? What's your status?"

"Land's with Adorite," he confirmed. "I'm headin' back to Coyote Ridge."

"You owe me one, Walker," Max said.

"Not in this lifetime, Adorite. You'll owe Reese for the remainder of yours. I'll see to it."

"Keep tellin' yourself that."

There was a click, which Brantley figured was Max tossing his earwig out the window. It made him smile.

"All's well that ends well," Atticus said. "Hartwood turned off the TV, muttered somethin' about good riddance and kudos to Adorite. I don't think he cared much for Toby."

Brantley laughed. "No, probably not."

"I do think Serendipity's gonna miss him, though," Jay noted. "She's torn up about it."

"I'm sure she'll move on."

"Oh, she is," Atticus said with a chuckle. "In fact, she's about to go on stage. I guess heartbreak's not always a long process."

Brantley was starting to like Atticus. In fact, he'd pulled this off so seamlessly, he might have to offer the guy a job.

"Nice work," Brantley told the team. "Finish up your part and meet at Moonshiners. That means you, Atticus. I've got an opportunity to talk to you about."

This time the chorus of confirmations came from every member, and Brantley couldn't help but feel pride for the team they'd built. They were a talented bunch, there was no doubt about it.

After all, they'd just convinced a wannabe mobster that his mark was dead and given a real mobster a man who was a myth.

All in a day's work.

Stay Tuned

I hope you enjoyed the eighth installment of the Off the Books Task Force. The team continues to morph and grow, and they'll continue to do so because it's not over for Brantley and Reese, JJ and Baz, and the rest of the task force. And while Trey is off on a different adventure, it looks like we might have someone new joining the task force.

Each book in this series is a full-length novel involving a new case and the continuation of the relationships between them all. And I promise not to keep you waiting long for each installment.

If you enjoyed *Bounty*, please consider leaving a review.

ABOUT NICOLE EDWARDS

New York Times and *USA Today* bestselling author Nicole Edwards lives in the suburbs of Austin, Texas, with her husband, their three fur babies, and the youngest of their three children, who has threatened never to leave home. When Nicole is not writing about sexy alpha males and sassy, independent women, she can often be found with a book in hand or attempting to keep the dogs happy. You can find her hanging out on social media and interacting with her readers - even when she's supposed to be writing.

BECAUSE NAUGHTY CAN BE OH SO NICE®

CONNECT WITH NICOLE

I hope you're as eager to get the information as I am to give it. Any one of these things is worth signing up for, or feel free to sign up for all. I promise to keep each one unique and interesting.

NIC NEWS: If you haven't signed up for my newsletter and you want to get notifications regarding preorders, new releases, giveaways, sales, etc, then you'll want to sign up. I promise not to spam your email, just get you the most important updates.

Ramblings of a Writer Blog: My blog is used for writer ramblings, which I am known to do from time to time.

NICOLE NATION: Visit my website to get exclusive content you won't find anywhere else, including sneak peeks, A Day in the Life character stories, exclusive giveaways, cards from Nicole, Join Nicole's review team.

Nicole Nation on Facebook: Join my reader group to interact with other readers, ask me questions, play fun weekly games, celebrate during release week, and enter exclusive giveaways!

Instagram: Basically, Instagram is where I post pictures of my dogs, so if you want to see epic cuteness, you should follow me.

Text: Want a simple, fast way to get updates on new releases? Sign up for text messaging. If you are in the U.S. simply text NICOLE to 64600. I promise not to spam your phone. This is just my way of letting you know what's happening because I know you're busy, but if you're anything like me, you always have your phone on you.

Naughty & Nice Shop: Not only does the shop have signed books, but there's fun merchandise, too. Plenty of naughty and nice options to go around. Find the shop on my website.

Website:	NicoleEdwards.me
Facebook:	/Author.Nicole.Edwards
Instagram:	NicoleEdwardsAuthor
BookBub:	/NicoleEdwardsAuthor

Acknowledgments

Brantley and Reese have become two of my favorite people on the planet, even if they're not real people. They still *feel* real, at least inside my head. Not to mention, JJ and Baz, and the rest of the task force. I spend a lot of time with them and each time I do, I get this giddy feeling inside.

I have to thank my husband, who puts up with me every single day. If it weren't for him and his belief that I could (and can) do this, I wouldn't be writing this today. He has been my backbone, my rock, the very reason I continue to believe in myself. I love you for that, babe.

Chancy Powley – As always, you keep me going. Your support and friendship is one of the best things to come out of this journey I am on.

Jenna Underwood – I always look forward to the random notes in the mail, especially when they have a return address of nowhere. Hopefully, you'll put down roots again soon and maybe you'll even invite me to come visit.

I want to thank my street team – Nicole Nation Street Team. Your unwavering support is something I will never take for granted even if I'm not the best leader due to my lack of time. But you still pull through for me when it matters, and for that, I am forever grateful.

I can't forget my copyeditor, Amy, at Blue Otter Editing. Thank goodness I've got you to catch all my punctuation, grammar, and tense errors.

Nicole Nation 2.0 for the constant support and love and for those of you who have my back. You've been there for me from almost the beginning. This group of ladies has kept me going for so long, I'm not sure I'd know what to do without them.

And, of course, YOU, the reader. Your emails, messages, posts, comments, tweets… they mean more to me than you can imagine. I thrive on hearing from you; knowing that my characters and my stories have touched you in some way keeps me going. I've been known to shed a tear or two when reading an email because you bring so much joy to my life with your support. I thank you for that.

By Nicole Edwards

The Walkers

Alluring Indulgence

Kaleb
Zane
Travis
Holidays with The Walker Brothers
Ethan
Braydon
Sawyer
Brendon

The Walkers Of Coyote Ridge

Curtis
Jared (a crossover novel)
Hard to Hold
Hard to Handle
Beau
Rex
A Coyote Ridge Christmas
Mack
Kaden & Keegan
Alibi (a crossover novel)

Brantley Walker: Off The Books

All In
Without A Trace
Hide & Seek
Deadly Coincidence
Alibi (a crossover novel)
Secrets
Confessions
Bounty

Austin Arrows

Rush
Kaufman

CLUB DESTINY

Conviction
Temptation
Addicted
Seduction
Infatuation
Captivated
Devotion
Perception
Entrusted
Adored
Distraction
Forevermore

DEAD HEAT RANCH

Boots Optional
Betting on Grace
Overnight Love
Jared (a crossover novel)

DEVIL'S BEND

Chasing Dreams
Vanishing Dreams

MISPLACED HALOS

Protected in Darkness
Salvation in Darkness
Bound in Darkness

OFFICE INTRIGUE

Office Intrigue
Intrigued Out of The Office
Their Rebellious Submissive
Their Famous Dominant
Their Ruthless Sadist
Their Naughty Student
Their Fairy Princess
Owned

Pier 70

Reckless
Fearless
Speechless
Harmless
Clueless

Sniper 1 Security

Wait for Morning
Never Say Never
Tomorrow's Too Late

Southern Boy Mafia/Devil's Playground

Beautifully Brutal
Without Regret
Beautifully Loyal
Without Restraint

Standalone Novels

Unhinged Trilogy
A Million Tiny Pieces
Inked on Paper
Bad Reputation
Bad Business
Filthy Hot Billionaire

Naughty Holiday Editions

2015
2016
2021

Because Naughty Can Be Oh So Nice®
NE LTD

Printed in Dunstable, United Kingdom

78693642R00147